BREATHE WITH ME

BOOK SEVEN IN THE WITH ME IN SEATTLE SERIES

KRISTEN PROBY

For Pamela:

I can never repay you, not just for everything you've done for me, but for your friendship as well. I love you.

PROLOGUE

Eleven years ago

-Meredith-

Meet u at ur place in 30. Luv u.

I grin and type back a quick *luv u 2* and snap my phone shut as I hurry home from dance class. I really wanted to skip dance today, but Mark insisted that I go. He said he understands how important dance is to me and that he would see me later.

We are celebrating my seventeenth birthday tonight. It's a week early because my mom will be home on my real birthday, but she's gone tonight on a business trip, and Mark told his folks that he's staying at a friend's house so he can stay with me all night.

I can't decide if I'm super nervous or super excited. Maybe I'm both.

Because tonight we are going to do *it*.

I grin and shimmy my butt in a little happy dance in the driver's seat of my 1995 Ford Escort. I just have enough time to take a quick shower and touch up my makeup before Mark gets to my house.

I hurry through the shower, but pay extra attention to shaving my legs and bikini line. I wipe the fog off the mirror in my bathroom and wrinkle my nose. My makeup did not survive dance *and* the shower, so I quickly scrub my face clean and just reapply my eyeliner and mascara and smooth some lip-gloss on my lips. Mark's seen me without makeup plenty of times, but I want to at least look like I'm making an effort tonight.

I pull the short black skirt and red-cropped sweater that shows off my belly out of the closet and after slipping into some lacy black underwear that I've been saving for this exact occasion, I shimmy into the cute outfit and take a turn before my mirror.

"You're so beautiful," I hear from behind me and smile when I turn to see Mark leaning his shoulder against my doorjamb. "So this is what it looks like."

"This is it." I open my arms wide and glance around my bedroom. Mom doesn't allow Mark up here with me when he comes over.

And, it's probably a good idea, given what we'll be using this room for tonight.

Nerves suddenly take hold and I wring my fingers as giant butterflies take flight in my belly.

"I like it." His eyes still haven't moved from me. I smile shyly.

"You haven't even looked at it."

He smiles and glances about my frilly room. My dance shoes are scattered about. Photos of my dance teams and friends clutter a cork bulletin board above my desk where my computer sits. A photo of him and I together at Pike's Place Market is framed next to my bed. The top of my dresser is littered with makeup and jewelry. My double-sized bed is made neatly. I changed the sheets before I left for dance this afternoon.

"I like it," he repeats. "Why are you standing way over there?"

I shrug one shoulder and glance out the window, watching the rain fall down the window pane.

"Hey, M." He walks to me and hugs me close. This is what I needed, the familiarity of his smell and the feel of his strong arms around my shoulders. He's so much bigger than me. His muscles are crazy defined, but it's his sweet smile and blue eyes that have done me in since the day I saw him in biology class last year.

When he smiles, it looks like he has a naughty secret.

I hope I learn all of his naughty secrets tonight.

"I'm making you dinner," he says before kissing my forehead and taking my hand to lead me downstairs to the kitchen.

"You are?" I giggle and bounce down the steps behind him. "What are you making?"

"Chicken parmesan and pasta."

"Holy calories, Batman!" I exclaim and mentally calculate how many miles I'm going to have to run to burn it off.

"It's your birthday, M, the calories don't count," he says and leads me to the breakfast bar in the kitchen.

"You brought me flowers!" I exclaim and immediately bury my nose in the beautiful red roses sitting on my kitchen counter. I yank the card out of the plastic holder and read it aloud. "To M, Happy Birthday. Love, M." I grin but in my head I'm bouncing up and down like a big dork and launch myself in Mark's arms. "Thank you."

"You're welcome." He kisses me hard before setting me down and getting started with dinner. "You'll get your real present later."

"There's more?" I ask and clap my hands excitedly.

"Yep," he replies. He pours me some bubbly water and I sit back and watch my man move about the kitchen.

"You're good at this."

"Mom makes us all take turns cooking," he replies with a shrug. "She says we have to earn our keep."

"I love your mom," I say and sip my water.

"She loves you too."

"I'm so glad that we like each other's parents. It would really suck otherwise."

"Did you have any doubt that I could charm your mom?" he asks.

"No." I giggle and shake my head. "You're quite charming."

"I'm just kidding. I like your mom a lot. I feel kind of guilty that we lied to her about tonight."

"I know." I bite my lip and look down into my glass.

"Hey, it'll be okay."

I nod and sit back to watch him bustle about the kitchen, enjoying the way he moves. He has a natural grace that appeals to the dancer in me. When we danced together at the junior prom, I didn't think that anything could get any better than that.

When dinner is done, he serves me first and we laugh all through the meal, talking about school and our mutual friends.

"How is Luke?" I ask casually.

"Good. He's about to audition for some movie project about vampires," he replies with a laugh. "Can you see my brother as a vampire?"

I laugh with him and shake my head. "He's too nice to be a vampire."

"Sam is enjoying college," he continues as he clears our dishes. "The house seems quiet without her."

"She doesn't like me," I reply and bite my lip. No matter how hard I try to talk with Mark's older sister, she just doesn't like me.

"Sam doesn't know you very well, and she's kind of stand-offish with strangers," he says and loads the last dish into the dishwasher, then takes my hand in his and kisses it gently. "Besides, I don't care if Sam doesn't like you. Sam isn't dating you."

"Thank goodness," I say with a grin and lean into him, hoping he'll kiss me again. I can't get enough of Mark's kisses. He rests his forehead against my own and rubs his hands up and down my arms softly, sending shivers through me.

"Are you sure about this, M? We don't have to do anything more than lie on the couch and watch TV if you want to."

"Is that what you want?" I ask with a small voice.

"No." He chuckles and if I'm not mistaken, blushes just a bit. "I can't seem to keep my hands off you, and I want nothing more than to make love with you, but it's a big step, and I just want you to know that it's okay if you're not ready."

I love him even more for that speech. With a renewed sense of confidence, I link his fingers with mine, toss a sassy smile over my shoulder and guide him up the stairs toward my bedroom. Once inside, he shuts and locks the door—just in case—and follows me to the bed. Keeping eye contact with him, I crawl onto the bed and, leaning back on my elbows in the most seductive pose I can come up with, I crook my finger in invitation for him to join me.

"I guess this means you're sure," he mutters and pulls his shoes off quickly and crawls onto the mattress with me.

"I guess so," I whisper. My stomach is doing crazy somersaults as he leans in and kisses my cheek and then down to my neck.

"You're so beautiful, M," he whispers. "I'm so lucky that you're mine."

I smile and close my eyes as he pushes his fingers into my hair and turns my head to meet his lips. He guides me to my back and hovers over me, kissing me for what feels like forever. My hands are all over his back and arms. God, I love the feel of his body, and I suddenly want to feel him naked.

Now.

I tug the hem of his shirt up and he pulls back long enough to yank it over his head and throw it on the floor and then returns to kissing me, but now his hands are wandering all over my body.

This I'm used to. We've done this countless times. He even got my shirt and bra off in the back seat of his car one night after a football game before we put a stop to it.

The rain is coming down harder outside, and it's gotten much darker. The only light is the sliver of light coming in from the streetlight on the corner. Mark's breathing is coming faster as he pushes my sweater up and sees my bra.

"Let's get you out of these amazing clothes," he says and watches me closely. I nod and sit up and let him pull my sweater over my head and unclasp my bra. His fingers are shaking so it takes him a few seconds to get the hooks loose. Next, I shimmy out of my skirt and panties, and when I move to put my hands over my breasts, he tugs them away and kisses my palms gently. "I've never seen anything more beautiful than you."

I'm lost in his blue gaze. I'm too skinny and my boobs haven't reached their full potential yet, but when he's staring down at me with so much love, I know he's telling me the truth.

"I love you, M," I murmur and cup his face in my hands. "I love you so much."

"I love you too, baby," he says and kisses me softly. I reach down for the button on his jeans and with some fumbling around and muttered curses, he manages to wiggle out of them and toss them aside and suddenly there he is in all of his glory.

"You're damn hot, Mark Williams," I say and watch my hand glide over his hip and that really sexy muscle there. My eyes move over to his… *thing* and I feel them widen in surprise. "Holy shit."

"Is that a good holy shit or a bad holy shit?" he asks with a laugh.

"That won't fit in me," I say and then feel my face flush hot. *Geez shut the fuck up, Meredith!*

"It will," he promises and nudges my gaze back up to his and kisses me some more. He knows I love the kissing. He lies on top of me and cradles my head in his hands and kisses me silly, nibbling my lips and nuzzling my nose with his. Just when my stomach muscles loosen, he nudges between my legs and I can feel him *there*.

"Oh God," I rasp with a panic.

"Hey, it's okay, baby."

"I'm really nervous," I say and bite my lip, watching his face.

"Are you still sure? Or just nervous about what it will feel like?"

"Just nervous about what it will feel like," I respond truthfully.

"Just look at me, M. It's just me." He eases inside just a bit and it hurts—*fuck, it hurts!*— but then it doesn't hurt so bad. "Breathe with me, Meredith."

He takes a deep breath and I follow him, watching his eyes with all of my attention, and as we breathe together, he slips even farther inside me. His brow is breaking out in a sweat and he licks his lips nervously, and I can see that he's just as nervous as I am.

"I love you, baby," he whispers softly.

"I love you too."

"Happy birthday."

"Thank you."

He links his fingers with mine and holds our hands against the bed next to my head. God, he's so damn *big*. And it's uncomfortable, but it feels really, different. Full. Our breaths are coming really fast, and then he starts to move, like he just can't help it. His hips pull back and then push back in, slow at first and then faster.

"Oh my God, this is so fucking amazing," he says with awe. "I'm so glad you're my first, M."

"Me too," I say, happy that he's talking. It seems awkward when we're quiet. We talk nonstop. "I'm so happy that we waited for each other."

"I want to be your *only*, baby."

"You do?"

"Oh, yeah. It's you and me, M and M, against the world." His hips are moving faster, and I can feel my eyes fill with tears as his whole body tenses. God, I've never felt anything like this in my life. It's as though we're not just connected physically, but in *every* way. "Oh God, baby. I'm going to come."

"Okay." I caress his face with my hands. "That's a good thing, right? Come, M."

"Oh, shit." His face contorts in this weird mask, like he's in immense pain, and I can't take my eyes off him. *Wow.*

"Are you okay?" I ask softly.

"I think I'm supposed to ask you that," he replies, breathing hard.

"I'm really good," I say and smile reassuringly. *But you need to pull out because...* *ow.*

"I love you, M." He leans his forehead on mine gently.

"I love you too, M."

***

One year later

I've never been this fucking nervous in my life. Not even that first time that Mark and I had sex. I grin as I think back on that night, and the many, many times we've had sex since then. My Mark is insatiable and we've learned so much about each other over the past year.

He's not going to be mine much longer.

I pull in a deep breath and let it out slowly as I see his car pull into my driveway. We graduated from high school last week. It was a proud moment for both of us, for our families, who threw us a huge party.

And we're supposed to leave for New York City together in two days.

"Hey, baby," he says with his signature naughty grin as he meets me on the porch and hugs me close. "Are you packing?"

"Yes," I reply and bury my nose in his neck, knowing this might be the last time I have the right to do this.

"What's wrong?" He pulls away and studies my face. He knows me too damn well. "M?"

"I don't think you should come with me to New York," I say it really fast, like pulling off a Band Aid.

He blinks and frowns. "What are you talking about? We've been talking about this for the past year."

"I know, it's just…" I push my fingers through my hair and barely hold on to my sanity. "I need to concentrate on dance, Mark."

"Okay." He shakes his head like he just doesn't get it. "Why the change of heart?"

"I've been thinking about this for a while, but I just didn't know how to tell you."

"How long?"

"A few months," I whisper. Since the day my instructor pulled me aside when she caught me daydreaming about Mark and yelled at me about responsibilities and how hard it's going to be in New York.

"*Months?*" He rubs his fingers over his mouth and begins to look a little panicked. "Mer, where is this coming from? Is there someone else?"

"Of course not!" I gape at him like he's lost his marbles. "You know I love you so much it hurts!"

"Then why?"

"Because I have to concentrate on dance, Mark. This is going to be the hardest thing I ever do. The days are super long, and it's so competitive."

"So you're saying I'll just be in the way?" He props his hands on his hips and glares at me and I feel the first tear fall.

"You'll be a distraction that I can't afford, M." I take a step to him, begging him with my eyes to understand, but he steps away.

"I don't want to do the long distance thing, Meredith."

"I don't either." It's a whisper, and his face pales when he realizes what, exactly this means.

"You're breaking it off?"

"I love you, Mark."

"But you're breaking it off."

"I just think that we're so young, and I have to focus on dance."

He takes another step away, blinking blindly, and I know I'm breaking his heart.

"So much for M and M against the world," he spits out.

"Mark, come inside and talk to me."

"No, you've said enough." He stops and stares at me as I cry, tears in his own eyes. "Good luck to you, Meredith."

With that he shakes his head and leaves, and I run inside to find my mom crying in the living room, having heard our conversation.

"Mom," I cry and fall into her arms.

"Oh, baby girl," she coos. "I'm so sorry for both of you."

"What did I just do?" I am crying uncontrollably, leaning on my strong mother.

"You made an adult decision, baby. But I know it hurts you. And it hurts him too."

"I love him so much."

"I know you do."

"How will I live without him?"

She strokes my hair and kisses my forehead. "One day at a time, my love."

***

Two days later.

I've never been on a plane before. I don't come from a poor family, but we just never went on vacations that required air travel. And now here I am, only a few months past my eighteenth birthday and on a plane.

Without Mark.

I pull my phone out of my pocket and reread his text from last night. The one I didn't respond to.

Please don't do this to us. We can make it work. I love u.

God, what did I do? I've cried nonstop for two days. Can I get off this plane? Shit, they just shut the doors. Maybe they won't card me if I order a drink. I've never drank a day in my life—too many calories—but I need something to calm my nerves now.

I need Mark.

I need Mark!

I am about to stand up and make a big scene when his voice fills my head. *Just breathe, M. Just breathe with me.* I take a deep breath and close my eyes and focus on his voice, wishing with all my heart he were really beside me, talking me through this.

Just breathe, M.

CHAPTER ONE

Ten years later

~Mark~

"Hey, man. Come on in." My brother, Luke, steps back as I walk through his door and see my beautiful sister-in-law, Natalie, snap her new son, Keaton's pants shut and lift him into her arms.

"Unca Mawk!" Olivia, Keaton's older sister exclaims and toddles toward me with her arms up and a wide smile on her perfect little face.

"Hi, troublemaker," I say and lift her high into the air, then snuggle her in my arms.

"My baby," she says and points to her brother.

"She's claimed him," I say with a laugh and lean in to kiss Nat's cheek.

"Indeed," she replies dryly. "Keaton is hers, along with all of his toys and clothes."

"It's okay, you can have anything you want," I tell her and blow raspberries in her neck, making her giggle.

"I'm just about ready," Luke says and pats his pants and suit pockets, looking about the room with a frown. "Where's my wallet, baby?"

"On the kitchen counter." She points it out to him and then laughs. "He's more forgetful since Keaton has arrived than I am."

Natalie is a gorgeous woman, with long dark hair and wide green eyes and curves that go on for days. My brother is a lucky, lucky man, and I make sure to do my part and flirt with her as much as possible, just to make him crazy.

"Run away with me," I say and wrap my arm around her shoulders, pulling her close to my side. "He's ugly and he stinks most of the time."

"Get your hands off my wife, dude." Luke scowls at me and shakes his head.

"She loves me. Don't you, darlin'?"

"I do." She pats my chest and I smile proudly. "But I love my husband more."

"Killjoy," I whisper loudly and sigh in mock despair. "What will I do now?"

"I'm sure you've got a few dozen women lined up who'd love the same invitation."

I smirk and nod, but the truth is, I don't have as many women on the line as they'd all like to think.

And I'm about to come face to face with the one woman who can bring me to my knees for the first time in ten years.

"I'm so sorry to hear about Adelaide Summers, Mark." Nat kisses my cheek and rubs my arm soothingly. "She was a good woman."

"She was." I nod as the pain pierces my heart all over again. Meredith's mom lost her fight with breast cancer just a week ago, and I'm going to her funeral today. "She sure was good to me."

"I would go with you guys, but I'm on baby duty today."

I grin down at her and kiss Livie's cheek again. "It's fine. Luke, you don't have to go either. It's no big deal."

"Yeah, it is," he says and frowns at me. He can read me too well. "I want to come. I liked Addie."

I nod, secretly relieved that I won't be going alone and set Olivia on her feet as Luke leads me to the front door. Halfway there he quickly turns back and pulls his wife in for a long, deep kiss.

Dear Jesus, you'd think they were still dating.

"You're going to see her in a couple hours, Romeo."

"Bite me," he says with a grin. "You're just jealous."

"I'm nauseated," I reply and lead him to my Jeep.

"How are you really?" Luke asks quietly as I pull out of the driveway of his new home toward Bellevue, where the funeral will be held.

"I don't know, man. I knew she was sick, so it's not exactly out of the blue."

"I mean about Meredith, Mark. Jesus, you're stubborn."

I shrug my shoulder and rub my hand over my face. I've had ten years to get used to the idea of seeing her again, and now I'm nervous as hell.

"She's probably married," I reply.

"We both know that isn't true," he says calmly.

"Look, it's been a long time. I'm just going to pay my respects to a woman who I loved. Seeing Mer is part of that." I swallow hard and Luke catches it.

"But?" he asks.

"But it feels like I'm finally saying goodbye to Mer for good too. Like it's closure on the whole fucking thing."

Luke sighs and slips his sunglasses on. "I'm sorry, man."

I shrug one shoulder and concentrate on the freeway. "It is what it is."

The funeral home isn't far from our childhood home. There are several cars parked in the parking lot and some people standing outside, talking. Others are coming in and out of the wide red doors of the funeral home.

"Here goes nothing," I whisper. Jesus, I haven't been this nervous in years. Luke and I both slam our doors and walk toward the entrance. Luke looks like the millionaire celebrity in a custom designer suit. I'm also in a dark suit with a purple tie. Purple was Addie's favorite color.

We walk through the front door and nod hello to a few people we know. Mom and Dad are quietly talking with another couple they know and wave at us when they see us then turn back to their conversation.

As we're walking into the chapel area, I hear her voice.

Her voice.

I stop in my tracks and stare at her, standing up near the closed casket that's covered in all of Addie's favorite flowers, talking with the pastor. She's dabbing at her eyes with a tissue and nodding. She hasn't seen me yet, so I take a moment and drink in the sight of her.

She's no longer the young woman I once knew so intimately. I knew every inch of her. I knew what turned her on and what made her squirm. What made her smile. What made her sigh in pleasure.

But better than that, I knew what made her laugh. What made her sad. How to cheer her up and even what she was going to say before she said it.

I knew *everything.*

She was my world, and even though I know I was too young, nothing will ever erase the way it felt to stand on her front porch and have her tell me she didn't want me any more. I've fought with that particular demon for years.

She turns and sees me, her bright blue gaze locks on mine, and she's suddenly coming toward me, walking quickly on those tall black heels. Her face crumples and to my utter shock, she launches herself into my arms and holds on with all her strength.

"I can't believe she's gone, M," she whispers and buries her face in my neck, the way she always used to, as if no time has passed at all and my heart feels like someone is stabbing it over and over with an ice pick.

"I'm so sorry," I whisper back and wrap my arms around her, holding her against me. "I'm so sorry about Addie, M."

"At least I got to spend Christmas with her," she says and sniffles. "She wanted to make it through Christmas and she did."

I nod and give in to the moment and kiss her head. Fuck me, she smells the same.

How is that possible?

"I don't know what else to say, sweetheart," I murmur and rub her back softly. She's still so slender. So small. Her hips and breasts seem to have filled out more with womanhood, but she feels just like she always did in my arms.

Like she was born to be here.

Stop it, asshole!

She seems to come to her senses and pulls herself out of my embrace, wiping her eyes. She smiles at Luke.

"Hi, Luke."

"Nice to see you, Meredith." He kisses her cheek and leans in to whisper in her ear. She smiles softly and nods up at him when he pulls away.

A man I don't recognize sidles up next to Mer and wraps his arm around her. "Are you okay, cupcake?"

Cupcake?

Luke and I glance at each other quickly, but a whole chapter of dialogue just passed between us.

Cupcake? Who the fuck calls his girl cupcake? *How can she stand that?*

And who the fuck is this asshole?

Meredith smiles at him and gestures to us.

"I'm fine, Jax. This is Mark and Luke Williams. They're both old friends of mine."

Right. Old friends. I spent the better part of a year inside you, sweetheart.

"This is Jax," she continues.

Luke and I both nod and suddenly, music starts and the service is about to begin.

We find seats in the middle near our parents while Mer and Jax walk to the front of the room. I watch her walk away, my eyes glaring holes through the arm still wrapped around her shoulders.

She lets him call her cupcake?

"So, she has someone," I whisper to Luke.

"He might just be a friend."

I smirk and shake my head. What was I expecting anyway? Some kind of fucking reunion? If that's what I expected to happen, I would have rushed to her side the minute I found out she was back in Seattle early last year.

Not gonna happen.

The service begins with music and then the pastor talks about Addie and her contributions to the community, her family, and prayers. After a few more words, he asks for volunteers to share stories about Addie. There are photos set up next to the casket. Photos of Addie and Meredith, and family photos from when Meredith was very young.

Meredith stands and walks to the podium, white tissues clutched in her small hand. I wish I were up there with her, to hold her hand while she struggles through this.

"Hi, everyone," she begins and clears her throat. "Thank you all so much for coming today. Mom would be proud and happy that you all thought so highly of her. She sure loved all of you."

I clench my hands in my lap and watch, my eyes trained on her face.

I'm so sorry, M.

"You all know that Mom and I lost Dad and Tiffany fifteen years ago," she begins, referring to the car accident that took her father and sister from them when she was only thirteen. "I guess I just keep reminding myself that Mom's with them now, and they're so happy to see each other."

She has to pause and take a deep breath, and as she does so, her eyes find mine in the crowd. She seems to straighten her shoulders and continue.

"My mom taught me to be a fighter. She always said, 'No one is going to chase your dreams for you, my love.' And she was right. She showed me what it is to be a good woman, and to fight for what you believe is the right thing."

She nods slowly, still watching me. "I will miss her. Every day. But I'm so happy that she's not sick anymore. She was always so strong, such a strong, strong woman, that being sick this past year just pissed her off."

We all chuckle and nod, knowing she's right.

"So, although it's so hard to say goodbye, I know in my heart that she's so much happier now. I love you, Mama."

She returns to her seat and several other friends stand to tell stories of Addie. Some are funny, others just nice.

Finally, I stand, button my jacket, and walk to the podium. When I glance down at Mer in the front row, the fucker Jax has his arm around her shoulders again, rubbing her arm soothingly.

I've never wanted to punch someone so badly in my whole life.

"I'm Mark Williams," I begin and smile wide, looking over at Addie's coffin. "I couldn't be here today and not share a story about my Addie."

Jesus, which story do I tell?

"I've known this amazing woman since I was a young man. She used to scare the hell out of me, mostly because I was dating her daughter."

Everyone chuckles with me, setting me more at ease. "But I quickly learned that Addie was a no-nonsense woman who never met a stranger. She was generous and loyal. And although my relationship with her family changed with time," I glance down to see fresh tears rolling down Mer's face and it makes me pause. I clear my throat and continue, "Addie never treated me any differently. I visited with her many times over the years. Cut her grass, or helped her out around the house. And every time I showed up at her house it was as if she hadn't seen me in years, and she always had a warm hug and a cold glass of lemonade waiting for me."

I bite my lip and glance to the back of the room, lost in my own thoughts of this special woman.

"Thanks, Addie, for making me feel like your family. You were one awesome lady."

I smile and return to my seat. Several more people stand to talk and soon another song is played as the pastor gives the benediction.

"Do you boys want to go with us to the reception?" Mom asks and takes my hand in hers when we stand.

"I don't think so," I reply. I can't bear the thought of watching Meredith with that man for the next few hours.

No way.

"I need to get back to Nat and the kids," Luke says and kisses our Mom's cheek.

"What you said was really nice, son," Dad says and claps his hand on my shoulder. "Addie would have liked that."

"Thanks, Dad."

I glance around the room one last time and see Mer wiping her eyes and hugging one of her former neighbors.

"Let's go, man," I murmur to Luke.

"You don't want to say goodbye?"

I shake my head and glance over at the most beautiful woman in the room. "I already have."

We say our goodbyes to our parents and make a hasty exit back to my Jeep.

"Well, that went better than I expected," Luke comments and sighs.

"It was a funeral, dude. What did you expect to happen?"

"Don't be an ass. Mer looks great. And she hugged you. That surprised me."

"She's grieving." I shrug like it's no big deal, but my stomach is still in knots. "I'm familiar. Had I seen her on the street two months ago, it wouldn't have gone like that."

"If you say so."

"What are you trying to do? Set me up with her? She has a man. Cupcake man."

"Who the fuck calls his woman 'cupcake'?" Luke asks with a laugh.

"My thoughts exactly. And how in the hell can she stand that?"

"It's pretty cheesy," he agrees with a nod. "You okay?"

"I'm fine."

"Come inside," Luke says when we pull up to his house. "Looks like Jules and Nate are here."

"I haven't seen the baby since she was born." We climb out of the Jeep and when we step inside, we hear Jules and Nat laughing. Nate is lying on the floor on his belly and Livie is climbing all over him.

"We buy her a state-of-the-art jungle gym out back, and all she wants to climb on is Nate," Luke mutters in disgust.

"I like climbing on Nate myself," Jules replies and wiggles her brows. "Hey, handsome." She stands and wraps her arms around me. "I'm sorry for your loss."

"Thank you, beautiful." I hug her hard and kiss her forehead before she pulls away then I make a beeline for the gorgeous baby girl in Nat's arms. "My turn."

"Who knew you'd be such a sucker for the babies?" Nate says and pushes himself up off the floor.

"I'm a sucker for the ladies," I reply and grin down at a newborn Stella Montgomery McKenna. "Hello, gorgeous girl."

"It's kind of hot to see you with a baby," Nat says thoughtfully.

"I'm glad you approve. It's good to know the woman I'm going to steal from my brother thinks I'm hot."

"Not gonna happen," Luke replies as he passes a sleeping Keaton to Nat then scoops her into his arms, then sits with her in his lap. "Get your own girl."

"I found one," I reply and grin down at Stella who is watching me with big, sober blue eyes. "God, Jules, she's awesome."

"I know." She sighs and leans on Nate's arm, watching us. Livie toddles between Nate's knees, begging to be held. Nat is holding Keaton.

"It looks like a daycare in here."

Natalie laughs and kisses her son's blond head. Where Livie was born with dark hair, her younger brother has light hair like Luke.

"Brynna's due anytime, right?" Nate asks Jules, referring to her sister-in-law.

"Yep, just a few more weeks."

"You're all a bunch of baby making machines. But thanks for taking the pressure off me with Mom and Dad." I wink at Luke who laughs and gently rubs his fingertips on Keaton's head.

"You're welcome. Anytime."

Stella's tiny pink lips pucker, and suddenly she lets out a loud wail.

"Oh, okay, this is my cue to leave." I gently pass the crying baby to her mama and back away with my hands raised in surrender. "I don't do crying women."

"Pussy," Luke taunts me.

"Call me all the names you want. I don't like to make a girl cry." I kiss each of the girls on the cheek and back away toward the front door. "Have a good afternoon, guys."

"Bye!" They all wave and I return to my Jeep and toward the house I recently bought in north Seattle. It's a fixer-upper, but I got it for a steal, and since I work construction for a living, I figure I can fix it up for a song and flip it for a tidy profit.

Win-win.

I wonder what Mer's gonna do with her mom's place? Will she keep it? Live in it? *With Jax?*

Why does the thought of that make me violent?

Because I still think of her as mine. After all this time, when I think of Meredith, she's *my* Meredith. Irrational? Yes.

Stupid? Most definitely.

But I don't give a fuck.

I take a deep breath and scrub my hand over my face and suddenly feel... *heavy.* As of right now it feels final. Over. Maybe I held out hope for all of those years that she'd come to her senses and come running back to me. Fuck, I don't know what I thought. But seeing her today, hugging her so tightly and hearing her voice in my ear call me *M,* then seeing the other man claim her, finally hammered it home.

She's not mine. She hasn't been mine in a very, very long time.

It's time to move the fuck on.

CHAPTER TWO

Three Months Later
~Meredith~

"Madison, not to be confused with Madeline, so we do *not* say Maddie, forgot her shoes at home," Jax says in a hurry as he bustles past me back stage. "So her mom is making a mad dash home to fetch them."

"It's fine, we have like thirty minutes," I say and prop my hands on my hips to survey the area. Little girls are admiring themselves in the mirrors, in their pretty dance tutus and makeup. "I can't believe we gave in to the tutus," I mutter.

"The moms like to see them in frilly dance clothes." Jax shrugs and then laughs when a little girl, while watching herself in the mirror, makes a complete turn, transfixed by the sight before her. "And the girls like it too."

I nod and then squat to help another girl with her shoes.

Before long, the excitement backstage is mounting. The girls are excited to show their mom and dads what they've learned. Or just show off onstage. We have girls of all ages dancing today.

"Ten minutes!" Jax calls out and the little girls all clap excitedly. "Hey, isn't that your Mr. Hot Tamale in the audience?"

I frown and glance out from the curtain and survey the audience. Sure enough, right there in the front row, is Mark with Luke and his family.

What are they doing here?

I glance back at Jax with what I'm sure is panic written all over my face. He laughs and pats my shoulder. "Go say hi."

"Oh God." I clutch my stomach and inwardly cringe when I think of the way I threw myself at him at Mom's funeral. I don't know what came over me. I saw him, and it was as if no time had passed at all and I just knew in that moment that he was the only one who could comfort me.

And then I realized what I'd done, and when I pulled away he was aloof and someone I didn't know.

He didn't even say goodbye.

I bite my lip and decide what the hell? "I'll be right back."

"No hurry, we're ready back here." Jax winks and turns his attention to a mom asking about adult classes.

I walk out from backstage and approach Mark and Luke.

"Hi, guys," I say with a bright smile. "What brings you here?"

It's then I notice the stunning blonde sitting to Mark's right, and the baby girl she's holding.

Holy Jesus, Mary and Joseph, he's married with a kid?

And that is the sound of my heart shattering and lying on the ground.

"Hi, Meredith," Luke replies with a smile. Mark's head jerks around as he takes the baby from his wife.

"What are you all doing here?"

"We're here to watch," Luke says and balances a toddler on his knee. "This is my wife, Natalie, and our children, Olivia," he points to the little girl on his lap and then to the sleeping baby nestled in his wife's arms, "and Keaton."

I smile and shake Natalie's hand and then turn my attention to Mark.

"I see congratulations are in order for you too, Mark."

He frowns for just a moment and then seems to remember that he's holding the infant. "Oh! This is Stella," he kisses her head and my chest aches. Oh God, he looks amazing with a baby in his arms. But it's not *our* baby.

Do not cry. Do not freak out. You can get through this. Keep smiling.

"She's beautiful," I choke out in the worst monotone voice I've ever heard. He's watching me carefully and the woman beside him is typing furiously on her phone, then looks up at me and smiles.

"Hi! I'm Jules. Sorry, I was just texting my husband. He's worried about Stella. He always worries." She laughs and tucks her phone in the Louis Vuitton sitting at her feet. "It's really very cute."

"Not your baby, then," I say to Mark and am mortified to hear the relief in my voice.

"No, Nate might have issues if I had children with Mark." Jules laughs and nudges him with her shoulder. "Mark might not survive Nate's wrath if that happened."

"I would be a dead man," Mark agrees with a laugh.

He kisses Stella's head again with that naughty smile on his lips that I've always loved. He looks delicious in a red T-shirt and worn jeans.

"Maddie, Josie and Sophie are my nieces," Jules continues and takes Stella back from Mark. "This is our family."

My eyes follow her gesture and then I feel them just about bug out of my head when about twenty people wave at me, including Brynna and Stacy, whose daughters are in my class.

"You brought the whole family to a dance recital?" I ask in surprise.

"Maddie and Josie pretty much guilt-tripped us all into coming," Mark replies. "Apparently, they'll be heartbroken if everyone isn't here."

"Extortionists," Caleb mutters.

"Hello, everyone. I'm Meredith Summers. I own this studio. Thanks for coming! I hope you enjoy the show."

I turn to leave and am just inside the curtain to backstage when a strong hand grips my arm and spins me around and I'm looking at a very sexy Mark Williams.

"Did you need something?" I ask as calmly as possible. His lips twitch, and I know I'm not fooling him.

"I don't have a wife and kid, Mer."

I shrug a shoulder and gaze blindly around, avoiding his face. "Okay. It's really none of my business."

"No, it's not," he agrees softly. "How are you, M?"

I bite my lip and cross my arms over my chest. "I'm fine. A little busy right now. I'm sorry that I flung myself at you at Mom's funeral, I was just really emotional and—"

"It's okay," he interrupts and shakes his head. God, he grew up nice. He's filled out, his shoulders are broad and strong and his biceps strain against the sleeves of his T. He's grown a couple of inches. His hair is a little longer than he used to wear it, just a little shaggy, like he hasn't had a haircut in a while.

"Well, enjoy the show." I turn to leave but he stops me again with his hand on my arm.

"How's Mr. Wonderful?" he asks abruptly. I scowl up at him.

"Who?"

"Hey, we go on in five, snowball," Jax says as he hurries past. He winks at me and smiles at Mark and hurries away.

"Him," Mark says with a cringe, and it occurs to me that he must think that Jax is my man.

"Jax is fine. He's my partner." Mark nods, and if I'm not mistaken, his eyes look hurt before he blinks and offers me a small smile. "He's my dance and business partner," I clarify.

He tilts his head, watching me.

"He'd be more interested in *you* sexually than he is me."

Mark blinks twice and when the realization of what I'm saying sinks in, a slow wide grin spreads across his handsome face.

"Can I see your phone, please?" he asks and holds his hand out expectantly. I pull my phone out of my pocket and hand it over to him. "You need to key in your passcode," he says dryly. I bite my lip and grin, take the phone back to key in the four-digit code and pass it back. He taps the screen with his thumbs, concentrating with a frown between his eyes.

I have to clench my hands into fists to keep from reaching out and smoothing my fingers over that frown.

"Are we still friends, M?" he asks, his face suddenly very serious and I'm suddenly as sad as I've ever been as my eyes travel over his handsome, familiar face. His deep blue eyes and square jaw. Full lips. Blond hair.

"We're not friends, Mark," I reply sadly. "We're strangers with memories."

He nods and looks down at my phone still in his grasp. He passes it back to me with a half-smile that makes my stomach and thighs clench. "Let's see what we can do about that. My number is in there. The next step is up to you."

He winks and turns away just as Jax pulls on my hand, catching my attention. "Come on, it's time."

I nod and shake my head, shaking Mark off as I stuff my phone back in my pocket and get back to business. I have twenty little girls who want to show off for their parents.

And apparently all of their aunts and uncles too.

"Come on, ladies! It's time to show 'em what you've got! Don't forget what Jax and I told you about breathing and focusing on me. I'll be out in the audience, helping you remember the steps, but you won't need me. Okay?"

They all nod with great big eyes and I smile encouragingly. This is one of my favorite parts of this job. Jax leads the girls to the stage and I take my place in the audience, standing near the stage so the little ones can see me. The music begins and camera flashes start going crazy around me as parents take photos of their little girls twirl and smile on stage, waving at their moms and dads. Sophie smiles big and says, "Hi, Daddy!"

They are so freaking adorable.

When their two songs are over, they wave and leave the stage and a few moments later the older girls replace them on the stage.

They're so funny as they try to act more sophisticated, remembering their steps and singing along with Kelly Clarkson as she sings about being stronger.

There are loud applause and whistles when the number is over, then all of the girls come back out on stage for one more dance.

When all is said and done, the girls are bursting with excitement, so happy about how their performance went. Jax and I are given lots of hugs and kisses on the cheek.

"I love you, Miss Mer," Maddie Montgomery says and wraps her arms around my neck. "I want to be a dancer just like you and Mr. Jax when I grow up."

"You do?" I chuckle and hug her back hard. "I know you can make that happen, sweet girl. You are a talented young lady."

"Really?" She braces her hands on my shoulders and gazes at me with wonder.

"Absolutely." I nod with confidence and smile widely.

"Will you help me?"

"I would love that."

She smiles again and runs to her daddy, Caleb, who is cradling a newborn baby against his big chest.

The man is massive, making the tiny baby look even smaller against him.

"Who is this?" I ask and point to the baby.

"This is our new baby brother," Josie says proudly and Caleb smiles kindly down at me.

"The program was great," Brynna says. The new mom looks fantastic.

"Thank you. When did you have him?" I pat his little diaper-covered bottom, but stay back. Babies kind of scare me.

"A month ago," she replies and gazes lovingly at her son.

"His name is Michael," Maddie says.

"That's a great name," I reply. "Congratulations, you guys."

"Thank you," Caleb replies and kisses his son's head. Geez, all these hot men with babies are making me squirmy.

I turn to look for Jax and instead find Mark walking toward the exit. He's going to leave without saying goodbye again? I shouldn't be disappointed, but I can't help it. But then, as if he can sense me, he turns back and smiles at me, nods and points to my pocket where my phone is, and disappears through the door.

***

"So, tell me about Mr. Hot Tamale," Jax says and passes me the vinaigrette dressing for our salads.

"Who?"

"Don't play coy with me. That tall drink of water you were talking with today. He was the same guy at the funeral."

We settle in the living room, me on the couch and Jax on the floor with our grilled chicken salad and water.

"That's Mark."

His fork stills midway between his plate and mouth and he stares at me. "He's *that* Mark?"

"The one and the same," I reply and take a bite of salad.

"I knew I couldn't get lucky enough for him to be gay." He shakes his head in disgust and continues eating. Jax is a hot guy. Tall with dark hair and eyes, chiseled face and body. He's perfect physically, even at thirty. He could have kept dancing another year or two but he chose to retire and come back to Seattle with me when Mom got sick last year.

He's also the best friend I've ever had. We met my first week in New York and we've stuck together ever since. We've been through everything together: Auditions. Gigs. Lovers.

All the drama that comes with the dance world.

He's my brother in every way that counts.

"He's definitely not gay," I mutter and drink half the water bottle in one guzzle.

"He's into you," he says and watches me closely.

"Used to be, Jax. Used to be."

"No, he *is*."

I raise my eyebrows and stare at him like he's crazy. "He doesn't *know* me anymore."

"He'd like to get to know you again, sugarbaby." He points his fork at me and keeps talking with a mouthful of food. "Trust me. I know what a man in lust looks like."

"I'm sure you do, man whore."

"That stings."

"Only because it's true."

Jax laughs and shrugs. "Okay, it's true. So, see? I know what it looks like."

I finish my salad and set the plate aside then pull my hair up in a ponytail with my hands and lean my head back on the couch.

"Mark and I were a long time ago." Yet when I'm standing next to him, it feels like yesterday. It feels like *home*.

"I saw that look of mutiny in your eyes today when you thought he had a wife and kid," Jax says and sets his plate aside.

"It was just a gut reaction," I insist but Jax shakes his head.

"You gave a shit about him, Mer. You still do. Just admit it."

I blow out a long breath and hate the heaviness I feel on my chest. "I do."

"Do you know how to contact him?"

"He gave me his number today," I reply absently and pick at a string in the cushion of the couch. "I don't know if I should call him. We were kids, Jax. Babies. It was forever ago."

"So what?" He shrugs. "You're not babies now. If you still feel something, why not call him? Get to know each other. Maybe you'll discover that he turned into an asshole and you can put the whole thing to rest."

"He's not an asshole," I reply with a laugh. "That I know for sure. Mom wouldn't have loved an asshole."

"Look, the way you explained it to me that time we got drunk and poured our hearts out to each other that night we both blew the *Annie* audition, you were the one to break his heart, not the other way around. So, if *he's* willing to give it another shot, maybe you should give it a shot too."

"Who are you? Dr. Phil?"

"I'm much better looking than Dr. Phil," he replies. "Don't insult me."

"I'm busy with the studio now. Business is crazy and I'm taking on more one-on-one clients too, and you're starting that choreography job at the university soon." I sound like an idiot to my own ears.

"Is it the sex you're worried about?" he asks with a smart-assy frown. "Here, I'll help. Sex 101."

"Stop it." I giggle and kick out at him, missing him by a good eight feet.

"How to give a hand job."

"Stop talking!" I am laughing hard now, loving Jax for being fun and hilarious.

"Step one: use your mouth."

"Oh my God!" I laugh and laugh and Jax joins me, flashing that perfect, white smile.

"I'm not worried about the sex." *Not very worried.*

"It's been a while for you. I understand."

I stick my tongue out at him and watch as he starts to laugh again.

"I'm so happy that I amuse you."

"You do, cupcake. You really do." He takes a deep breath and then sobers. "Call him. You could use a little excitement in your life."

"Maybe." I pull the throw pillow against my chest and sigh. "I'll think about it."

"Think about getting some new throw pillows while you're at it. Those are hideous."

"I told you that we could go furniture shopping whenever you want."

"Okay, we'll go this weekend then."

I nod, then climb to my feet and stretch my arms over my head. "I'm going to take a shower and call it a night."

"Running with me in the morning?"

"Yeah. Wake me up."

"Set your fucking alarm. You throw shit at me when I wake you up."

I wave at him and walk away without answering. He'll wake me up. He does every morning.

The shower is hot and perfect and I stay under the water a good ten minutes longer than I need to before washing my face, shaving my legs and turning the water off.

I dry my body, blow my hair dry and pull on a tank and short shorts before climbing onto my bed and tug my iPad to me to go over the schedule for the rest of the month.

My phone is mocking me. Mark's number is *right there*. How many times over the past ten years did I lie in bed at night and wish with all my might that I could call him and hear his voice just once?

After two years I mustered up all of the nerve I could and dialed his number, but it had been disconnected.

And now I have his number and he *encouraged* me to call.

I bite my lip and lift my phone, staring at his number in my contacts. He not only punched in his number, but instead of typing in his whole name, it just says, *M*.

I swear I can hear my mother in my head saying, "You only live once, baby girl. Just call the boy."

Before I can second-guess myself, I press the green *send* button and hold my breath as I wait for him to answer.

But he doesn't. An automated voice comes on the line saying that the person at this number isn't available.

I end the call rather than leave a message. My shoulders sag in disappointment, but I shrug one shoulder and set my phone aside then return my concentration on my iPad.

Less than one minute later, my phone rings.

M.

"Hello?"

"Tell me this is Meredith," he says. He's panting and I can't help but wonder what he's been doing.

Or who.

"What if I say it's *not* Meredith?" I ask with a grin.

"Then I'll be pissed that I ran away from remodeling my bathroom to call this number back. I need my shower back."

I have a shower you can use.

I almost say it out loud but catch myself. We're not there yet.

"Remodeling your bathroom, are you?"

"So this *is* Meredith then?"

"Like you couldn't recognize my voice."

He chuckles and I hear him swallowing. God, I bet his throat looks amazing when he drinks water.

"You said I should call," I begin a bit uncertainly.

"Yes, I did. Do you have plans tonight?"

I look around my bedroom and laugh in spite of myself. "Yes, I'm in bed working."

"Hmm, dancing in bed is always fun."

"No, the business side of it, funny guy." Oh, how I've missed this funny side of him. "I was going to call it an early night."

"Running in the morning?"

"You remember my running routine?" I ask in surprise.

"I remember everything, M."

I bite my lip as tears fill my eyes. "Me too."

"I work tomorrow," he mutters and I can just hear the wheels turning in his head. "But I am free tomorrow night and I have the day after off."

"My schedule is the same," I reply.

"I'll pick you up tomorrow evening around seven?"

I pause, the words *come over now* hovering on my tongue, but I suppose I can wait until tomorrow to see him.

I've waited for ten freaking years.

"Mer?"

"Yes, that's fine."

"Great. I'll see you then."

"Wait, I need to give you my address."

"You're not at your mom's?"

"No, I sold the house. I'm in Seattle. Jax and I share an apartment not far from the studio. It's easier."

"You share an apartment with Jax?" His voice is suddenly harder and I can't help but smile in satisfaction.

I'm not the only one who's jealous.

"Yes, we do. Different bedrooms, M."

"Okay. Text me your address and I'll see you tomorrow night."

"Are you sure about this?" My voice is quiet.

"Never been more sure."

"Okay." I nod once. "It's a date."

CHAPTER THREE

~Mark~

Twelve hours. I only have to get through the next twelve hours and I'll have Meredith all to myself.

Jesus, I'm so fucking nervous it's ridiculous. I've been with my share of women over the past decade, and not one of them made my palms clammy or my stomach clench.

Because they didn't matter.

And Mer matters.

I pull up to the construction site and park. I'm early, as usual. I want to check the site, progress and quality of work being done before the rest of the crew arrives.

I've worked as a site foreman for Isaac Montgomery since I moved back home almost two years ago. I love my job. I'm fucking good at my job. I have an excellent crew, but I don't put up with bullshit, and they know it.

It works well for us.

Just as I make a full circle around the outside of the multi-million dollar home we're building just north of Seattle on the coast, Isaac pulls up in his truck.

"Not in your office today?" I ask and cross to him. He's holding two Starbucks cups and passes one to me.

"On site today. Brynna has the office covered." He shakes my hand and glances up to the house. "This is coming along nicely."

"Thanks. I was just about to go inside. Want the grand tour?"

"Let's do it," he agrees and follows me through the front entrance. The door hasn't been hung yet, and when I glance around the inside of the great room, my eyes narrow menacingly.

"Fuck," Isaac whispers.

Someone snuck in during the night and spray painted one of the walls with gang graffiti. Thankfully, the drywall hasn't been hung yet either, and we can easily cover this up.

"Fucking kids," I growl and shake my head.

"I'll call Matt and have him arrange to have this neighborhood patrolled more regularly," he says grimly, referring to his younger brother, one of Seattle's best detectives.

"I'll make sure the doors and windows are installed today so it'll be locked up from now on," I reply.

Isaac nods and follows me as I walk through the eight thousand square foot home.

"This is going to be impressive," Isaac says.

"I agree. It's one of the biggest I've ever built, that's for sure." When we walk back out through the front entrance, we both sit on the temporary concrete steps and sip our coffee. "How are the other sites coming along?"

"No complaints today," he replies and then shakes his head. "Except that remodel at Alki. The owner has changed her mind on the master shower four motherfucking times."

"Seriously?" I laugh and sip my coffee. "That sucks."

"It's her money." Isaac shrugs as if he just can't figure her out. "I'd like to wrap that one up so we can move on to the next."

"How are Stacy and the kids?"

"Perfect," he replies easily with a satisfied grin. For the first time in my life,

I'm jealous of Isaac and our brothers and their families. "Stacy is beautiful and busy with Soph and Liam."

I nod and watch as some of the crew begins to pull in, gathering their tool belts and other gear from the beds of their trucks.

"You coming to Will's on Sunday?" Isaac asks.

"What's happening on Sunday?"

"Last minute family cookout." He shrugs and then chuckles. "The weather is heating up, so I think everyone wants to take advantage of being outside."

"Sounds cool." I pause and then decide *fuck it*. "Think it's cool if I bring someone?"

Isaac's head whips around and his eyes are surprised when he asks, "Who?"

"An old friend," I reply softly and then swear under my breath, uncomfortable as fuck at the way he's watching me. "Meredith."

"Since when do you bring women to family functions?" he asks incredulously then laughs. "I so want to bust your balls about this, but I'll be the mature one and simply say, yeah. It's fine. Will and the others will not let you off the hook so easily, my friend."

"I don't care."

And it's true. I don't. I just want her with me.

Jesus, I'm getting way ahead of myself here. We haven't been out on a date yet.

Patience never was a virtue I possessed.

"I'll invite her," I say and crush my empty coffee cup in my fist.

"Is she the reason?" he asks softly and doesn't turn his head to look at me. He doesn't clarify, not that I need him to. He just sits quietly and waits for me to answer, watching the cup in his hands.

"Yeah." My voice is quiet and I sigh deeply. "Once upon a time, she was everything."

"Good luck, man."

I nod and stand with him as the others join us on the steps.

"What's on tap for today, boss?"

"Doors and windows," I begin and push thoughts of Meredith aside for later as I get to work.

***

I knock on Mer's apartment door and shift back and forth on my feet. I haven't been this nervous since the very first time I picked her up for a date early in our Junior year.

I've come a long way since then.

Suddenly the door is wrenched open and Jax is standing there with a wide smile.

"Hey," he says.

"Hi. I'm here to pick up Meredith."

"Mr. Delicious is here for your date, tootsie roll!" Jax yells.

"I'm right here, dork," Meredith says as she slips under his arm out into the hallway. "Ignore him. He has horrible manners."

"Have fun," Jax continues, leaning on the doorjamb with his arms crossed and watching us walk to the elevator. I brace my hand on the small of her back and feel the electricity travel up my arm and down to my groin. After all this time, the chemistry is still here. "You have her home at a decent time, now. I'll leave the light on."

"Shut up, Jax," Mer says with a laugh.

"Use condoms!" He calls just as the elevator arrives.

"Oh my God! Shut the hell up, Jax!"

He laughs as the doors close and I can only smile in delight down at her. Her cheeks are pink with embarrassment. Her hair is pulled up in one of her signature messy buns and she's in jeans and a blue sweater the same color as her eyes.

Jesus, she's fucking gorgeous.

"You look amazing," I say and rub a large circle over her slender back.

"So do you," she murmurs and looks up and down at my plain black T-shirt and jeans. I threw a plaid button down over the T, but her eyes travel to my arms anyway.

She always did have a thing for my arms.

"Thanks for coming out with me tonight."

"Thanks for inviting me," she replies with a grin. "Where are we going?"

"You'll see." I lead her out to my Jeep, help her in and jump in the driver's side. Before pulling away, I look over at her and consider pulling her in for a quick kiss, but I know that once I start kissing her, I won't want to stop, and there's too much to say before we go there.

If she's interested in going there.

"What's wrong?" she asks as she clutches her black handbag tightly in her lap, as though she's as nervous as I am.

"Nothing at all," I reply with a shake of my head and pull out into traffic toward our old neighborhood. We drive in relative quiet, both lost in our own thoughts, and maybe a little nervous about what we should say. I have so many questions, but for now I'm content to have her next to me as I pull into our special place and cut the engine.

"Our pier," she whispers softly.

"Yeah," I reply and turn to her. "I brought dinner. I thought we could sit out here and talk, if that's okay."

"It's going to get cold," she begins, but I cut her off with a shake of my head.

"I brought extra blankets. We'll be warm."

She bites her lip, looks out at the water and the homes along the lake and then back at me with a watery smile. "I love it."

I brush my knuckles down her cheek and then reluctantly pull away. Jesus, I just want to keep touching her. Everywhere.

I grab the cooler full of dinner from the back and lead her to the end of the dock that we sat on for hours on end more than ten years ago.

"God, how many hours did we spend out here?" she asks, mirroring my thoughts.

"Hundreds," I reply and spread a thick quilt over the wooden pier, right at the edge and gesture for her to sit. It's just starting to get dark and the lights around the lake are twinkling. A sailboat drifts by slowly and we wave at the captain. "Are you hungry?"

"Starving," she says with a smile. "What did you bring me?"

"Salmon with salad and water and chocolate cupcakes for dessert."

"Gimme."

I chuckle and plate her meal, then my own and we eat in silence, watching the water.

"Still quiet out here," she says.

"Mm." I nod and watch her as she finishes her fish and salad and sets her plate back inside the cooler then takes my empty plate to join hers. "How are you, M?"

Her hands still for a moment, then she turns to me, pulls her knees to her chest and wraps her arms around her legs. "I'm getting better. It's been a rough few months."

I nod and frown. "I miss her too. Did she ever tell you that I still came to see her over the years whenever I was in town?"

"No." She shakes her head sadly. "She knew that talking about you hurt me, so she never brought it up."

I blink and watch her beautiful face. "I saw her at least once a year. I'd make repairs on the house and help her out in any way I could."

"Thank you for that," she whispers. "Mark, I'm sorry for the way it ended—"

"Stop." I take her hand in mine and kiss her knuckles. "There's nothing to apologize for, M. It was a long time ago."

She nods and bites her lip but then shakes her head and presses on. "No, I need to say this. It's important to me." She squares her shoulders and clears her throat and I just lean back on my hands and listen. "I know it's been a long time, but we never talked after that day, M. I didn't *want* to break it off. I knew that that's what I was doing, but it killed me. I'd been in dance class one day, and I wasn't concentrating, and the teacher called me out on it. She knew I was daydreaming, and explained that I needed to get my head in the game." She frowns and shifts like she can't get comfortable, then shrugs. "I just knew that we were so young, and that if dance was what I wanted, I had to go for it."

"I get it, Mer." I push a piece of hair that's fallen out of her bun behind her ear. "We were young. Chances are we would have broken up eventually. It hurt like crazy at the time, but hindsight is 20/20, right?"

She nods and releases her legs, crossing them in front of her.

"Tell me about New York," I say unexpectedly, surprising us both, but I realize, I want to know everything about our time apart. Every detail. "Start at the beginning and tell me everything."

"Really? You want to know?"

"Absolutely." I let her hand go and take a sip of my water as I watch her gather her thoughts.

"I didn't want to get on that plane," she begins softly, her eyes off in the distance, watching the lights of the boats on the water. I can't look away from her. Fuck, I'm still pulled to her in a way I've never been able to explain. It was there when I was seventeen damn years old, and it's just as strong now. "It was torture, knowing I was leaving you. The first week was scary and so much harder than I ever thought it would be."

She swallows and glances at me, then back at the boats, like she's nervous, so I scoot next to her and link her fingers with mine.

"I found an apartment and started dancing right away. From day one, it was twelve to fourteen hour days, dancing pretty much nonstop. I met Jax that first week too." She smiles as she thinks back on that time. "He was a couple years older, but also new to the area, so we bonded. He has quite the story to tell." She frowns suddenly and then turns those baby blues up to mine. "Maybe someday he'll tell you about it. Anyway, we worked pretty much all the time. Classes went late into the evening, so sometimes we'd just sleep there at the studio and then get up in the morning and start all over again."

Holy shit. I knew it would be a lot of work, but I had no idea it was all-encompassing. Is this what she tried to tell me that day on her porch?

"I thought my body was conditioned for it, but I hurt everywhere for a year solid. My feet, my joints, my mind. I was constantly exhausted. The auditions were nerve-wracking. I ended up in some small parts in shows. I did the Grammys and Tonys and began to make a name for myself in the community." She smiles proudly and I squeeze her hand.

"I'm so proud of you, M."

"Thank you. It was a lot of work. Physical and mental. So much fucking competition. And oh my God, the things girls will do for parts! They'll sleep with anyone!"

I immediately tense up and she laughs. "No, M, not me. But I admit, as I got older and the younger ones would come along, sniffing around a director or producer, my back immediately came up and I was like, 'Oh no you don't. You're not going to sleep your way into my part.'"

"How did you end up touring?" I ask.

"You knew about that?"

"I paid attention," I reply.

"Jax. He's an awesome choreographer. The best there is. He choreographed shows for Justin, Beyonce and Pink. And then one day, Starla called."

She smiles, lost in thought. Starla is a megastar, and I know that Mer toured with her for quite some time.

"Starla wanted Jax to choreograph her *Belladonna* tour, and he insisted that she hire us both, since we usually work together, especially when it comes to couples choreography, and she agreed. We had that gig for about four years." She grins and takes a sip of water. "We traveled the world, M. I didn't see much of it, because we worked so much, but it was fun to perform in front of all of those people every night. And Starla is just spectacular. What a performer. She works just as hard, if not harder than the rest of us."

"You became friends."

"We did." She nods and shivers. I check my watch and realize that we've already been here for a couple hours. I grab a blanket for each of us, wrap one around Mer and then one around myself and sit, ready to listen to more. "And then Mom got sick." Her voice turns softer and more distant, and she's still watching the water like she's watching it all play out like a movie. "I knew I had to come home. At first she didn't want me to. She insisted that she was okay, and honestly if she'd still had Dad or Tiff here, I probably wouldn't have come home when I did, but she had no one, M."

I nod and rub her back soothingly, letting her talk.

"I was close to retirement age anyway."

"You were twenty-seven." My voice sounds exasperated to my own ears.

"Most dancers peak at twenty-five." She shrugs, as if it is what it is. "Touring life gets old after a while, and Mom needed me."

"Why did Jax come with you?"

"He's older than me, and we'd been together since week one." She bites her lip and watches me quietly for a moment. "Jax is the closest thing I've had to a sibling since Tiff died, M. We'd talked about opening a studio for a long time, and it felt like this was the time. And I'm glad we did. The studio is doing really well."

"One more thing that I'm proud of you for," I reply and kiss her knuckles again. "Keep going," I say.

"Well, that's pretty much it. The CliffsNotes version, anyway."

"Will you go on tour again?" I hold my breath, waiting for her answer. *Please say no.*

"No," she shakes her head. "That time of my life is done. We have been asked to choreograph Starla's routine for the VMA's next month, so we'll be in LA for a few days for that, but things like that will be hit and miss. Our business is here."

"Why does Jax call you all of the crazy nicknames?" I ask.

"Oh." She swallows and cringes. "Well, eating disorders are pretty common in the dance world. That's no secret."

My hands fist in spite of myself and my whole body stills as I think of her hurting herself that way.

"Don't worry, I didn't get caught in that trap. Well," she cringes again and bites her lip. "There was one director who was just a hard ass. More so than anyone else. He told me I was too big in the boob area." She rolls her eyes. "I can't help that I have boobs. But I thought that if I went on a diet, I might loose some weight. Jax caught on and gave me a verbal tongue lashing."

"Good for him," I murmur, pissed that anyone would even *think* that Meredith is fat. If anything, she's always been too slender.

"That director made snide comments about my chest almost every day. It was hell. But I was determined that he wasn't going to make me quit. I worked my ass off on that job. Years later, he called and asked me to audition for another role, and I turned him down."

"I bet that felt good." God, she's so fucking amazing. She's turned into such a strong, confident woman.

"It was awesome to tell him to kiss my fat ass." She giggles and leans her head on my shoulder. "So, ever since then, Jax calls me things like twinkie and cheesecake. It's just a joke."

"He seems like a funny guy."

"One of the reasons we're friends," she says with a grin. "He makes me laugh. And he puts up with my moody shit. And there's no chance in hell he'll ever hit on me."

"And for that, he's *my* new best friend as well."

She laughs and then grows quiet. The boats have slowed down and the crickets and frogs around us are talking. It's late in the evening now, but I have no intention to leave any time soon.

"And you? What are you doing with that impressive science degree of yours?"

"How did you know I got a science degree?"

"We still know a lot of the same people, you know."

I take a deep breath and nod. "I'm not doing a damn thing with it. I worked on fishing boats in Alaska for a while, and now I'm working construction."

"Okay, that's the extreme CliffsNotes version. Expand, please."

I sigh and push my hand through my messy hair. Fuck, I need a haircut. I always need a haircut.

"My degree was in aerospace engineering."

"Holy shit," she replies with wide eyes. "You're a fucking rocket scientist?"

"No, I'm not. Haven't you been listening?"

"That's just semantics. You could be a rocket scientist. How did you manage to do that so quickly?"

I shrug and watch an owl fly over the lake. "After you left, all I did was study. I worked my ass off to get through college as quickly as possible. I was consumed with formulas and algorithms and if I was exhausted from school and work, I couldn't concentrate on missing you."

I cringe and look over to see her eyes fill with tears again. "It's okay, M," she whispers. "It's the truth. I did the same with dance."

"So, I got my undergrad and master's in five years and then decided I didn't want to live in a lab. I went to Alaska with a buddy of mine from college one summer. He worked the boats to put himself through college. I liked the solitude of it. I made good money."

"Isn't that dangerous?" Her eyes are wide as she watches me.

"It can be." I'm not about to tell her about the times that I was so scared my bowels wanted to give out on me. No need to burden her with that.

"What brought you back to Seattle?" She lies on her side, her head supported on her elbow and watches me silently.

"My brother got married to Natalie and it just seemed like there was a lot going on with my family that I'd be missing."

"Luke has a beautiful family," she replies, that wistful tone back in her voice.

"They're amazing," I reply softly and let my eyes travel over her beautiful face. "The Montgomerys have become part of our family too. So, I decided I'd been away from home long enough and came back a couple years ago, around the time Jules and Nate married. Jules' oldest brother owns a construction company and I run one of his crews."

"I'm surprised."

My eyes find hers as I cock an eyebrow. "Why?"

"You loved science."

"I loved you more," I reply without thinking and then wish I could pull the words back and throw them in the water.

Real smooth, Williams.

She clenches her eyes closed and then sits up and gazes over at me. "Do you know, *whenever* I got nervous, whether it was in an audition, or right before a show... whatever, it was your voice I heard? *Breathe with me, M.* I clung to that more times than I can tell you. You were with me, every day. Even when I tried to forget you."

"Were there other men?" I ask with a steel in my voice I can't hide.

"It's been ten years. Are you going to tell me you never slept with anyone in ten years?"

I blink at her and then look out at the water myself. "No, I can't tell you that."

"I'm not going to give you a play by play, M, because I don't want that from you either. It would fucking kill me." Her voice is strong and sure when I turn my gaze back to hers. "But I'll say this: you will never know how much I wished for you. Even though I knew it was selfish and wrong, I just wanted *you.*"

I open my blanket and pull her against me, rest my lips on her forehead and relish how it feels to have her in my arms. She buries her face in my neck, the way she always did, and takes in a long, deep breath.

"Do you still want me?" I ask, not sure if I really want to hear the answer.

"Every. Day. It's hard to forget someone who gave you so much to remember." She burrows deeper, clinging to me. "What about you?"

"There were days," I begin softly and rub my nose against her soft hair, "that

I would have exchanged a year of my life just to touch you one more time. You are my biggest *what if*, M."

We sit in silence, clinging to each other for a long time, breathing each other in and enjoying the night around us.

"How is it possible that you still smell the same?" she finally asks brokenly. I smile against her temple and then kiss her there.

"I thought the same exact thing when you hugged me at Addie's funeral."

"Mark, where do we go from here?"

I tip her chin back to look in her eyes. They're full of unshed tears and confusion. Fuck, I'm confused too.

"Do you want to start over? Get to know each other again?" I swallow hard and watch her bite that gorgeous lower lip. "We're not the same people we were then, M."

"The chemistry is still here," she replies dryly.

I nod, but I can't help but wonder, is it chemistry? Or is this just simply meant to be?

"I would like that," she replies. "I'd like that very much."

Her eyes fall to my lips, and I can't stand it any more. Those lips would tempt a saint. I lower my head and brush my lips over hers softly. Once, twice, then nibble the corner of her mouth. She sighs and moans softly, cups my face in her small hands and kisses me back. God, she feels so fucking good pressed up against me, her nipples puckered and rubbing against my chest as she pushes against me, trying to get closer.

She opens her mouth for me, and my tongue tangles with hers and suddenly we're kissing as if no time has passed at all. My hands remember where to hold her and her hands plunge into my hair and hold on tight, the way they always did. She sighs as my hands glide down her back to her hips and back up to her face as I pull back reluctantly.

"God, I missed kissing you," I murmur.

She kisses my nose and then tips her forehead against mine. "It's late enough that no one is out here to see us," she says with a naughty smile.

"Jesus, you'd tempt an angel into hell." I growl and push my hands under her sweater, gliding them up and down her bare back, over the thin strap of her bra. "But I'll be damned if the first time I make love with you again is on this fucking pier."

"When did you get such a potty mouth?" she asks with a laugh and kisses my cheek, still pushing her fingers through my hair.

"Many years on a fishing boat with a bunch of men," I reply with a chuckle. "Plus, now I spend a lot of time with the Montgomerys and they're nothing but potty mouths."

"They seem like a great family." I pull back to look into her eyes at the wistful tone of her voice.

"We're all getting together on Sunday. Come with me."

It's not a fucking request.

She blinks rapidly and shakes her head. "Um, we just—"

"I want you there," I whisper and drag my fingertips gently down her cheek. "Please."

"This is moving fast."

"We're just making up for lost time, baby."

She wraps her arms around my neck and hugs me tight, buries her face in my neck and squeezes. "I'll go."

I grin and hug her back. "Look." She pulls back and follows my outstretched arm. "The sun's coming up."

"Holy shit, we were out here that long?"

"We had a lot of catching up to do," I reply and lie back on the dock, cradling Mer on my chest. I wrap the blanket tightly around us and kiss her head as we watch the sky begin to wake up.

"I should get home. Jax probably tried to call. I left my phone in the Jeep."

"You're a grown woman and Jax can stay out of it," I reply. "But you'll need your sleep."

"Come home with me," she says spontaneously. "No sex, I swear."

"Well, that's no fun."

She laughs and pinches my arm. "Let's take a nap and then I'll cook you breakfast and we can go to a movie or something. Unless you had something else planned for your day off?"

I think of all the things I need to get done today, including the touch up work on my bathroom, and then shove it all aside.

"I don't have anything more important planned than that nap and catching a movie with you."

"Let's go." She stands and helps me fold the blankets.

"How firm are you on the no sex part of this plan?" I ask her with hope in my eyes.

"Meh." She shrugs and tilts her hand back and forth, as if to say *so-so*.

"So you're saying there's a chance," I reply with the most charming smile I can muster.

"I always loved that naughty smile of yours."

"Oh, baby, just wait until you see all the other naughty things I can do."

CHAPTER FOUR

-Meredith-

I wake slowly and blink at the sunlight falling over my face. I'm warm. Too warm, but I realize it's not just from the sunshine.

There's a very big, very warm man pressed up against my back, his arm wrapped around my waist, holding me tightly to him even in sleep. As warm as I am, there's no way in hell I'm moving out of his arms.

Last night rushes back to me, and all I can do is sigh. It's as though a heavy burden has been lifted. We've put the past behind us and can look forward. He's a rocket scientist. He's lived in Alaska and had so many amazing experiences since I last saw him.

He's grown up. But so have I, and I can't wait to start getting to know each other all over again.

There were days I would have traded a year of my life to touch you again. My eyes fill with tears again, and I can't help but turn to face him, waking him up. He inhales deeply, his eyes still closed, and kisses my forehead.

Is he really here?

His chin is covered in stubble, begging for my hands to rub over it. His lips are full and soft, and his blond hair is a riot of mess, even messier than normal.

We're both still fully dressed. Even as exhausted as we were, I didn't trust myself to sleep in my skivvies with him. I'm finding it impossible to keep my hands off him. I've always been attracted to Mark, from the moment our eyes met across that science classroom all those years ago. But Mark as a grown man is a sight to fucking behold.

I sweep my hand down his neck, over his shoulder and down his arm, pausing where his T-shirt ends over his biceps.

Jesus, the man's arms should come with a warning label. May cause panties to spontaneously combust.

"Go back to sleep," he whispers and kisses my forehead again. I lift my eyes to his to see his bright blue gaze peering down at me through heavy eyelids.

"You have great arms."

He growls and quickly rolls on top of me, resting on his elbows at either side of my head, brushing my hair off my face with his fingertips lazily. He sweeps his nose against mine and kisses me softly, still not quite fully awake.

"You're gorgeous in the morning," he says and nibbles his way down my jawline. I feel his dick grow hard against my core through his jeans and I can't help but wiggle, just a bit, trying to get closer. "And if you keep that up, we won't leave this bed today."

"I want to cook you breakfast." I glance over at my alarm clock. "Make that lunch. And I want to go to the movies."

"I want to strip you naked and kiss every inch of your incredible body." My nipples pebble and I bite my lip as he pushes back to look down at me. "I want you, M."

"I know, and trust me, I want you too." I bury my fingers through his hair and smile up at him softly. "Let's just take today and play. I want to laugh with you today. We used to laugh all the time."

"That's because you're silly," he says and kisses my palm twice before rolling us back to our sides.

"I'm not going anywhere," I say seriously. His eyes jerk back to mine, and I know that there is doubt there. I drag my fingertips down his rough cheek, over his bottom lip. "I'm not going anywhere. I'm all yours, M."

"Fuck yes, you are." He kisses me with dominance, claiming me like he never did before, and it makes my body come alive against him, but he slowly backs away and glides his hand down my neck, to my breast, over my nipple and to my ribcage. "We'd better get out of this bed before I say fuck it and strip you naked, baby."

I smile wickedly and bite his chin gently. "Yes, sir."

He slaps my ass playfully as I roll away and step out of bed. I immediately stretch, like I do every morning, reaching my arms up to the sky, then bending to press my palms flat on the ground next to my feet.

"Showing me your perfect ass isn't helping, Mer."

I toss a smile over my shoulder and shake my head. "Do you only think of sex?"

"No, sex is not all I think about." That naughty smile spreads across his handsome face. "I also think about you naked."

"Come on, horn dog. I'll make BLT's."

"You eat bacon?" he asks in surprise as he pulls himself out of the bed.

"Turkey bacon."

"What the fuck is turkey bacon?" He wrinkles his nose like I just told him it was tofu bacon.

"It's bacon made out of turkey."

"Then it's not bacon." He props his hands on his hips and I start to salivate. *Jesus, Mary and Joseph the man fills out a pair of jeans nicely.*

"You'll like it."

"Just call it a TLT," he insists and follows me out to the kitchen.

"A what?" I laugh.

"A turkey, lettuce and tomato."

"Whatever makes you feel better," I reply and smile when I see Jax sitting in the kitchen sipping water and reading a fitness magazine. "Good morning."

"It's afternoon. What time did you get home?" he asks and eyes Mark suspiciously.

"Does she have a curfew?" Mark asks coldly, glaring at Jax.

"No, but she does require respect, and keeping her out all night and then sleeping with her isn't respecting her, dude."

"No one," Mark replies with fire shooting from his eyes as he advances on Jax, pushing his face close to his, "respects Meredith more than I do. You don't know our history."

"I know plenty," Jax replies softly, never breaking eye contact with Mark. "And I know I'm watching you."

Surprisingly, Mark sticks his hand out to shake Jax's. "Thank you for protecting her," he says quietly.

"I love her," Jax replies honestly.

Mark nods, glances at me and then leans in to whisper something to Jax that I can't hear.

"Fair enough," Jax replies with a nod.

"Uh, can we forgo the pissing contest, boys?" I ask dryly. "No need to worry, Jax. We got in early this morning." I pin him with my best *butt out, everything is fine* glare and turn to the fridge to find what I need to make lunch. "We're going to a movie later. Wanna go?"

"I'd love to, lollypop, but I have a date." He grins and throws his magazine on the countertop, then leans back and crosses his arms.

"I haven't got my *Men's Fitness* in the mail yet," Mark says and reaches for the magazine, but I put my hand up, halting all conversation.

"Wait. Back up. A date with who?"

"You don't know him." Jax shakes his head and starts to walk out of the kitchen, but I grip his T-shirt in my fist from behind, bringing him to a stop.

"Wait. I need details. I can't just let you go out with some guy off the street."

"I don't think he's homeless, Mer," Jax replies sarcastically and Mark snickers.

"You know what I mean."

"Leave it alone. If it turns into anything other than sex, I'll tell you more."

I cross my arms over my chest and glare at my friend. We always talk about who we're dating. "Use condoms."

"Always." He winks and saunters out of the kitchen, then turns back abruptly. "Don't forget, we have rehearsal for Starla's piece Monday before class."

"I won't forget," I reply and wave him off. "What did you whisper to him?"

"Guy stuff," Mark replies and leans his hips against the granite countertop, watching me slice a tomato.

"You're not going to tell me?"

"Nope."

"Fine." I roll my eyes and assemble our sandwiches. "Do you want some watermelon with yours?"

"Sure."

We eat in silence, watching each other. When he swallows, his neck muscles flex, and I can't help but want to lick him there.

I'm so gonna lick him there.

"What are you thinking?" he asks as he tilts his head to the side.

"Nothing."

"You just blushed and blinked fast. You were thinking something."

I lick my lips and then just smile and shrug. "I was thinking about licking your neck."

He stops chewing and stares at me for a long minute, then swallows hard, like the food in his mouth is suddenly dry and tosses the rest of our lunch in the garbage.

"We need to get out of here."

"Why?"

"Because I'm two seconds away from carrying you back to your room and saying fuck the movie. Let's go." He holds his hand out for mine, and when our fingers lace, he leads me out of the apartment and down to his Jeep.

"What movie do you want to see?" he asks as he drives into downtown Seattle and finds parking.

"Hmm... something either funny or full of action."

"No chick flicks?" he asks in surprise.

"No way. Nothing mushy."

"You're my kind of girl."

"I'm so glad to hear that," I reply with a laugh and follow Mark into the movie theater. He buys our tickets for something called *Waterfall*.

"I've heard good things about this one! It's the new action movie with Mark Wahlberg, right?"

"Yep," he confirms. "Luke produced it."

"He did? Holy shit, that's cool."

Mark smiles proudly and waits in line with me for some popcorn. "Do you still mix M&M's in your popcorn?"

"Of course," I reply.

We gather our snacks and choose seats toward the back of the theater.

"So Luke's been producing for a while," I comment casually and pour my plain M&M's into the bucket of popcorn. "You used to bring me M&M's to school every single day."

Mark grins and steals one and pops it in his mouth. "I thought I was so clever, coming up with that play on our first initials."

"You were clever," I insist. "I thought it was incredibly romantic."

"You were easy to please."

"I was sixteen." I shrug. "Tell me about Luke."

"Yes, he's been producing for a long time. He mostly recruits the lead actors and finds funding for the projects, so he can work mainly from home."

"That's awesome." I shove some popcorn in my mouth.

"You're such a lady," he says with a laugh.

"It's popcorn," I say, but it comes out sounding more like *it'sh pocorn*. "I saw Luke's *Nightwalker* movies."

"Did you have his poster hanging on your wall too?"

"No, I was too old for that, and I'd already slept with his brother," I reply without thinking then gasp and stare at Mark in horror. "I'm sorry."

"No, I'm glad you didn't have his poster on your wall, and that you'd already slept with me."

I laugh and shake my head. "I still have no filter around you. What is that all about?"

"I like it that way." He leans in just as the previews start. "We don't have secrets, M."

I meet him halfway and press my lips to his, then sit back to enjoy the movie.

***

"Sam's gonna be here, isn't she?" I can't bring myself to open the Jeep door. Mark just parked in front of one of the biggest homes I've ever seen, in an exclusive neighborhood of North Seattle.

I'm at Will Montgomery's house. The *football player*. The super sexy and talented Will Montgomery.

Holy fucking hell.

"Yeah, she's going to be here."

"She hates me."

"No, she doesn't." He cups my chin in his hand and makes me meet his gaze. "Sam's mellowed a lot over the past few years. Besides, I don't give a shit what Sam thinks. Remember?"

I nod and look back to the house, swallow hard, and try to think up a viable excuse to go home.

"It's gonna be fine, M."

I nod again. I can just nod. Why am I so fucking nervous? I've danced before audiences of thousands. Tens of thousands. The super rich and famous and everyone in between.

But these people matter to Mark and in the past forty-eight hours, Mark has grown to matter more than anyone else ever has before.

After the movie, we went back to my place and watched TV all evening. At around midnight, he kissed me thoroughly and then went home.

He went home without making love to me.

Because we're getting to know each other again.

I don't want to screw this up with the people who mean the most to him.

"Okay, your brain is moving way too fast, baby." He jumps out of the Jeep, jogs around to my side, and pulls me into his strong embrace. "Take a deep breath, M."

"I'm breathing."

"No, you're not. Just breathe. You'll have fun. You've already met almost everyone here."

I nod and smile bravely. He's right. This is no big deal. I'll make conversation and the next few hours will pass quickly and then I'll have Mark all to myself again.

"Better?"

"Yeah. Sorry."

He takes my hand and leads me around the side of the house to the back yard. The view of the Puget Sound is breathtaking. It's a gorgeous spring day, warmer than usual for this time of year. Tables with umbrellas are scattered about the yard, and children are laughing and running around.

"I thought you said this was a small family thing," I whisper to Mark in a new panic.

"It is." He smiles apologetically. "This is all family."

My eyes widen at the number of people here. I recognize Jules holding Stella, gazing lovingly up at a tall, dark man wearing a black T-shirt and jeans. His right arm is covered in tattoos. Luke and Natalie are standing with them, laughing at something Jules is saying.

"Hold on," I say and tug Mark's arm back. No one has seen us yet. "Before you start introducing me, point out who we're looking at so I have my wits about me."

"Okay."

"I recognize Luke, Natalie and Jules. That must be Nate?"

"Yes. Over there is Sam and Leo."

"Holy shit, the rags were right. Sam's with Leo Nash."

"She is. He's really cool. That redhead with them is Meg. She and Leo grew up together and Meg is Will's fiancée."

"I've seen her photo before," I reply with a nod. "And I've met Leo before too."

"You have?"

"Yeah, he and Starla are, um, friends." I bite my lip, not wanting to tell him that Leo and Starla were much more than that way back when.

"I think Sam mentioned that before. Small world. Okay, let's see." Mark scans the back yard. "Over there is Caleb and Brynna with Isaac and Stacy."

"Yep, I know them from class."

"That's right. You know my parents." He points to one of the tables where it looks like all of the parents have gathered. Some are holding babies. The women are talking and the guys are laughing. "There are also Gail and Steven Montgomery, and Brynna and Stacy's parents."

"That's right, Brynna and Stacy are cousins, right?"

"Yep. And that's Matt with his girlfriend, Nic."

"Lots of people."

"I think that's it."

"Who's the hot Italian guy?" I ask without thinking, earning a cocked brow from Mark.

"That's Dominic. He's a half brother to the Montgomerys. I'll tell you that story later. I'll also be watching you around him. He's the last single one among them."

"Hey, you're here!" Jules jogs over to us and hugs us both. "I'm so glad you came," she tells me.

"Thanks for having me," I reply.

"Come on, I'm going to introduce you to everyone." She smiles widely, looking beautiful in her red sundress and sandals. "Don't you just love this weather?"

"Yes, I'm so ready for summer," I reply and smile as Jules introduces me to everyone in the back yard. When we make our way to Sam and Leo, I feel my heart rate pick up and the nerves go crazy in my stomach.

Fuckity fuck fuck fuck.

"Hey, Leo and Sam, this is Meredith. She's here with Mark."

Sam's face goes pale in shock. Her jaw drops and then she blinks and looks around for her brother.

"Hi, Leo," I say lamely.

"Meredith." He pulls me in for a hug and smiles happily. "It's been a while. You must be the Meredith that teaches dance class for the girls."

"One and the same," I confirm.

"You two know each other?" Jules asks.

"Yes, I used to tour with Starla," I reply. "The music community is a small one."

"Ah yes, the bimbo you banged years ago, right?" Sam asks with a smirk and rolls her eyes.

"According to you, I banged everyone," Leo replies with a smile.

"I know for a fact you banged Starla."

"There's no video proof," Leo replies and Mark laughs next to me. Holy shit, these people are funny. At least, I hope they're being funny.

"That we know of," Sam replies and watches me with narrowed eyes.

Fuck.

"How is Starla?" Leo asks.

"She's great. She's getting married in Paris this fall and goes back on tour next year."

"Good for her. I'm glad to hear it." Sam walks away and Leo pats my arm before following her. "It's great to see you, Mer."

"You too," I reply and nod, then feel myself blush under Jules' stare. "What?"

"You have gossip," she accuses me. "Admit it."

I laugh and shake my head, finally feeling myself begin to relax. "I've signed nondisclosure agreements, Jules."

"Oh, honey," she says as though I'm a child with so much to learn. "I'll give you liquor. That'll loosen those lips right up."

"I'll have to remember not to bring Jax around. Pretty girls and liquor will make him spill his guts every time."

Jules leads me back to Natalie and Luke, who both hug me tightly. I've felt Mark's eyes on me the whole time, and he smiles at me from Luke's side.

"Meredith has gossip. We need to take her with us on girls night out to liquor her up and make her spill the beans."

"I'm telling you," I insist. "Jax is better at that than me."

"Is Jax your partner?" Natalie asks.

"Yes, he's been my dance partner for years and now we're business partners."

"He's hot," Jules informs everyone. "I saw him at the recital."

"Is he now?" Nate asks calmly and kisses a sleeping Stella's head. Holy hell, Nate is one fine specimen of man. He's all dark and toned and... *wow.* "Something you need to tell me?"

"Don't get your panties in a twist, ace."

"No worries," I assure him as well. "Jax is very gay."

"Oh my god," Natalie exclaims. "We're bringing you both out for girls night out."

"We'd love that."

"Miss Mer!" Josie and Maddie both run over to me and throw themselves in my arms, hugging me tightly. "You're here!"

"I'm here," I say and hug them back just as Sophie joins them. My arms are full of little girls.

"This is our baby cousin Livie," Maddie says, introducing a tiny little dark-haired girl who smiles up at me shyly.

"I remember you from the recital. How old are you, Livie?"

"She's two," Natalie says with a smile.

"She's beautiful." Livie giggles and holds her arms up for me to lift her into my arms. I can't resist her. "Hello, gorgeous girl. Don't you have the prettiest hair?"

"She has hair like her mama," Luke says and kisses Natalie's forehead.

"Will you dance with us?" Maddie asks hopefully.

"Dance!" Livie exclaims, making us laugh.

"Maybe later, sweetie." Someone has piped music outside, and Kelly Clarkson is currently singing through the speakers.

"Yes!" Josie yells and the girls run away. Livie squirms in my arms, wanting to follow her cousins, so I set her on her feet and she toddles away.

"At what age can we put her in class?" Natalie asks.

"I recommend after three, after potty training."

"Hold a place open for us."

"There is always space for you guys," I assure them and feel Mark slip his hand possessively on my lower back. I lean into him and sigh in contentment.

Over the next few hours, I make the rounds with Mark around the party, speaking with Will and Meg and the other siblings. Jesus, the Montgomerys are gorgeous. Every single one of them. It's a visual feast that I don't mind in the least. Mark's parents hug me warmly. I've never been welcomed so quickly by a group of people in my life.

I walk over to a cooler by the back door and pull a fresh bottle of water from the ice and turn in time to run smack into Dominic.

"Oh! Excuse me."

"My fault," he assures me and grips my arms to make sure I don't fall backward. "Sorry about that."

"I wasn't watching where I was going. I don't think we've met yet. I'm Meredith." I hold my hand out to shake his, and he raises my hand to his lips, kisses it softly and then lets go.

"I'm Dom. Welcome."

"Thank you."

"Who are you here with?" he asks and turns to scan the yard.

"Mark."

He turns back to me with a raised brow. "Really. Very interesting." He takes my hand again kisses it, then winks before pulling away. "It's a pleasure to meet you, Meredith. Good luck."

He leaves me standing here, confused. What did he mean by *interesting*? Suddenly, I realize the condensation from the water bottle has dribbled down my shirt. I walk into the kitchen to dab at it with a towel, and just then, Sam walks into the kitchen behind me.

When she sees me, she turns abruptly to leave, but I stop her.

"Wait. Sam, can we talk?"

She stops mid-stride and sighs deeply before turning back around and facing me. Her face is completely sober, but I can tell this is not the conversation she wants to have.

"What's up?" she asks.

"I swear, Keaton eats more than I do," Natalie says as she bustles into the kitchen and pulls a bottle out of the fridge, then turns to us and her eyes go wide. "I'm sorry, I didn't mean to interrupt."

"You didn't," Sam replies. "What do you want, Meredith?"

"First of all, I hope I didn't cause any trouble by mentioning Starla earlier."

Sam laughs and shakes her head, surprising me. "Trust me. Starla is not an issue. I've known about her for a long time, and not that it's any of your business, but Leo and I are just fine."

She begins to walk away, but I stop her again.

"Well, I guess I want to clear the air. I know you've never liked me."

She holds her hand up for me to stop talking. "I didn't know you. I was away at college when you dated my brother all those years ago. But I do know that you broke his heart."

"I don't want you to hate me—"

"I don't hate you. I just don't trust you."

Well, there you go.

"Sam," Natalie says softly. "You didn't trust me either."

"I didn't know you either, but you didn't see Mark after she broke it off," Sam reminds her, then glances back at me and pulls in a deep breath before letting it out slowly. "People grow up. They change. I know that." She props her hands on her hips. "I love my brothers more than just about anything, so I'll be watching, Meredith. I don't hate you. I don't even dislike you. I don't trust you."

"I get it." I nod and shrug.

"What the hell is going on?" Mark asks from the doorway.

CHAPTER FIVE

~Mark~

I saw Mer walk through the back door a few minutes ago, and Sam followed her, and neither has emerged.

I don't have a good feeling about this.

"Hey," I say to Luke quietly. "I'll be back."

He nods and I make a beeline for the open door, and just as I'm about to walk through, I hear Sam say, "I don't trust you."

"What the hell is going on?" I demand. Natalie is holding a baby bottle in her hand, biting her lip. Sam's hands are braced on her hips and Meredith is leaning her hands on the countertop, but she looks fine. She's not crying or breathing heavily, and I send up a silent prayer of thanks.

Sam can be ruthless. But Mer is holding her own.

My strong girl.

"I'm just clearing the air with Sam," Mer says and smiles brightly. "No problem."

I glance at Sam who continues to watch Meredith before she turns to me and shrugs. "We're fine, Mark."

"There's no blood?" I ask, trying to lighten the mood.

"Not yet," Sam says and cocks a brow at me.

"Geez, no need to be violent, slugger."

"We'll see," she replies and turns to leave.

"I'm going to take this to Keaton," Natalie says, but stops by Meredith on her way by. "I'm glad you're here. Just give it time."

Mer smiles and nods and I immediately cross to her and tilt her chin up. "What happened?"

"Nothing dramatic," she replies. "She doesn't dislike me. She doesn't trust me, which I can work with."

"What does that mean?"

"It means that it's better than I thought." She smiles and hugs me tightly, wrapping her arms around me and nuzzling her face against my chest.

"I know Sam can be ruthless, so if she said anything to make you…"

"Stop." She lays her hand on my chest and looks up at me with those blue eyes, shining with unshed tears. "Do you know what I would give to be able to grill my sister's boyfriend? To make him squirm a little?" She shakes her head and bites her lip and I tighten my arms around her. "I can handle Sam."

"Okay." I kiss her head and hug her close. "Do you want to leave?"

"No, let's go back out." She smiles bravely and my heart melts a little more. She's here because of me, because she knows it's important to me. She leads me outside and we quickly join a conversation with Meg, Will, Matt and Nic.

"Vegas," Meg says.

"What's happening in Vegas?" I ask, keeping Mer's hand in mine. Matt and Will both notice and exchange a glance.

Yeah, I'll be getting ribbed later. I don't care.

"We're all going to Vegas," Will says. "We're just going to do a big group bachelor/bachelorette party."

"Fun," I reply. "When?"

"In a few weeks," Meg says and smiles. "We're making all the travel arrangements. All you guys have to do is show up."

"I like the sound of this trip," Matt says. "How are the wedding plans coming?"

Will groans, but Meg lights up, clearly excited to talk about wedding plans. "Great! Alecia is the best."

"Alecia is planning this one too?" I ask. That woman plans every event for this family. She might as well just marry someone and officially become part of the gang.

"Yes, and she's brilliant."

"When is the big day?" Meredith asks.

"June 9th," Meg replies.

"That's only about six weeks away," Nic replies. "I'll need you in the shop this week so we can look at cake ideas."

"Okay! Fun!" Meg agrees. "It took us a while to choose a date," she tells Meredith.

"It's because she's lazy," Will informs us all with a smile. Meg slaps his arm and rolls her eyes.

"I am *not* lazy."

"I can't wait to marry you," Will says and nuzzles Meg's ear, making her laugh. "Let's go right now."

"It's Sunday," Meg replies and pushes against Will's chest. "Nothing is open right now."

"I'll make some calls," Will replies with a smug smile.

"Miss Mer!" Josie interrupts, pulling on Meredith's hand. "We love this song! Come dance with us. Please?"

Meredith laughs. "You like Starla, do you?"

"Yes, please come dance."

"Okay." She smiles up at me. "My dance card just filled up. I'll be back."

"Have fun."

She lets Maddie take one hand and Josie take the other as they guide her to the open lawn area where the kids have been playing. She starts to move her body, showing the girls some new moves, laughing with them. Maddie concentrates, watching Mer with an intense look on her sweet face.

"She's great," Nic comments and sips her water.

"You brought a woman to a family function," Will states soberly.

I just nod and watch as Livie joins the others and Meredith lifts her in her arms and twirls her around, dancing effortlessly with the toddler.

"He's not even listening to us," Matt comments.

"I can hear you, asshole."

"She's so good with the kids," Isaac says as he and Caleb join us. I nod and shove my hands in my pockets as Mer glances up and winks at me, sending a punch right to my gut.

"Brynna rarely drops the girls off with anyone," Caleb says, "but she and Stacy have no qualms about leaving the girls with Meredith while they go get pedicures during dance class."

Sophie tries to turn and falls on her butt. Her little lip sticks out, but before she can start to cry, Mer squats next to her, Livie still in her arms, and calms her, then helps her back to her feet so she can continue dancing with the others.

Christ, she's magnificent. She kisses Liv's cheek and then sets her on her feet so she can dance in that awkward way that toddlers do, and finishes the song with the others.

"She's clearly in the right job," Matt says quietly. "Most of us can't deal with two of them at once, and she has all of them around her effortlessly." He points as baby Liam toddles over and grips her jeans, pulls himself up on his feet and bounces on his legs, dancing with the others.

"Mark's a goner," Meg says. I glance over at her and grin.

"I'm bringing her with me to Vegas." I'm bringing her with me *everywhere*. If I'm invited, she's invited.

"We wouldn't have it any other way," she replies and pats my arm. "I like her already."

I'm fucking in love with her again already. I'm never letting her go. Never again.

She comes running back to us, out of breath and a wide smile on her beautiful face.

"They would dance all day," she says with a laugh. "Maddie's amazing. If she wanted to, she could go pretty far in the dance world."

"She's eight." Caleb growls.

"Well, not today," Mer agrees. "But someday."

"She asked me if we could sign her up for one on one classes with you," Brynna says as she pats Michael on the back. "Isn't she too young for that?"

"Maybe a bit," Mer says and purses her lips as she thinks it over. "You could add a second class a week for now. If she's still interested when she hits about thirteen, I can take her on one on one and work with her."

Brynna nods thoughtfully and glances up at Caleb who's just gone pale. "What do you think?"

"I think I don't want to even think about the day she turns thirteen."

"Oh! That reminds me, I have something for Mom. I brought her birthday gift along with us, but it's in the car. Meredith, will you hold Michael for me?"

"Oh, I..." Mer begins, but Brynna places the sleeping baby in Mer's arms and hurries away. Mer looks at each of us with panicked eyes and then back down at the oblivious baby. "I'm not good with babies. Here, his dad should hold him."

"You'll do fine," Caleb says with an amused grin.

"Here," Stacy says and helps Meredith settle Michael on her shoulder. "There you go. He's not going anywhere."

"You were just swarmed by children and looked just fine, sweetheart," Will says.

"I'm good with kids, but tiny babies scare the hell out of me. I'm afraid I'll break them." Meredith immediately sways back and forth, patting Michael's diaper-covered butt and rests her cheek on his head. "Is this okay?"

"Perfect," I reply quietly. Her eyes find mine over the baby's head and she smiles softly.

"Wow," someone—Meg?—says. I can't look away from the gorgeous woman before me.

My woman.

Mine.

She looks amazing wearing that baby. I can see her holding *our* baby. Grandbabies.

Fuck, this is forever. She's it for me.

"I'm going to need someone to take that baby," I say calmly.

"Why?" Mer asks and frowns. "Am I doing it wrong?"

"No, I need to get you out of here. Now."

"I got it!" Stacy takes Michael from Meredith and I immediately grip her hand in mine and tug her along behind me to the gate at the side of the house.

"Goodbye everyone!" she calls with a laugh and waves. "I had a great time! Thanks for including me!"

"Goodbye!" I can hear the guys laughing, and I don't give a shit. I need her. I need to claim her, to remind her that she's mine. To lose myself in her for hours, rediscovering everything about her.

"Mark?" she asks with another laugh. "Slow down, babe."

"No."

I yank the Jeep door open and wait for her to climb in but she stops in front of me and cups my face in her small hands.

"Stop. What got into you?"

"I can't wait another minute." Her eyes darken as she watches me. "I know it's nuts and my brother will most likely never let me forget dragging you out of there like a caveman, but I can't share you with them any longer. I need you naked and wet and moving beneath me for about the next two days."

Her eyes dilate and she licks her lips as she watches my mouth move. Her hands are braced on my biceps and I smile as I flex them on purpose, making her eyes widen and that pulse point in her throat thrum in anticipation.

"Well, when you put it like that," she says softly. "Are you taking me home?"

"I'm taking you to my place," I reply and tip my forehead down onto hers. "No interruptions. I'm going to make you scream and laugh and come undone, and I don't want you worrying about who can hear us when I do."

"Fair enough," she says. "Can we stop talking about it in Will's driveway and just go do it now?"

"That was the idea."

CHAPTER SIX

~Meredith~

"Where do you live?" I ask and nervously bounce my knee in a fast staccato.

"About ten minutes from here," he replies and takes my hand in his, pulling it to his lips to kiss my knuckles. "Too far."

I can't stand it anymore. Telling me he needs me *now* flipped a switch inside me and I need to touch him. He stops at a red light and I slip out of my seatbelt and crawl over the center console, grip his face in my hands and kiss him. Demandingly. He growls and buries his fingers in my hair, holding me to him as he kisses me back with a hunger I've never seen from him before.

Suddenly, a car honks behind us, alerting us of the green light.

"Too fucking far," I say and sit back in my seat.

Mark keeps my hand gripped tightly in his as he maneuvers the Jeep through the neighborhood to his house and comes to a quick stop in the driveway.

"Home sweet home," he murmurs, jumps out of the Jeep and jogs around to my door to help me out.

"I like your house." It's in an established neighborhood, on the bigger side, with a huge blooming cherry blossom tree in the front yard.

"Thanks," he replies and leads me through the front door. "I'll give you the tour later." He throws his keys on a nearby table, and turns to me, pins me against the closed door at my back and devours my mouth, kissing me hungrily. He cups my cheek with one hand and with the other, lifts my right leg up around his waist and grips my ass in his palm.

"God, you feel good, M," he murmurs against my lips. Suddenly he spins us around and pulls my top over my head just as I dive for the button on his jeans. We can't get each other naked fast enough. We are a tangle of clothes and arms and laughter as we strip each other quickly and trip and stumble our way up a set of stairs and into his bedroom. He's still in boxers when he tears my panties from my body. Fuck, his arms are flexing, the muscles jumping beneath his bronze skin and I'm about to come undone.

I reach for his boxers, but he suddenly stops cold, grips my wrist to stop me from touching him.

"Mark, hurry," I begin, but he interrupts me.

"Don't talk."

"What?"

His eyes are roaming up and down my naked body like he's a starved man at an all you can eat buffet.

"Just the sound of your voice is going to make me come right now, M. Fuck me, you're so…" He shakes his head as if he just can't find the right word.

"I thought you were going to fuck me," I pout and then grin at him but his eyes meet mine and they are on fire. His face is tight, his jaw clenched as he closes the gap between us, lifts me easily in his arms and lays me on the bed. He kisses up my body, from my belly, between my breasts, up my neck and finally covers me completely and kisses me softly.

"Trust me, I'm going to fuck you. I'm going to fuck you blind, but I'm not going to fuck you right now, baby." He strokes my hair and nudges my nose with his. "I've waited such a long time for this moment. I'm going to make long, slow love to you. I'm going to explore every inch of this amazing body. I have to relearn you, M."

Tears prick my eyes at his sweet words. His fingers are infinitely gentle as they stroke down my cheek. My hands can't stop roaming up and down his back, down his arms and then over his back again. His skin is warm and smooth and the muscles jump beneath my touch.

"I love touching you," I whisper.

He grins and lowers his lips to my lips, then drags them down my jawline to my neck and begins a slow journey down my body. He doesn't leave one inch untouched. He pauses at my breasts and pulls back to admire them, and I can't help but giggle.

"So you're a boob man."

The naughty smile spreads over his lips and he leans in to circle his nose around one tight areola. "Your breasts filled out nicely."

"Told you," I murmur and push my fingers through his hair.

"Your body was always magnificent. You kept me in a perpetual state of horniness for a long time, but my God, Mer, seeing you as a woman, it's just breathtaking."

"You're getting laid, M. You don't have to shower me with pretty words."

His eyes find mine and I know he's not kidding. "I'll give you all the pretty words I want to, and you should know that I mean every single one of them."

His hands glide down my stomach, over my hips and between my thighs, but he doesn't touch me where my body is begging him to. My hips come up off the bed, begging for his attention.

"Beautiful skin," he continues and kisses the path his hands just took, down my belly to my hip. "What is this?"

"A tattoo." I grin down at him and laugh when his jaw drops. "You don't like it?"

His fingers dance over the ink. "It's tiny."

I glance down where he's looking and nod. It's a simple eighth note, and in the middle of the circle part of the note is an *M*.

"I kept two things with me while I was dancing," I begin and bite my lip. "Music..." I take a deep breath. Jesus, I'm laying myself bare here.

"And."

"You."

His eyes connect with mine. "You're unbelievable."

He brushes his thumb over the ink as he watches me quietly for a long moment, then places several kisses over my hip, nuzzles my small tattoo, and then travels farther down my thigh.

"You're killing me," I tell him and wiggle my hips.

"Settle in, baby, because you're in for a long ride."

"Jesus Christ, what did you just do with your finger?" I boost myself up on my elbows and stare down at him as he kisses my knee.

"Who says that was my finger?"

I laugh and fall to my back and then moan when he reaches my foot and begins to rub it in strong circles.

"Oh God."

"Your feet have taken a beating."

"Don't look directly at them. You'll run screaming."

He chuckles and kisses the top of my foot then moves to the other one and repeats the process.

"I'm not going anywhere, baby."

He moves up my leg to make me writhe and moan as he pays extra attention behind my knee and just when I think he's going to dive into the sweet spot, he avoids it completely, kisses up my hip, belly and teases the other breast.

"Mark?"

"Yes, love."

"Take your shorts off and let me have a turn."

"You got very bossy," he murmurs and kisses my jaw. "I'm clearly not doing my job right if you're still able to string words together."

"You're doing fine."

"I'm going to do a lot better than *fine*, sweetheart."

His hand drifts down my belly and his fingers finally slide between my folds and into my wet core.

"Holy fuck," he whispers against my lips. "You're so fucking wet, M."

"Need you," I reply and gasp when his fingers move slowly in and out then up to circle my clit.

"Is this what you need?"

I shake my head and lift my hips, pushing against his hand. Dear God, he's good with his hands.

"What do you need?"

"You!"

"I'm right here," he replies. I can feel the bed shift as he shuffles out of his shorts then kneels between my thighs. "I'm going to eat this pussy before the night is out."

"Fuck," I whisper.

"No?"

"Yes!"

He chuckles and I hear the rip of a condom wrapper.

"Look at me, M."

I open my eyes and look directly into his dark blue gaze. He takes one of my hands in his, links our fingers and holds our hands over my head while guiding himself to my entrance. His eyes never leave mine as he begins to push inside me. His fingers tighten on mine. I cup his face with my free hand, and I've never loved him more than I do in this moment.

I love you.

He pushes in all the way and stops, every muscle tight with the effort of holding still, panting, watching me.

"So tight." He kisses me softly and nibbles his way to the corner of my mouth. I hitch my thighs up higher around his hips and he growls. "You're going to make me lose it."

I grin and rotate my hips, watching with fascination as he bites his lip. I love watching him struggle to keep his composure.

"Mark," I whisper and pull my fingertips down his face. "You feel so good."

He begins to move now, slowly at first and then faster, as though an outside force is pushing him on. He grabs my other hand in his and pins it above my head as our bodies take over, moving in perfect tandem.

Fuck, he's so *big*. I can't help but grip him hard as he thrusts in and out until finally he swears a blue streak as I come apart beneath him, crying out as the orgasm consumes me.

"That's it, baby," he says and watches with hungry eyes as I shiver beneath him. "Fuck yes." He groans and comes hard, rocking his hips against mine as he empties himself inside me. He's panting as he releases my hands and rests his forehead against mine. I can't move my arms, so I leave them resting on the bed where he left them.

"Do you know what I whispered to Jax yesterday?" he asks suddenly.

"Uh, I wasn't really thinking about Jax while you're still inside me," I reply and chuckle making him flinch as my pussy squeezes him with the movement.

"Smart ass," he whispers and kisses me softly then brushes loose tendrils of hair off my cheeks. "I told him that I love you more than I can say."

I still and feel my eyes widen as I stare up at him. "You did?"

He nods and continues to watch me soberly. He looks like he's going to say something more, but before he can, I wrap my arms around him and bury my face in his neck and murmur, "I love you so much."

He rolls us so he's beneath me and I push up onto my elbows so I can see his face while I continue. "But I never stopped, M. I gave you my heart all those years ago, and I never took it back."

"I'm not giving it back," he replies.

"Good."

"But I believe I made you a promise." His face is completely serious as he stares up at me and I frown.

"What?"

"I promised," he says and kisses my palm. "To fuck you."

My lips twitch as I try to stay serious and nod gravely. "You did."

"I'm a man of my word, you know."

"Yes, you do have that reputation."

He sits up and pulls me from the bed then tosses me over his shoulder and carries me into his master bathroom. It still smells of sawdust, and the new gleam of fresh countertops and tile makes me smile. "This is beautiful."

"I finished it this morning."

"Did you stay up all night doing this?"

He nods as he sets me on the countertop and discards the condom.

"You wanted to go to the movies yesterday," he says.

"You were supposed to do this instead?"

"No, I was supposed to go to the movies with the woman I'm in love with." He starts the shower and then returns to me.

"I'm still on the pill, M. We don't need the condoms."

He cringes and shakes his head, glances down and then meets my gaze. "I haven't been a saint, Meredith. I've always, *always* used condoms, but I won't take any chances with you. We'll use them until I see a doctor this week."

The thought of him with other women makes me want to claw someone's eyes out, but I take a deep breath and remind myself of what I told him the other night on the pier. It's been ten years.

I haven't been a saint either.

"Okay," I reply. "Starla required us to get check ups every year, and I haven't had any partners since the last one. I'm good."

"You're amazing and I don't deserve you."

"This is probably true."

He laughs and wraps his arms around me, hugging me tight. His bare chest feels fantastic against my cheek and we stay like this for a long minute while we wait for the shower to heat up. When steam begins to fill the room, Mark helps me down and leads me into the gorgeous blue-tiled shower big enough to have a floor show in.

"Did you plan to host parties in here?"

"Just the two-person kind with you," he replies and begins soaping me up with my brand of shower gel and a fresh shower puff.

"You bought my shower gel? Pretty sure of yourself."

"Hopeful," he says and draws circles over my belly and down over my bare pubis. I grab a washcloth and return the favor, loving the feel of his naked body beneath my hands.

"Your body is incredible," I murmur.

"Glad you approve."

"I might never stop touching you."

"That's the plan."

I grin up at him as he rinses us both off and suddenly his eyes turn hot again and he backs me up against the cool tile and kneels before me, lifts my left leg and throws it over his shoulder, opening me up to him.

"I'm going to slip and fall." I gasp.

"I've got you," he replies and watches my face as he slips his fingers through my lips. "God, Mer, you're so fucking wet."

"You turn me on." I grip his hair in my hands and hold on as he growls and leans in to tease my clit with his tongue and lips. He sinks two fingers inside me and wraps those lips around my clit and that's all it takes, I come apart, crying out his name while leaning against the wall of the shower.

He stands, flips the shower off and doesn't even bother drying us off as he tugs me behind him back to the bed.

"Um, Mark? I'm wet here."

"Fuck yes, you are," he says and tosses me—*tosses me!*—onto the bed then spreads my legs wide and dives back in. "You taste so fucking good." He's lapping at my labia, licking every drop from me, then pushes his fingers back in and jerks them quickly, tipping me over another ledge into a mind-numbing orgasm.

"Holy shit!"

He licks and bites his way up my body, sheaths himself in a condom and plunges inside me, fast and hard.

"Fuck, Mer," he growls and begins pounding in and out of me. The sounds coming out of him are primal and gritty and I love this side of him as much as the man who made sweet love to me not thirty minutes ago.

Suddenly, he pulls out and flips me over, yanks my hips up and plunges back inside me from behind, smacks my ass and rides me in earnest.

Holy fucking hell, it's the hottest thing I've ever experienced.

"Mark, oh my God!"

"Mine," he growls and leans in to press his lips to my ear. "You are *mine*."

I grip the sheets in my fists and hold on for this wild ride with this crazy, amazing man.

"Say it," he commands.

"Yours," I reply breathlessly. "Always."

"Fuck yes, always." He grips my hips and pounds into me for several long minutes then stops, balls-deep, and shouts as he comes hard, sending me over with him.

"Jesus Christ, I won't survive you," he says breathlessly as he falls beside me in a heap.

"That one was all you, babe," I reply and crawl onto his chest. "Wow. You're definitely better than *fine*."

"You're magnificent," he whispers and kisses my forehead. "I love you, M."

"I love you too."

***

I wake alone. It's dark, still the middle of the night, and the bed is cold where Mark was lying.

Where did he go?

I wrap the sheet around me and set out to find him. The house is still, but when I glance out the window, his Jeep is still in the driveway.

I search the whole house and come up empty, but then see a glow coming from the back yard. I open the French door to the patio and step out into the mild night to find Mark sitting on a chaise lounge, watching the flames in a brick fireplace.

"What are you doing?" I ask and cross to him. He's shirtless, clad only in loose sweats that hang in that way that show off the V muscles in his hips.

Delicious.

And just like that, I'm wide awake and my body is humming in anticipation.

"I didn't want to wake you. I couldn't sleep." He holds his hand out for me then pulls me into his lap. I snuggle up against him and watch the fire.

"Aren't you cold?"

"I'm good," he replies and kisses my head.

"Why can't you sleep?"

He shrugs and I lean back to watch his face. "Mark?"

"I just keep thinking that this is going to be a dream." He chuckles ruefully and shakes his head. "I think I just lost my man card."

"I get it." I wiggle out of his lap and shed the sheet, then tug his sweats down around his thighs, unleashing his thick erection before straddling him and sinking down onto him.

"No condom." He gasps and grips my hips as I rock back and forth slowly.

"It's fine," I whisper and kiss him sweetly. "This is no dream, babe."

He closes his eyes and I lean my forehead on his as I ride him steadily. "This is you and me, M."

His mouth closes around my nipple and I throw my head back as the electricity zings down to my core, making me clench around him harder.

He pushes a hand between us and circles my clit with his thumb, and I'm lost to him, biting my lip as I come around him.

"Fuck," he whispers and comes with me, then pulls me down to him, kissing me and holding me close. Finally, I rest my head on his chest, content to sit and watch the fire beside us.

"It's no dream. It's better," I say quietly.

"So much better," he agrees.

CHAPTER SEVEN

"Okay girls! It's our favorite time! Free dance!" Jax announces and the girls in class clap and jump up and down. This is our older class, over fourteen, so Jax chooses a brand new Pitbull song and the girls begin to dance about the floor. The part the girls love the most about this time of class is that Jax and I join them, dancing with them as if we were at a school dance.

Jax grabs my hand and spins me into his arms, then boosts me up into a lift and back down into another spin, making everyone cheer.

He's such a show-off.

When the song is over, the girls change their shoes and gather their book bags and jackets, waving goodbye as they leave.

"That Melissa is good," Jax mentions as he locks the glass door.

"She's really good," I agree and drop down in the chair behind the desk. "You should work with her one-on-one."

"Me? I thought that was your area." He leans his hip on the desk and guzzles a bottle of water.

"She responds well to you, and she doesn't have a crush on you, so it would work well."

"I'm hurt that she doesn't have a crush on me." He pretends to pout. "I must be losing my touch."

"You're getting old," I tease him and laugh when he flips me off. "I'll talk to her mom next week."

"Her mom will jump all over it," he says with a shake of his head. "Some of the moms get more excited about it than the dancers do."

"My mom always loved watching me dance." The pain is swift and sharp, settling heavy in my heart.

"She would be so fucking proud of you, shortcake," he says and pulls me in for a hug. "She was always proud, and seeing you start this studio made her glow with it."

"I'm glad she got to see it," I say and blink hard against the tears that always threaten when we start talking about my mom. "She enjoyed watching the little ones dance."

"She enjoyed watching you teach them," he replies softly.

I bite my lip and stare up at my friend for a long minute and then decide fuck it, and let the tears come. "I miss her. Why do people I love die?"

"I'm sorry," he says as he pulls me into his arms and rocks me back and forth.

"You can't die on me," I cry and bury my face in his chest. "I tried to shake you off years ago, but you wouldn't leave, so you can't die on me."

"Silly woman, thinking you could shake me off. I showed you." He tips my face up and wipes my cheeks dry with his thumbs. "I'm not going anywhere."

"Okay." I nod and take a deep calming breath. "Thank you for tolerating my hysteria."

"I'm used to it." I glare and punch him in the arm.

"Ow! I'm also used to the violence." He rubs his arm and doesn't look me in the eye when he says, "Going out with Mark again tonight?"

"We had planned to." I check my phone and smile when I see a text from him. *What are you wearing?*

"So you won't be home again tonight?" His face is neutral, but his voice sounds annoyed.

"Are you keeping score? I doubt you've been home much more than I have since you've been seeing your new guy."

"I'm home more than you know," he says.

"Who is this guy, by the way?"

He shrugs and takes another drink of water.

"Why don't you want to talk about him? We always talk about who we're dating."

"Like you've been talking to me about Mr. Hot Tamale?"

"That's not fair. I haven't seen you."

"That's my point, Cherry Garcia."

"What do you have against Mark? He never did anything wrong in the first place."

"It feels like you're moving fast. I heard you tell him that you love him over the phone yesterday. Are you sure he has good intentions? Maybe he's got some vindictive plan to hurt you so he can get retribution for you dumping him back in the day."

"Uh, hello, drama queen." I shake my head in exasperation. "No, I don't think that."

"I'm just saying it's a possibility."

"You don't know him, Jax. He's not like that."

"Okay, it's your heart." He shrugs and moves to walk away, but I stand and stop him.

"I know it's fast," I admit and chew my lip as he stands and watches me with worried eyes. "You think I don't know it? It's scaring the shit out of me."

"If he's pressuring you into something..."

"Oh, get real." I roll my eyes and shake my head. "No one pressures me into anything. You know that better than anyone. I don't feel pressured, I feel... drawn to him. I can't stop it. It's stronger than it was when we were teenagers, and it's not just the sex, although, hello, the man has sure as hell honed *that* skill, and he was good ten years ago."

"Oh good. That's exactly what I want to hear about, your sex life."

"Am I making a mistake? Am I letting myself fall back into love with him and setting myself up for heartbreak when it all falls apart?"

"Why is it going to fall apart?"

"Why wouldn't it?"

"Boy, we're both pretty cynical, aren't we?" He smirks and then runs his hand down my ponytail. "As long as you're on the same page, don't walk away from him. I watched you pine for him for years. If this is your time to be together, reach for it, Mer."

"Wow, that's very romantic coming from you."

He laughs and backs away. "Or just fuck him until you have him out of your system and kick him to the curb, but I don't see that happening this time."

Neither do I.

"Either way, keep me posted." His smile fades and he checks his phone. "I have to go."

"Don't walk away, Jax. Something is off with you this week. Is it this Mr. Lovey Pants you're seeing?"

He busts out laughing and then pulls me into a big hug. "Mr. Lovey Pants?"

"What's going on?"

He sighs and kisses my head then pulls away and sits on the desk, swinging his feet. "His name is Logan. I thought it would be a quick fuck, as usual, but it's… not." He shrugs as if he's at a complete loss, and I take his hand in mine and squeeze.

"What is it?"

"Hell if I know. The sex is crazy. He's thoughtful and nice and I stayed the night with him. Twice."

"Wow," I reply with raised brows. "That's very un-Jax."

"Yeah, you're usually the only one I like to cuddle with." He grins and tweaks my nose with his fingertip then his face sobers. "It's been hard to slide into second place on your priority list."

I blink at him in surprise. "Do you think that's what's happened since I've been back with Mark? I've been sleeping with him less than a week."

"That *is* what's happened, cheesecake. But it would have happened sooner or later, no matter who you're seeing. I get it. It just doesn't feel good."

"I'm sorry," I whisper. "I love you, Jax. You're always going to be important to me, no matter what."

"I know. I'm stuck with you. It's a burden I bear bravely."

I laugh and shake my head at him, but I can't help but feel guilty. I haven't spent any time with Jax outside of being at the studio, and we're always working when we're here.

"Do you have plans with Logan tonight?"

"Yeah."

"Well I'll tell you what. I'll cancel with Mr. Hot Tamale and you'll cancel with Mr. Lovey Pants and you and I will go get mani/pedi's."

He looks surprised for a moment, then tosses his head back and forth like he's contemplating my offer. "Hmm, hot sex or mani/pedi's. That's a toughie."

"If you're good, we can go home and eat ice cream and watch *Pretty Woman*."

"I'm not that much of a girl," he replies, offended. "We'll watch *Pitch Perfect*."

"Not that much of a girl, huh." He flips me off again and I laugh. "Go call Logan."

He hugs me and grins down at me. "Thank you."

"If you don't beat me to the Blu-ray player, I'm putting in *Pretty Woman*."

"You're a bitch."

"Absolutely."

He laughs and pulls his phone out of his pocket as he walks away. I lift my own phone and dial Mark's number.

"Hey, gorgeous," he answers.

"Well hello there," I reply with a grin. "Hey, I have to cancel on you tonight."

"Cheating on me already?" he asks with a laugh.

"Yes. I'm so relieved you understand."

"Wait. I don't like this game anymore."

I chuckle and throw my sunglasses and scarf into my handbag. "Jax has some stuff going on, and he kind of misses me, so he and I are going to have GGN tonight."

"What is GGN?"

"Gay Girl Night."

Mark laughs in earnest over the phone for several seconds before clearing his throat and saying, "What, exactly, does that involve?"

"The spa, ice cream and chick flicks."

"Have fun," he says quickly, as though he's afraid I might invite him along.

"Sorry for the short notice. Rain check?"

"No problem. Why don't I bring you coffee in the morning?"

"Jax and I have an early rehearsal tomorrow. We're gearing up for the LA trip. I have a break before the first class at about 9:30, but you'll be at work by then."

"I'll take a break. That's one of the perks of being the boss."

I grin and feel my stomach tighten at the tone of his voice. "I'd like that."

"See you then, sweetheart."

"Bye." I hang up just as Jax returns from our changing room. "Ready?"

"Let's go." He holds the door open for me, locks it behind us and takes my hand as we walk down the street to the nail place.

***

"Why don't we do this more often?" Jax asks as we sit and wait for my nails to dry. Our feet and hands are soft and rested.

Well, our hands are soft. Our feet will never be soft again.

"I'm tipping our pedicurists extra. No one should have to ever touch our feet."

"Good call," he says and sighs contentedly. "Do we have ice cream at home?"

"Yes. I think that's all we have in the freezer right now."

When my pink nails are all dry, we set off to the apartment, drop our bags inside the doorway and race to the Blu-Ray player. Jax beats me by two steps.

"Ha! *Pitch Perfect* it is!"

"Just don't sing along this time. For someone with such great rhythm, you are completely tone-deaf, my friend."

"I am not."

"Starla paid you extra to make you stop singing. You do the math."

I settle on the couch, flopped back in the cushions, my feet on the coffee table and hands folded over my belly as Jax heads to the kitchen for our dinner.

"Ice cream," he says with a grin and joins me on the couch with two pints and two spoons. "Dinner of champions. Do you want Chubby Hubby or Chunky Monkey?"

"Yes." I reach for the tub closest to me, take the spoon offered and press play on the remote. "We'll switch when we're halfway through."

"Jesus, this is a lot of calories."

"Calories don't count on GGN. Besides, we're working our asses off, literally, on Starla's routine. You're kicking my ass with this one."

"It's good, though. It'll be the best routine at the VMA's."

"Obviously," I reply and roll my eyes. "You're the best there is, Jax."

"This is why I love you. You feed my ego."

I kick him and take a big bite of Chunky Monkey. When both containers are empty, we lie in sugar comas and watch the movie, cuddled up on the couch. Jax's body is hard. Broad. Lean.

He's a hottie. I hope Logan isn't going to try to screw him over. I'd have to kill him.

Just as the movie ends and the credits begin to roll, Jax's phone rings.

"Is that Mr. Lovey Pants?"

"Yeah." He looks torn as he glances at me. "But it's GGN."

"Answer it. I'll call Mark and then we'll snuggle up in my bed and sleep."

He grins and swipes his finger over the phone, answering, "Hey. Yeah, I'm still with Mer. We'll be hanging out all night."

"Hi, Logan!" I call into the phone. Jax grins.

"He says hi."

"I want to see a photo of you!" I yell.

"Yeah, I'll show her one when we get off the phone."

"You have photos and I haven't seen them?"

"Can I talk here?"

I grin and walk into my room, giving Jax privacy as I call Mark.

"What are you wearing?" he answers.

"Just a smile, sexy man," I reply and giggle.

"Well put on some clothes. You're hanging out with Jax, and even if he is gay, I'm not comfortable with you hanging out naked together."

"Well you're no fun." I giggle again and collapse back on the bed. "What are you doing?"

"I'm painting the downstairs bathroom."

"So, you work construction all day and then go home and keep working?"

"If you were here, I'd be working on something far more exciting."

"Yeah? What's that?"

"Well, it's almost ten, so you'd be well on your way to your third orgasm by now."

"Damn Jax," I murmur, making Mark laugh.

"I'll make it up to you tomorrow night."

"Yay me!"

"I thought this was super secret gay girl time. What are you up to?" I can hear clanking in the background, and I picture him pouring more paint into a plastic pan.

"Jax got a call from the guy he's seeing, so I decided to take advantage of it and call you. I kind of miss you."

"Kind of?"

"Just a little bit."

He chuckles and then I can hear him swallowing something. "I can come over later."

"It's okay." I sigh. "Jax and I are going to snuggle up in my bed and go to sleep."

The line gets quiet and I think I've lost him there for a minute.

"M?"

"You and Jax are going to snuggle up in your bed? All night?"

"Um, yeah?" I phrase it as a question because I'm not entirely sure why he sounds suddenly jealous.

"You're sleeping in your bed with another man?"

"With Jax," I clarify. "Clothed. I was just kidding about the whole being naked thing. Sleeping. He snores. I'll probably kick him out at some point."

"Now would be good."

I frown and bite my lip. "Jax and I have slept together—*just slept*—for ten years, M. It's nothing new."

"It's new to me." He sighs and I can picture him rubbing his forehead in exasperation.

"If it makes you this uncomfortable, we won't."

"Why does my caveman come out full blast with you?" His voice is gritty and I grin. It's sexy as hell.

"I love you," I whisper. "I will sleep alone tonight."

"This is my own issue, baby. Do what you've always done. I'm fine. I'll see you in the morning."

"Are you sure?"

"I want to say no. I want to say the only man who will ever share your bed again is *me*. But that's irrational. If Jax was a woman, I wouldn't care."

"Let's snuggle," Jax announces as he barges into my bedroom. "But I'm not staying. Logan says he's staking a claim on sleeping privileges."

I blink at Jax, who is smiling smugly, as he climbs into my bed and opens his arms. "Come on. Bring Mark with you. It'll be a Chunky Monkey sammich."

"What is he talking about?" Mark asks with a laugh. "Who is Logan?"

"His boyfriend," I reply and crawl under the covers to snuggle up to Jax. "And apparently, you and Logan just laid down the law that we can cuddle, but there will be no more sleeping together."

"I like Logan," Mark replies.

"I like Logan too," Jax says. "Say goodnight, Meredith."

"Goodnight, Meredith," Mark says with a laugh.

"Goodnight, Meredith," I reply and giggle again. "Love you, handsome."

"Love you too," they both say at the same time.

"I'll see you tomorrow, baby." Mark hangs up and I toss my phone to the foot of the bed.

"So, if Logan is staking a claim on sleeping privileges, he's definitely your boyfriend."

"He wants to invite you and Mark out to dinner with us this weekend."

"Wow! Okay! How fun!" I grin and kiss Jax's cheek. "We've never been on a double date before. Show me the picture."

He finds a photo on his phone and shows it to me. A smiling, brown-haired man is staring back at me. He has a scruffy face, but it suits him. His teeth are just a bit crooked on the bottom, and his eyes are green and kind. He's wearing a red beanie and black thick-rimmed glasses.

"Hello, Mr. Hottie Lovey Pants."

"Right?" He takes the phone back and stares at Logan's photo for a long minute before shutting it down and setting it aside. "He's seriously hot."

"What does he do?"

"He's an architect." His eyes light up with pride as he thinks about Logan. "You should see some of the buildings he's designed."

"He and Mark will have something to talk about."

Jax nods and yawns. "I feel like I'm waiting for the other shoe to drop."

"Why?"

"Come on, Mer. You know my history with men. It's not exactly what romance novels are made of."

"Me neither," I reply with a shrug. "But that doesn't mean we don't deserve that. You deserve to be happy with a hot guy who's kind and loves you."

"No one said anything about love," he replies quickly.

"Whatever. You know what I mean."

He grows quiet, lost in his own thoughts and I leave him be, enjoying this quiet time with him. I admit, I've missed him too. I've spent every night this week with Mark, and while it's been pure bliss every night, I can't forget that my relationship with Jax is important too.

"I think I'm just going to take things with Logan day by day and see what happens," Jax finally murmurs.

"I think that's a good idea."

He nods. It's hard for Jax to trust, so the fact that he's willing to try with Logan means the man must be very special.

"I'm sleepy," I whisper.

"I'll go to bed." He slips out from under me and kisses my cheek. "I love you, moon pie."

"I love you too, best friend."

***

"You're trying to kill me." My chest is heaving as I try to drag air into my lungs, glaring up at Jax from the floor. I'm on my ass after falling during rehearsal.

"You're sloppy today," he replies, his voice hard.

"I am not. Starla can't do moves like this, Jax. She's a singer, not a dancer."

"She'll do it."

"I'm telling you, she can't. I haven't landed that throw once and we've done it two dozen times."

"Let's do it a dozen more."

"Fuck you. It's not your ass that's getting bruised." I stand and plant my hands on my hips as I glare at him. This is why he's the best. He's so fucking stubborn, he'll hammer this over and over again until I stick it, just the same way he'll do with Starla.

"You're fine. Let's do it again."

"I need a break." I walk to the desk and guzzle some water as I check my phone. There's a text from Mark.

Can't meet this morning. Trouble at job site. Will pick you up tonight.

Great. I'm already in a pissy mood, and I was looking forward to seeing Mark. I saw him twenty-four hours ago, but I miss him.

I'm pathetic.

"Problem?"

"Yeah, my ass hurts." I scowl at Jax and type a message to Mark.

No worries. See you later.

"God you're whiny today," Jax says and resets the music. "Let's do this."

We move through the routine again. It's an excellent routine. Fun to dance, but when we get to the lift and the throw, I fall again.

"Mother fucker!" I yell and pound the floor with my fist.

"Okay, you're overthinking it. Let's run through it one more time without the lift and call it good."

I nod and take a deep breath, then dance the routine with Jax, satisfied that besides that evil lift, we're ready for LA next week.

When we're done, there's a knock on the glass door. I whip around, hopeful that it's Mark, but it's Nic, Matt Montgomery's girlfriend, standing at the door with a wide smile. I jog over and open the door.

"That was amazing," she says and steps inside. "I was at a Starla concert a couple years ago and remember seeing you guys."

"Thanks," I reply and glance down at the white box with red bow in her hands. "What can we do for you?"

"Oh! Mark called me this morning and said that he was supposed to bring you coffee but he can't make it, so he asked if I'd bring you some cupcakes instead. I own Succulent Sweets, the bakery just a few blocks over."

"I'm in love with you," Jax informs her and takes the box from her hands. "Of course, these will go straight to my hips."

"Whatever." I wave him off and roll my eyes. "He never gains a pound. This is Jax, my partner."

"Nic," she says and shakes his hand. "Jules was right. You are hot."

"I love Jules already," Jax says with a wink and salivates over the cupcakes. "There are some with M&M's on them!"

"Yeah, Mark asked me to make those today's special." She rubs her hands on her thighs as if she's nervous of what we'll think of them. "Jax is going to be a great addition to girls night out," Nic says with a laugh. "I have to get back to the shop. Oh! Mark included a card." She pulls a white envelope out of her back pocket. "See you soon!"

She waves and leaves and I open the card.

M-
Miss you. Sorry I had to cancel.
Love,
M.

"Oh my God, these are amazing." Jax hands me a cupcake with M&M's on the top. I sigh as I glance up at him.

"Okay, I feel better."

"Cupcakes make you feel better?"

"No, Mark makes me feel better."

"You are in trouble, sugar baby."

"You have no idea."

CHAPTER EIGHT

-Mark-

"I'm going to put Keaton down for a nap," Natalie says and kisses the baby's head where he's resting in my arms.

"He's fine here," I offer, enjoying the feel of the baby in my arms. He's growing so fast.

"He'll sleep longer in his crib, and you guys can talk," she replies easily and takes the baby from my arms. "Come on, Livie, we'll put Keaton to bed and I'll read you a story."

"Ferdinand!" Livie exclaims as she holds her mom's finger and walks with her out of the room.

"Liv's on a Ferdinand kick," Luke informs me. "I think Nat's going to redecorate her room based on the book."

"That's fascinating," I reply, ribbing my brother. "What other tid-bits do you have to share?"

"You're an ass." Luke laughs. "This is my life, man. Nap times and fictional bulls and the sexiest woman I've ever seen."

"Nat's great," I reply seriously. "You couldn't have done better than marrying her."

"You're damn right. If she ever tries to leave me, I'm going with her. This life doesn't work without her."

When his words sink in, I cover my mouth and try not to laugh too loudly, afraid of waking the baby. "'If she ever tries to leave me, I'm going with her.' That's awesome."

"And completely true." Luke offers me some pineapple from a bowl, and I take a slice, the juice reminding me of Mer's pussy.

God, I fucking love her pussy. So sweet, so addictive.

"How are things with Meredith?" he asks, as if he can read my mind.

"Good." I shrug like it's no big deal.

"What's on your mind?"

"Nothing."

He chews on a slice of pineapple. "You don't show up at my house in the middle of the afternoon on a Friday for no reason."

I chew the pineapple slowly, trying to verbalize the words that keep floating around in the back of my head.

"Spill it, for fuck's sake," Luke says with exasperation.

"Things with Mer are great..."

"But?"

"If something seems too good to be true, it usually is."

Luke grows quiet. I glance up to find him watching me thoughtfully with narrowed eyes. "Do you think it's too good to be true?"

"I think it's happening fast, but I can't seem to slow it down."

"You've been in love with her since you were sixteen, man."

"She's not the same girl she was when she was sixteen, and I'm not the same either."

"So you're getting to know each other, and learn what's changed, but at the heart of it, you're still fundamentally the same people. Trust yourself. Trust your girl." Luke shrugs as if it's the easiest thing in the world. "I'm not saying be stupid about it. Keep your eyes and ears open, but you've found each other again after more than ten years apart. If it's what you want, enjoy it."

I nod thoughtfully and take another bite of the sweet fruit. "I know you're right, but I can't help but wonder when the other shoe is going to drop."

"Why does it have to?"

"It doesn't it's just…" I push my hand through my hair and scrub my scalp with my fingertips. "What if something happens, like a job or *something* that takes her away again?"

"You still think she'd choose dance over you."

Hearing Luke voice my deepest fear makes my mouth go dry. All I can do is jerk one shoulder up in a shrug.

"Part of learning each other is also learning to trust each other. Only time will do that."

"I'm not a patient man."

"I don't know, you've been more patient than I would have been." Luke grins and leans on the counter. "Enjoy her. Bring her for dinner some time. I always liked her."

"I like her too," Nat says as she joins us in the kitchen. "I got to page five in Ferdinand and Livie fell asleep too, so I get to have a grown up conversation now."

"How are you, beautiful girl?" I ask and kiss her cheek. Luke's eyes narrow and I can't help but sling my arm over her shoulders and grin smugly at him.

"I'm good," she says and hugs me around my waist.

"She likes me more," I inform Luke.

"She tolerates you," he says. "Like we all do."

"Pshaw. I'm everyone's favorite." I kiss Nat's head and then back away when Luke growls.

Even I know where the line is.

Natalie stands on her tiptoes and kisses Luke, wrapping her arms around his neck and holding on tight. When he comes up for air, she grins and says, "You're the sexiest man I've ever seen."

"She's just saying that."

Luke flips me off and kisses his wife, and I'm suddenly aware that with two sleeping kids, this is an opportunity for them to have some time for just them.

"I'm gonna head out. Mer should be just about ready."

"Bring her for dinner next week. Monday?" Nat says.

"She'll be in LA early next week," I reply and ignore the way my stomach clenches with nerves. "Then we have Vegas next weekend."

"Well then I'll get to chat with her in Vegas."

"Sounds good. Bye guys."

They're giggling before I even close the front door. They've been together for a few years now, and are as much in love today as they were the day they got married.

My brother's a lucky bastard.

But so am I.

I park on the street outside the studio and walk inside and the sight before me steals my breath.

A popular Starla song is blaring on the speakers and Jax and Mer are dancing, perfectly synced with each other, looking into each other's eyes.

They didn't hear me come in. I lean back on the desk and watch avidly as they sway and drift around the floor, watching themselves in the mirror.

"Watch your arms!" Jax calls out, scrutinizing Meredith.

Her arms look good to me.

The song is haunting, about love gone horribly wrong, and the dance has been translated to reflect it, portraying abuse and betrayal. The choreography is flawless, and when Jax moves like he's hitting Mer across the face, it looks almost real.

My hands and jaw clench as they continue through the dance, and suddenly Jax lifts Mer up over his head and throws her, and she falls on her ass.

"Son of a mother fucker!" she yells, surprising the hell out of me.

"You're not concentrating," Jax says and stops the music. "We did this same move four years ago during the "Love's Kiss" routine."

"Not with the combination that comes before it. I can't get my bearings in time for you to throw me like that, Jax, and I'm telling you, Starla won't either."

"What if we cut the half turn right before it?"

She leans her elbows on her knees and thinks it over for a minute. "Yeah, that could work."

"Again." Jax holds his hand out for her and lifts her to her feet. The music begins from the top, and they begin the routine again.

They are magnificent. The love and friendship they share shines through in their dance. They trust each other.

Part of me is jealous that I'll never have this connection with Meredith, and the other part of me is just so fucking proud of her and thankful that she's found this with Jax.

They approach the throw and change up the steps leading up to it, so when he throws her this time, she lands on her feet and they finish the routine flawlessly.

"Yes!" she yells and runs into Jax's arms, hugging him tight.

"There we go," he says and hugs her back. "God, you're so good, cupcake."

I begin to applaud in earnest, smiling wide and they glance over in surprise.

"Oh my God!" Mer runs to me and jumps in my arms, her arms and legs wrapped around me and kisses me hard. "I didn't see you come in."

"You were busy," I reply.

"I landed the throw!"

"I saw. It's awesome."

"I can't wait to show Starla. She's going to go ape-shit," she says excitedly and kisses me again then buries her face in my neck and takes a deep breath. "You smell good."

"You... *don't*," I reply with a chuckle.

"I know. I'm going to go take a quick shower and then I'll be ready." I set her down and she jogs to the back of the building.

"It's a great routine, man," I say to Jax.

"Thank you. She's a dream to work with." Jax wipes his face and bare chest with a towel then loops it around his neck. "Gonna keep her out again all weekend?"

I prop my hands on my hips and watch the man before me for a long moment. "Yes."

He nods once and begins to walk away, but I decide to confront this here and now.

"What's the problem?" I ask quietly.

He stops in his tracks, his back to me and slowly turns to face me. "I don't know you," he begins and keeps his eyes trained on mine.

I have to respect a man who maintains eye contact and isn't afraid to stand his ground.

"I don't know what your intentions are. You say you love her. You spend every waking moment that you aren't working together." He frowns as though he's searching for the words and I cross my arms over my chest, waiting. "She's consumed by you right now and—"

"And you're jealous?"

"I'm concerned."

"About what, exactly?"

"What are your intentions with her?"

"I'm going to be with her until the day I die," I say honestly without even thinking about it. He blinks, clearly surprised by my response and then sighs deeply.

"I'm fucking jealous, yeah," he says and wipes the towel over his hair. "Not because I want her the way you do, but because for a long time, it was just her and me, dealing with life and we were doing just fine. You need to know, man, I'm here for the long haul. Meredith is my only family, and I'm hers."

I nod, but he keeps talking.

"Don't misunderstand me. I have living relatives, but do you know what happens to a gay kid who loves to dance in the Deep South?"

I raise a brow. "Enlighten me."

He swears under his breath and paces away then paces back. "They get the shit kicked out of them every fucking day. Their parents disown them and claim they're a blasphemous abomination." He laughs humorlessly and shakes his head. "Meredith is my sister. She's my best friend. She's the first person who has accepted and loved me just the way I am. She's my confidant, and I trust her implicitly, and you need to know, I don't trust many. And over the past ten years, I've been that for her too. She missed you every fucking day. Every time she got drunk, which I think was exactly four times, she did nothing but talk about *you*." He points at me and I just don't know what to say. "The guys who made their way into her pants were worthless assholes, and out of her life before the sheets cooled. It's only been you for her, and I'll be Goddamned if I'm going to stand by and watch you let her fall in love with you all over again unless you plan to also be around for the long haul because she doesn't deserve anything less."

He's panting now, his eyes feral with protective anger and frustration. I've respected few more than I respect him in this moment.

"I don't deserve her. I'm not good enough for her because no one will ever be," I reply calmly. "But I missed her every fucking day too. I don't know if I believe in soul mates, but she belongs with me. She belongs *to* me." I shrug and hold my hands out as if in surrender. "I don't know what else to say to you. I can tell you that I would take my own life before I'd ever deliberately hurt her."

There are tears in Jax's eyes as he watches my face and finally he nods and scrubs his face with the ends of the towel. "Fine. I don't have any reason not to believe you."

"I'll never give you one."

"I smell so much better!" Mer exclaims and comes running out of the back, then stops and looks between us. "Am I interrupting?"

"Nope, just more guy talk," I reply and smile down at her as I tuck her against my side.

"What are you doing tonight?" Mer asks Jax.

"Logan and I are going out to dinner," he replies and checks the clock on the wall. "I'd better hit the shower myself."

"Why don't we all go out together?" I ask. Jax's head whips up in surprise. "If you don't mind us crashing your dinner."

"Yes!" Meredith agrees and nods. "We talked about doing dinner this weekend anyway."

"Are you sure?" Jax asks.

I nod and kiss Mer's hair then smile at Jax. "I could use some guy time."

"Your girlfriend accused me of being a girl the other night. She almost made me watch Pretty Woman."

"No man should have to endure that," I reply with a shudder.

"I know, right? I'll call Logan and take a quick shower."

"Cool."

He jogs away and Mer looks up at me, searching my face.

"What just happened?"

"I think I just bonded with your best friend."

"Really?" She grins widely, ridiculously pleased.

"Yeah, we should hang out with Jax more often. He's cool."

"Okay." She frowns and searches my face again then shrugs and walks behind the desk to collect her handbag. "I haven't met Logan yet. But he sounds really nice."

I circle the desk and pull her into my arms, burying my nose in her hair. "After dinner, I'm going to take you home."

"Oh?"

"Yes. And then I'm going to strip you out of these clothes and fuck you until you can't remember your own name." I slide my hands down her back to her ass and tug her against me so she can feel my cock against her stomach.

"Let's skip dinner," she mutters.

"That's too easy." I grin and tuck her hair behind her ear. "But all during dinner, I'm going to remind you how much I want you."

"How?"

"You'll see." I lower my lips to hers and sweep them across, gently, barely touching her skin, then nibble the corner of her mouth before sinking in and claiming her. She wraps her arms around me, anchoring herself to me and surrenders to me beautifully. Every time she does this, it makes me fall in love with her all over again.

"Seriously?" Jax asks as he walks into the room, freshly showered and dressed in jeans and a red button-down. "Are y'all going to do this all night?"

"Maybe," Mer replies and nuzzles my nose with her own before pulling away. "Are you and Logan gonna be mushy?"

"You know how I feel about PDA," Jax replies dryly.

"How does Logan feel about it?" she asks.

"Logan feels good about it." We all spin in the direction of the voice coming from the front door. He must have just walked through.

"We need to put a bell on that door," Jax murmurs.

"Hi!" Meredith immediately walks to him and gives him a hug. "I'm Meredith."

"I figured," he replies and hugs her back then smiles down at her. "I'm Logan."

"I hope so," she replies, then loops her arm through his and leads him over to Jax and me. "This is my boyfriend, Mark Williams. You've met Jax."

"Once or twice," he agrees with a laugh as he shakes my hand. His grip is firm. As he pulls away, Mer steps back to my side and Logan takes Jax's face in his hands and plants one right on him.

"Oh my," Mer murmurs.

"Logan is fine with it," Logan says again, his eyes locked on Jax's, before turning back to us with a smile. "I'm also hungry. Where are we going?"

"You're adorable," Mer says honestly as Jax watches Logan with lust-filled eyes. He's clearly falling in love with the other man.

"So are you," he says with a wink. "Your man's not bad either."

I feel my cheeks go red as all three of them watch me with sober faces and then burst out laughing at my expense.

"Thanks, I think."

"Come on. Mexican food is calling our name." Mer takes my hand and leads us all to the door.

***

"So you both leave Monday morning?" Logan asks as we eat chips and salsa and wait for our meals to be served.

"Yeah, really early," Mer replies. "I'm glad it's only a two hour flight."

"The VMA's are next Sunday, right? How long are you staying?"

Holy shit! Will they be gone almost a full week?

"We have rehearsals until Wednesday, then we come home and they'll rehearse each day before the performance," Jax replies.

"You're not dancing in the actual show?" Logan asks.

"No," Mer replies. "We'll teach Starla and her dance partner the routine and then they'll rehearse until the show on their own."

"So you'll be home Wednesday?" I ask Mer softly.

"Yeah, mid-afternoon."

"My whole family is taking a celebratory trip to Vegas on Friday for the weekend. I want to take you with me."

Her eyes grow big and then she bites her lip.

"That'll be fun," Logan says. "What's the occasion?"

"My brother-in-law is getting married, so it's a combined bachelor/bachelorette party." My eyes haven't left Mer's yet. "You don't want to go?"

"I don't want to leave Jax with all that work…"

"Jax is coming too," I reply.

"He is?" Mer and Jax reply at the same time.

"Sure. Just close the studio for the week. You'll love the girls, man. They're a riot, and they're already excited to have girls night out with you."

"I am good with the ladies," Jax agrees and nods with mock seriousness. "It's a shame."

"It sounds like fun," Mer says with a smile.

"Can I trust you in Vegas?" Logan asks Jax. "Liquor and beautiful women and all that debauchery and shenanigans?"

"I may come home married, but those are easily annulled. You know, it's Vegas."

Logan leans in to whisper in Jax's ear and Mer's jaw drops when Jax's cheeks flush and he clears his throat then coughs into his hand.

"Point taken," Jax says and rests his chin in his hand, unable to look anyone in the eye, but looking very smug.

I lean over and whisper into Mer's ear, "Go take your panties off."

She raises a brow but wipes her mouth with her napkin and excuses herself from the table. When she returns, she sends me a wicked smile and under the cover of the tablecloth passes her panties to me, which I immediately tuck into my pocket.

"Good girl," I murmur and kiss her hand.

"So, Logan, Jax tells me you're an architect," Meredith says after our food arrives.

"Yes, ma'am," he replies. "Going on almost fifteen years now."

"Good for you," she replies, and I can see that she's trying to figure the age difference in her head. "Would I have seen any of your work in Seattle?"

"Probably," he says. "My firm has worked on several of the buildings downtown."

I offer Mer a bite of my carne asada and while she chews, I lean in and whisper, "I'm going to spend about an hour with my face planted between your legs tonight."

She gasps and coughs, and I pass her a water glass. "Are you okay, baby?"

She nods and swallows the water and then narrows her eyes at me. "I'm fine."

I chuckle and resume eating my meal, enjoying the way Mer's cheeks have flushed and the pulse in her neck has sped up.

She's fucking turned on.

Of course, that's the point.

"How long have you been dancing?" Logan asks Meredith.

"Since I could walk," she replies with a laugh. "I've always been in a dance class of some sort. I danced professionally for just under ten years."

"Good for you. I'd love to watch you and Jax dance sometime."

"Come to the studio tomorrow," she replies. "We have rehearsal early in the morning."

"On a Saturday?" I ask with a frown. "You usually take weekends off."

"Not this weekend. We have to make sure the routine is perfect before we head to LA on Monday," Jax replies. "You can come watch if you want," he tells Logan.

"I do," Logan says.

"Hopefully you won't have to witness me land on my ass anymore," Mer says and glares at Jax. "This one likes to throw me around."

She shifts her legs, uncrossing and recrossing them under the table, and the thought of her bare pussy under those jeans makes my cock throb.

"Will you excuse us, please?" I stand, pulling Meredith with me. "I have to talk to Meredith about something."

I turn and lead her away from the table without waiting for an answer. We walk into a dark hallway that separates the restaurant and the bar and when we're out of sight from nearby tables, I cage her in against the wall and press my thigh against her pussy, cup her face in my hands and kiss her hard and deep. No lead in. No softness, just hot kisses.

She clamps her hands on my arms, holding on tight when I drag my nose down her jaw to her ear and growl. "I need to get you home and bury myself inside you for hours. The thought of how wet you are right now is making me crazy."

"Let's go—" she begins but I interrupt her.

"No. We're going to spend some more time with Jax and Logan and make small talk and you're going to know the whole time how fucking hard I am for you. Just you." I kiss her again and boost her up on the wall with my thigh, making her moan softly. "You make me nuts."

"I'm feeling a little nutty right now myself," she whispers and pushes her hands through my hair. "I like it."

"You're going to fucking love it."

CHAPTER NINE

~Meredith~

"Everything okay?" Jax asks when Mark and I return to the table. My pussy is throbbing in anticipation and my cheeks feel hot. It's a wonder I don't have I'M ABOUT TO GET LAID tattooed on my forehead.

"Fine," I reply and sit in my chair, then squirm a bit in my seat, trying to relieve the ache between my legs. Mark is trying to kill me.

Death by horniness.

Mark lays his hand on my thigh and it slowly drifts up to rest just below the juncture of my legs. I cover his hand with mine and squeeze out of pure self-preservation. His lips twitch when I glance up at him.

"That was delicious," I announce and push my plate away, ready to get the hell out of here.

"You barely ate anything," Jax says.

"I'm full," I insist.

"Did you save room for dessert?" Logan asks and gazes at the dessert menu. "The churros with chocolate sauce sound good."

"Yes, let's get dessert," Mark agrees and squeezes my thigh. "We have time."

I'm going to torture him later. I'm going to suck his cock until he's begging me to let him come and then I'm not going to. I'm going to keep him on the edge for as long as possible.

I grin at my new plan and nod. I'll play his game.

I slide my hand under the tablecloth to rest over his hard erection and give it a little squeeze through his jeans. Mark's face doesn't change a bit, he just takes my hand in his and lifts it to his lips to kiss my knuckles then rests our hands on the table.

Jax places our dessert order then jerks his head toward Logan in surprise when Logan also lifts his hand and kisses his knuckles. Logan's face is calm and happy and he winks at me across the table before pinning Jax with a hot look.

"Problem?"

Jax blinks and glances down at their linked hands then returns his gaze to Logan. "No."

I smile widely at my friend as he stares back at me with a *what in the hell am I supposed to do now* look.

Dessert is delivered quickly. The sugary pastry is delicious, especially when Mark drenches it in the warm chocolate sauce and offers it to me then licks his fingers clean.

I can't wait to lick *him* clean.

Finally the check comes but Logan is fast, snatching it up before anyone else can react.

"Dude, that's mine," Mark says and reaches for his wallet.

"No, I don't believe it is," Logan replies and drops his debit card in the plastic tray.

"At least let me cover mine and Mer's," Mark tries again but Logan shakes his head no.

"You can grab it next time," he says.

"Thank you," I say and grin at the kind man. I'm pleased with this first meeting. Logan is smart and good-looking and clearly into my best friend. Jax chose well this time.

I hope he doesn't fuck it up.

We all walk out into the cool spring evening and stand on the sidewalk for a moment, taking a deep breath, ready to part ways for the night.

"Thanks again for dinner," Mark says and shakes Logan's hand, then Jax's. "We'll do it again soon."

"Absolutely. Nice to meet you," Logan replies, then turns to me and hugs me tight. "Have fun," he whispers.

"Goodnight," I say and grin at Jax. His eyes widen because he knows what's coming, but he can't stop me before I call out, "Use condoms! Be safe!"

"Goodbye, Meredith Agatha," Jax replies, making me gasp.

"You promised never to tell anyone my middle name!"

He grins as Logan takes his hand and begins to pull him away. "No I didn't."

"Yes you did! We were drunk! We even took a shot to seal the deal."

"Shot deals don't count, lemonhead. You know that." He laughs loudly as Logan leads him away and I glare at his back, wondering how I can get vindication.

"Let's go home, baby," Mark says and kisses my hand as he leads me to his Jeep.

"He yelled out my middle name for everyone to hear."

"I heard. I was here. How did I never know your middle name?"

"I never tell anyone."

"Except Jax," he replies with a laugh. I love that the jealousy over Jax seems to be fading.

"We were drunk one night and were trying to one-up each other on the embarrassing story scale, and I told him that *in confidence*. He wasn't supposed to blab it. Now his boyfriend knows it too!"

Mark laughs and shakes his head as he drives onto the freeway, headed north out of downtown Seattle. "I'm quite sure there are worse middle names out there."

"I'm quite sure there aren't."

"What else did you tell him?" Mark asks and lays his hand on my thigh, waking my body up again.

"I told him about that time I almost lit the chemistry lab on fire in high school."

Mark laughs and squeezes my thigh. "I thought we were all done for."

"I'm sorry you had me for a partner. I was hopeless. I never should have paid John Stevens to switch with me."

"What?" His head jerks around in surprise.

"I paid John to switch lab partners with me so I could be yours. I had such a crush on you, but I couldn't get your attention."

"You had my attention, I just didn't think you were interested."

"Why did you think that?"

"Because I'd asked you out for ice cream after school a couple of times but you turned me down."

"I had dance after school."

"I didn't know that yet," he reminds me then chuckles ruefully. "From the moment I saw you I knew there would never be anyone else for me. How much did you pay John?"

"Fifty bucks." I grin as I lean over and kiss Mark's shoulder. "It was worth every penny."

He parks in his driveway.

"Why don't you ever park in your garage?"

"I have too many tools and building supplies in there right now," he says and pushes his fingers through my hair. "You are so beautiful, M."

I pull his hand to my mouth and plant kisses on his palm, then rest my cheek in it. "Thank you."

"Come on, I have stuff to show you."

"I thought you were gonna fuck me? I kind of had visions of us tearing each other's clothes off and having sex against the front door."

Mark grins as he gets out of the Jeep and waits for me by the front porch. "That's not a bad plan, but we'll have to try that another time. I'm going to show you some of the projects I've finished around here over the past few days."

"But I'm horny," I whine and stick my lower lip out.

"Haven't you figured it out?" he asks as he unlocks the door and leads me inside, then pulls me in his arms and tips his forehead against mine. "Anticipation is the best foreplay there is."

"I'm going to spontaneously combust," I whisper, my eyes closing as he combs his fingers through my hair and nuzzles my nose with his, then glides his fingertips down my cheeks to my neck. My nipples pebble and I clench his shirt in my fists. "I feel like you haven't been inside me in weeks."

"It's been hours, baby."

"Too long."

Suddenly he backs away and clears his throat, licks his lips and shakes his head. "Nice try. Follow me."

"I want to suck your cock," I grumble and walk right into his back as he comes to an abrupt stop then spins and cradles my face in his hands, kisses me madly, his tongue colliding with mine and then shuts it down just as fast, panting and eyes on fire.

"Enjoy this. Trust me."

And with that he turns away again and leads me through the living room, furnished sparsely with a simple loveseat and recliner, to the downstairs bathroom.

"Wow, this is gorgeous." The walls are painted a rich gray, set off by a fresh white pedestal sink and toilet. The mirror is framed in black, and the black shelves above the toilet are full of white towels, tissues and an old, broken clock.

"Thank you."

"You did all of this the other night?"

He nods, watching me with hot eyes.

"What else have you done?"

He takes my hand again and leads me down a hall, but before we reach another room, he cages me against the wall, pins both my hands above my head with one hand and with the other cups my sex through my jeans as he buries his face in my neck and nibbles, not quite gently but not hard enough to leave marks.

"I'm going to make you scream later, Meredith. How do you feel about that?"

"Can't wait," I whisper and feel him grin against my skin, which turns me on even more.

Everything he does is so fucking sexy.

"Good," he says, plants one more kiss on my chin then releases my hands, links his fingers with mine and continues to lead me down the hallway.

I'm going to fucking kill him.

My body is humming in lust and anticipation. I need him inside me *yesterday*.

He gestures for me to follow him into the spare bedroom, but my heart stops as my eyes take in the beautiful, bright room. The floors are gleaming blond hardwood, the walls mocha and the windows are wide and let in ample light.

Lining three of the walls are floor-to-ceiling bookshelves. Speakers are mounted in two corners of the room, and a sound system is mounted near the doorway.

"A library?" My eyes meet his. He's watching me closely as he nods. "I've always wanted a library."

"You have?"

I nod and wander through the empty space, imagining hundreds of books filling the shelves and deep, soft furniture and throw rugs sprinkled around the space.

"Aside from dancing, reading is my favorite thing."

"I'm surprised you find time to read," he says and watches me wander the room.

"I don't often anymore. When we were touring, it was either find a corner to yourself and read or drive each other crazy. This would be the perfect room to escape to, curl up in a chair with a good book and waste an afternoon." I stop in front of the windows and look out on the back yard, the fire pit and lounge where we made love in the middle of the night, the grassy lawn that's just starting to turn deep green, and I know in my heart that this is where I want to be. After more than ten years of touring and working and not having a true home, I want *this* home with *this* man.

"What are you thinking?" Mark asks as he slides up behind me and wraps his arms around me, kissing my cheek.

"This is a beautiful home, M."

"Thank you. I hope someone will be happy here."

"What are you talking about?" I spin in his arms and frown up at him.

"I'm going to finish remodeling it and sell it."

"You bought it to flip it?" I ask and gaze about the beautiful room.

"Yes."

"But…" Why do I suddenly feel like all of my hopes and dreams were just snatched out from under me?

"But what?" He grips my chin in his thumb and forefinger and catches my gaze in his.

"I just thought you planned to live here."

"Do *you* want to live here?"

"Pshaw," I roll my eyes and pull out of his arms, trying with all my might to cover my disappointment. I'm being ridiculous! "We're nowhere near ready to move in together."

"Then why do you look so sad?" He pushes his hands in his pockets and watches me quietly.

"I'm not sad." I walk toward the doorway, my shoes clicking loudly on the floor. "Show me the rest."

I turn and wait for him, one eyebrow raised, but he hasn't moved. He's still watching me silently until I feel my cheeks flush.

"Talk to me, M."

"I just like your house, Mark. It's just a house."

A house that I'd started to think of as ours, which is completely ridiculous.

He slowly walks to me and cups my cheek in his palm and kisses my forehead tenderly before taking my hand in his and leading me out of the room and up a back stairway that I didn't know was here.

"This house is bigger than it looks."

"It's deep, so yeah, it's bigger than it looks from the street," he replies. "I've been remodeling it with a family in mind, hoping that it'll attract a young family to buy it."

He guides me to a bedroom and walks through ahead of me. The room has been painted baby pink with white filmy curtains and gray carpeting. It's clearly a little girl's room.

"This bedroom is attached to the other bedroom through a jack and jill bathroom." He slides a door open, revealing a bathroom with fresh colorful tile and countertops, leading through the other side to another bedroom, the same size as the last. This one is painted blue with white curtains and the same gray carpet.

"Very cute," I say with a smile.

Holy shit, I can imagine our kids in these bedrooms. What the fuck is wrong with me?

He's still watching me soberly, and I can see that he's not buying my bright smile.

"Are you going to tell me what the hell is wrong with you?"

"Why would anything be wrong?" I shrug and turn my back on him to walk out into the hallway toward the other end of the house where the master suite is. Until I saw that library downstairs, this was my favorite room. The bed is big and comfortable, the carpet deep and soft under bare feet, and instead of regular windows, there is a wall of glass with a door that opens onto a small balcony.

I can picture myself sitting on that balcony every Sunday morning for the rest of my life, drinking coffee while I listen to birds sing in the trees. Or rock my babies to sleep out here while I listen to crickets and watch the stars.

And in every scenario, Mark is in the chair next to mine.

I'm so jumping ahead of myself here. I didn't really think about it too much before, but now that he's said that he's going to sell the house, it feels like I've lost something… important.

"Okay," Mark says abruptly and lifts me in his arms, then lies on the bed with me. "Something's up. Speak."

"I'm fine."

"You're sad, M. We went from hot horniness to sadness in the blink of an eye, and I want to know why."

I shrug and bite my lip, feeling ridiculous.

"It's stupid. Forget it. Let's have sex." I dive for his jeans but he rolls over me, pinning me beneath him.

"No. This won't work if we don't talk, so talk."

"You talk." I pout.

His lips twitch and his eyes light with humor, making me feel better.

"Okay. I love you. Your turn."

"I love you too. Your turn."

"I want to know why you suddenly withdrew from me."

"I didn't, I just…"

"What?" He rests his lips on mine for a moment, kisses me softly and pulls up, stroking my cheeks with his thumbs.

"I don't want you to sell this house." I bite my lip and cringe.

"Why?"

"I just don't."

He growls and laughs as he leans his forehead on mine. "Am I going to have to torture the information out of you? I have ways of making you talk, you know."

"No you don't. I'm a vault."

He cocks a brow in that arrogant way he does and his naughty smile spreads over his mouth and I know I'm in deep trouble.

"Oh, sweetheart," he murmurs, his lips tickling mine. "Challenge accepted."

He nibbles my lips and rips the buttons completely off my button-down shirt as he spreads it apart and buries his face in my cleavage.

"That was a new shirt," I inform him dryly.

"I like it," he replies, not deterred in the least. He pushes back on his knees, pulls me up to take my shirt and bra off, then covers me with his broad body again, kissing my shoulder and down to my breasts, pulling the nipples into his mouth.

"Holy shit," I whisper, burying my fingers in his hair then raking my nails down his back, gathering his shirt in my hands. "Take your shirt off."

He grips his shirt and tugs it over his head then throws it on the floor with my ruined clothes and returns to kissing down my torso to the waistband on my jeans. He rubs his nose on my skin along the top of the denim, sending goose bumps over my skin.

"Mark," I whisper and wiggle beneath him.

"Yes, love," he says.

"I'm too turned on to go slow."

He pops the button on my jeans and watches my face as he slowly lowers the zipper, making me bite my lip and moan in frustration.

"I'm frustrated too," he says.

"I can help with that." I reach down for his jeans but he takes my hands and pins them to the bed at my hips.

"Not that."

I glare at him, not enjoying this game anymore. "I don't want to tell you this, Mark. Just leave it be and fuck me."

His eyes flare in anger. "No. It's a simple question."

"Not for me."

He peels my jeans down my hips and legs then tosses them over his shoulder.

"Did you like it when I told you to take your panties off at the restaurant?"

"Yeah, it was fun."

He kisses my belly, just below my belly button and takes a deep breath.

"You smell like you need to be fucked."

His words make my entire body clench in anticipation. "I do."

"God, you're so fucking sexy, Meredith." He's panting now, watching me with molten blue eyes. "I'll never get enough of you."

He parts my thighs and gently spreads my lips with his thumbs.

"Your pussy is amazing. Small and pink." He nudges my clit with his nose, making me gasp. His tongue swirls around my opening before he sinks a finger inside.

"Oh God."

"Why don't you want me to sell this house, Meredith?"

"I don't know." I bite my lip and then cry out when he backs away from me completely. "Hey!"

"Anticipation," he reminds me as he kisses my inner thigh. I glare down at him and he laughs, the jerk.

"I'm so glad I'm entertaining you while I *need* you inside me," I reply angrily. Suddenly, his face changes. He's no longer amused. He's... *I don't know.*

For the first time ever, I can't fucking read him.

"Mark?"

He lays his forehead on my belly, grips my hips in his hands and holds on to me for a moment before looking up at me again with love and fear and... *hope?*

I sit up, cup his face in my hands and kiss him passionately, breathing him in. God, he always smells so good. His arms wrap around my waist, lifting me against him. I wrap my legs around his hips and press my center against his denim-covered cock, kissing him with everything I have.

I hate that I saw fear in his eyes. What could he possibly be afraid of?

"I don't want you to sell the house," I whisper as I place soft kisses over his cheeks, "because I love this house. I could see us living here, having kids here. This is a family house, but the family I see in it is *ours*. That's why I don't want you to sell it." I press my face to his neck, unable to look him in the eye. "I didn't want to say that because this is still so new, and kind of scary, but I couldn't read you just now and I can't stand that."

He's hugging me fiercely. I expect him to make me look him in the face, but he doesn't, which is very un-Mark. Instead, he cradles my head gently; brushes my hair with his fingers and rocks us soothingly. Finally, he lays me on my back, shucks out of his jeans and covers me completely, resting his pelvis against my own.

His heavy cock pulses against my core, the tip tickling my clit and I can't help but circle my hips in invitation. Mark's eyes are intense, hot, and I can't look away from them. Finally, he pulls his hips back and slides inside me, infinitely slowly and reverently, making tears form in my eyes.

"Don't cry, sweetheart."

"You feel so good," I whisper roughly.

He hasn't said anything in response to me spilling my guts, which worries me. Maybe he's not ready to hear about my clingy need to someday live with him? Maybe this *is* just sex for him and I'm jumping to conclusions?

Maybe I'm an idiot.

He begins to move, rhythmically making love to me. One large hand glides up my side to cup my breast, his thumb tweaks over my tender nipple, making me bite my lip. His lips turn up in a half smile as he watches my body's reaction to his touch.

"Do you have any idea," he whispers and brushes his cheek against mine, barely touching me. His stubble tickles me, but makes my body clench even more. "Any idea how often I've wondered what it would sound like to hear those words come from you?"

He shudders and closes his eyes and I brush my fingertips up and down his back. A light sheen of sweat covers his strong body as he begins to move, his pubis pumping against my clit, sending electricity zinging through my body, all the way to my fingertips.

"Oh my God," I whisper and close my eyes as he makes love to me, pounding into me while whispering words of love and forever and I can't take it. It's just too much. I erupt beneath him, crying out his name as I see stars explode around us.

"That's right, baby," he whispers. He reaches over me and grips his headboard as he thrusts into me harder, his mouth forming an O as he comes hard, jerking over me and watching me with wonder.

Finally, he scoops me into his arms and rolls us to the other side of the bed, cradling me in his arms.

"I'll keep the house and we'll take it one day at a time. Is that okay?"

"Yes. Thank you."

He kisses my forehead and suddenly grins. "I guess you'll have to help me shop for furniture."

"I will?"

He nods and gives me that naughty smile again. "Now that I've finally got you to admit that you'll want to live with me one day, you should have a say in how your house is furnished."

"It's not my house," I insist quickly with a shake of my head, pushing against his chest.

He rolls his eyes and pulls me back in his arms effortlessly. "Will you make up your mind? It either is or it isn't."

It so is.

"It's *your* house that I don't want you to sell."

"We'll work on it."

CHAPTER TEN

For the first time in as long as I can remember, I don't want to go to work. I want to stay here, in my bed with my man still sleeping and wrapped around me and pull the covers over our heads and pretend that the rest of the world doesn't matter.

But I have a plane to catch and I don't think Jax ever came home last night. Good for Jax.

My bag is packed and I'm ready to go, so I just lie here and watch Mark sleep for a while, enjoying the way his face is soft in sleep, the whiskers on his cheeks and how messy his hair is.

Of course, his hair is always messy.

He rolls onto his back and flings an arm over his head. I'm not stupid. Like I'm going to pass up this opportunity.

I slide down his body and before my movement can wake him, I take his semi-hard cock on my hand and lick him from the root to the tip in one fluid motion then take him in my mouth, wrap my lips around him and pull up firmly.

"Holy shit," he mutters and sinks his hands in my hair. "Good morning."

"Good morning," I reply with a smile and circle the head of his cock with the tip of my tongue. "You can go back to sleep. I'm just gonna play down here for a little while."

He chuckles and then groans when I cup his balls in my hand and massage them while sucking up and down on his now very firm dick. It's so damn big, almost too big for my mouth, so I lick and kiss and even graze the tip of my teeth down the shaft.

"Damn, you're good at that, baby." His voice is still thick with sleep, his body warm and completely at my mercy.

Sexy as fuck.

"I can feel your heartbeat right here," I say and rub my fingertips over the thick vein on the under side of his dick. "It's moving a little fast."

"I'm sure it is."

"Why is that?" I suck on the head and jerk him with my hand as I wait for his answer.

"Because the sexiest woman alive is sucking me off," he replies with a growl and pushes his hips off the bed. "Jesus fucking Christ, M, your lips should come with a warning label."

I laugh and lick down his shaft to his heavy balls and lick them both, then lick each one in turn while slipping my finger over that super sensitive spot right beneath them.

"You're going to make me fucking come."

"I think that's the point," I say and smile smugly as his legs begin to move restlessly and his hands clench in the sheets at his hips. "Like this, do you?"

"Just a bit," he says through gritted teeth. I lick up the shaft and suck on the tip again, knowing he's close as I pump my fist over him and feel his entire body clench. His balls tighten and lift and suddenly he's coming in my mouth. I swallow quickly and watch his face as he pants and combs his fingers through my hair.

"Best way to wake up ever," he says and laughs as he collapses back on the bed.

"That was fun," I say and kiss my way up his body and lie on top of him. "Good morning, handsome."

He kisses my forehead and wraps those amazing arms around me, holding me tightly to his chest.

"When do we have to leave?" he whispers.

"In about thirty minutes," I say. "Are you sure you don't want to come with us?"

"I think that's the fourth time you've asked me that since Friday night," he says as his fingertips glide up and down my bare back. His heartbeat is beginning to return to normal beneath my cheek.

"I know. I'd kind of like having you there."

"I have to work too. It's only a few days." He rolls us on our sides so he can see my face. "I'll pick you up from the airport on Wednesday."

I nod and cup his face in my palm. "I'll call you whenever I can."

"Do your work, enjoy Starla and Jax for a couple days, then come back home to me."

I smile widely and lean in to kiss him. I know he's nervous about me leaving. I've felt it from him every time we've made love this weekend, in moments when I've caught him watching me quietly. I don't know how to assure him that there is nothing to worry about.

"Want me to bring you back something?" I grin and sit up, letting the sheet pool in my lap and scrub my hands over my face. "A T-shirt? Coffee mug? Post card?"

"Just my woman, thanks," he says as he climbs from the bed and walks naked to the bathroom. Good God it's not a hardship to watch him walk away in the least. That ass is just… delicious.

I could bounce a quarter off that ass.

I blink when I hear the toilet flush and then feel my face heat when he walks back in the room.

"What were you thinking?"

"That I could bounce a quarter off your ass."

"I thought you liked my arms?"

"Your ass isn't half-bad either." I shrug and climb from the bed, searching for my clothes, avoiding eye contact. For God's sake, I had the man's penis in my mouth ten minutes ago, but telling him that I think he has a nice ass makes me shy?

What the fuck?

"Come here." It's not a request. I drop the shirt and leggings I plan to wear on the plane to the bed and cross to him. He loops his arms around me and hugs me tight, gently rocking back and forth and plants his lips on my head. He takes a deep breath when I press my palms to his back and hold on tight.

"I like looking at you," I whisper.

"Good. I like looking at you too." He chuckles and kisses my hair then rubs my back soothingly. "Is Jax here?"

"I don't know. I never heard him come home." I cross to the bed and check my phone. "There aren't any messages from him."

Mark and I have just finished pulling on our clothes when I hear the front door burst open.

"My bags are ready!" Jax calls out on his way past my bedroom to his.

"He's home now," I say and laugh as I jog out into the hallway. "Are you okay?"

"Yeah. Logan and I... uh... overslept."

"Right."

"Shut up."

"I like him." I lean my shoulder on his doorjam and cross my arms over my chest as he gathers his toiletries and throws them in a bag. "He's nice. And he's hot."

"I heard that!" Mark calls from my bedroom, making me laugh.

"He's not as hot as you!" I call back.

"We're gonna be late," Jax mumbles and stops in the middle of the room, looking stressed and rushed, with his hair standing on end, stubble still on his cheeks and the clothes that I'm sure he was wearing yesterday.

"No we're not. You have time to at least change your clothes. You're in a relationship with the man, Jax, no need to be doing the whole walk of shame thing."

"I'll shower and change when we get to the hotel."

I roll my eyes and walk back to my room. "Thank God it's only a two hour flight!"

"I don't smell!" I hear him loudly sniff his armpit and then mumble under his breath about finding a clean T-shirt.

Mark is sitting on the edge of my bed checking his phone. He's also wearing the same clothes from yesterday.

"Looks like Jax isn't the only one doing the walk of shame today," I say with a chuckle. "You should just bring some extra things here for when you stay with me."

"You should just move in with me and we won't have this issue," he says, still staring down at his phone.

"I'll make room for you in *my* closet," I reply without acknowledging his suggestion because frankly, I don't know how in the hell to respond to that.

"I'll make room for you in my closet," he says, still typing furiously on his phone.

"I'm ready!" Jax says as he hustles past my room, then backtracks and pokes his head around the doorjam. "Hello? Flight? LA? Job? Are you coming?"

"Yes. Ready, babe?"

"I'm ready."

The drive to the airport is quiet as all three of us are lost in our own thoughts. It's early enough that traffic isn't too thick yet and we make it to the airport with plenty of time.

"You don't have to pay to park, M. Just pull up at the drop off area."

"I'll go in with you," he says.

"It's a waste of money," I insist, but he takes my hand in his and kisses my knuckles gently, making me go all gooey inside.

"No it's not. I'm not going to be able to touch you for more than forty-eight hours, Meredith. I'll take every minute I can now."

"Damn, you have it bad, man," Jax says with a laugh from the back seat earning a grin from Mark.

"And you don't?" Mark challenges him.

Jax shrugs. "I said all my mushy stuff in private this morning."

"Aww, you're mushy?" I squeal and bounce in my seat. "I've never seen you be mushy before."

"And you won't see it now," he replies dryly. Mark parks the Jeep and the guys pull our suitcases out of the back and pull them behind us as we walk into the terminal.

We print our boarding passes, check our bags, and Jax shakes Mark's hand. "Thanks for the ride, man. I'll meet you at the gate, tootsie roll. I don't want to witness any more of the mush." He winks and walks away, leaving Mark and me alone.

"I'll text you when we get in."

"Good. I'll worry." He links our fingers on both hands and loops them around my back then leans in and kisses me, not giving a shit who might be watching. Finally he releases one of my hands and cups my neck, his thumb making little circles on my cheek as his lips nibble and make me forget where I am.

With one kiss, he can completely disarm me.

"Be safe," he whispers against my lips.

"You too," I reply and brush my fingers through his hair. "I'll see you soon."

He nods and frowns slightly, but then smiles widely, in that naughty way and winks down at me. "I love you, Meredith Agatha."

"I love you too. But Jax is gonna die."

***

"Christ on a cracker, Jax, you're trying to fucking kill me." Starla growls before guzzling half a water bottle. I raise my brows at Jax and plant my hands on my hips.

"I told you."

He glares at me and shakes his head. "Trust me, you'll get it."

"Oh, I'll get it alright," she agrees. "But it doesn't change the fact that you're a sadistic asshole."

"I've missed you," I say and wrap my arms around Starla's shoulders. "I love that you can tell Jax he's an asshole."

"You tell me I'm an asshole all the time," he reminds me.

"I've missed you guys too. This routine is stellar. Seriously perfect for the song. Thank you for doing this."

"It's all him." I point to Jax and wink at him. "I'm just his puppet."

"You're a gorgeous puppet," she says. "I want you guys to come back to my place tonight for dinner and to chat. It's been too long."

"I'm up for that," I reply. "Thank you!"

Jax nods and then turns at the sound of his name. Brian Kellogg, the dancer who will be dancing Jax's part in the routine just came in from taking a phone call.

"Let's get back to it," Starla says.

***

"God, I'm exhausted," Starla says and exhales deeply. We're settled in her family room, sprawled over couches and chaise lounges, stuffed with fresh fish and salad.

"You worked hard today, baby," her fiancé, Rick, murmurs and kisses her temple. Rick is great. He's not in the music business at all. He's a racecar driver, of all things, and they met at a charity function about two years ago. He's tall and thin and all tattooed up, even on his neck.

He looks like he could be a rocker.

"How do you know? You weren't there."

"You always work hard."

"You guys are too cute," I say and smile at them. "How are the wedding plans coming?"

"I hired a girl," Starla replies and rolls her blue eyes. Starla is stunning, with chin-length platinum blond hair, smooth white skin and her signature bright red lips. She's in fantastic shape. She always danced just as hard as the rest of us. Starla isn't just a singer, she's one of the top entertainers in the world, and she works her ass off. "I like her ideas and she's great about checking in with me on stuff, so it's working for us."

"Good."

"And you guys are coming," she says while pointing at us.

"We wouldn't miss it," Jax assures her.

"How is Brian doing with the shows?" I ask and pick a hangnail on my right hand.

"He's fine. He's a damn good dancer, but he's no Jax."

"He's a drama queen," Rick says with a roll of the eyes.

"Yeah, he is that," Starla agrees. "But he's hot and the audience loves him, so as long as he doesn't piss me off too bad, I'll keep him around. Until I can talk Jax into coming back, that is."

Jax laughs and shakes his head, but Starla isn't laughing. She sits up straight and leans her elbows on her knees.

"Actually, I wanted to talk to you guys about something."

Jax and I share a look and then watch her quietly.

"Mer, I'm so sorry about your mama. I'm sorry I couldn't come to the funeral. I was stuck in a blizzard in New York and couldn't get a flight out."

"Oh, Star, it's okay. Thank you for calling that day. I knew you were thinking of me."

She nods and then sighs. "Geez, why am I nervous?"

"What's up, little girl?" Jax asks. He always called her little girl because Starla is so petite.

"I miss you guys. We toured together for so many years, you're just a part of this whole family that we have going here. I want you to come back on tour with me next year, and choreograph the whole tour too."

"That would mean that I'd have to start working on that as soon as we get back to Seattle," Jax says in surprise. Starla nods, watching us both.

"We have a studio now, Star, with clients and kids who depend on us." I'm shaking my head slowly as the possibilities run through my head.

"You can hire people to take care of the studio while you're gone," she replies. Rick continues to watch us silently. "Think about it. I'll give you both raises of course. And I'm now offering a benefits package too."

"You're so generous," Jax says dryly.

"It's tax deductible," she says.

Do I want to go back on tour? Never knowing what time zone I'm in, not to mention what city. The long hours on planes and buses. The grueling, constant rehearsal. Late nights. Weird sleep patterns.

No Mark.

No way.

I shake my head and look Starla in the eye as I answer her honestly. "Thank you for this opportunity, Star. I'm going to pass. I've only got a year or two left in me before I start getting injured from the rigorous routines, and honestly, I'm happy with my life in Seattle."

"You met someone," Rick guesses.

"I've reconnected with someone," I reply. "And I love him. I'm done touring. But I love that you thought enough of me to ask me back."

"Keep in touch," she says. "I'll need regular updates on how it's going with your man."

"I'll do that."

"I'm going to pass too," Jax says with a sigh. "I'm happy at the studio, and I have some choreography opportunities with the university dance team as well."

"You met someone too, you bitch!" Starla cries and throws a pillow at him.

"He did," I say and clap my hands. "And he's *hot.*"

"Why did you all have to leave me and find sexy people to have sex with and not want to come back with me?" She sticks out her lower lip in a pout before burying her face in another pillow. "Moo haff me."

"What was that?" I ask with a laugh.

"You hate me."

"We love you." I blow her a kiss and grin widely. "But I love Mark more."

"Well, then, let's get all our gossiping in now while I have your undivided attention." She clears her throat and begins telling us stories of the band and their sexcapades and which celebrity fell backstage at the Grammys.

I settle back in the cushions and listen, laughing, and counting the hours until I can go home to Mark.

***

"Hey," I whisper as I borough down into the covers and cup the phone to my ear.

"Hi, sweetheart. Why are you whispering?"

"Because it's late and I'm tired and it seems appropriate."

"How was your day?" His voice sounds tired. I wish he was here, cuddled up next to me where I could smell him and feel him.

"Busy."

"Tell me."

"Well," I begin and turn onto my back so I can stare at the ceiling. "We checked into the hotel, which you know because I texted you. After Jax showered and we both changed, we went directly to the studio and worked with Starla and Brian until about six this evening."

"Who's Brian?" he asks and then I hear him chewing something crunchy.

"The male dancer. What are you eating?"

"Popcorn."

"This late?"

"I worked through dinner."

I can't help but be sad at the thought of Mark working alone in his big house all evening, skipping dinner and eating only popcorn.

"Do all women have the undeniable urge to take care of their men?" I ask aloud and bite the inside of my cheek.

"What are you talking about?"

"I suddenly wish I was there to make sure you didn't forget to eat dinner."

"I wish you were here for far more interesting things than dinner," he says with a dry voice, making me giggle. "What else happened today?"

"Starla invited Jax and I back to her place for dinner with her and Rick, her fiancé."

"Was that fun?" More chewing, and now I'm suddenly craving popcorn.

"Yes. They're both really cool people, and she filled us in on all of the gossip we've been missing out on. She wants us to come to the wedding in Paris this fall."

"That'll be fun for you guys."

I frown and look at the phone and then press it back to my ear.

"It'll be fun for *all* of us. She invited all four of us, silly."

"Wow. Okay. I'm glad you're having a good time."

"It's fun, but I'm ready to come home."

"So, what are you wearing?"

"You always ask me that," I reply. "What are *you* wearing?"

"Well, I took my shirt off a while ago because I was getting too warm, so no shirt and jeans."

"Can you see the elastic of your underwear over the top of your jeans?"

"A little bit, yeah."

"Holy fuck," I whisper. "That's so fucking hot."

"Seriously?" He laughs and crunches on more popcorn. "Why do women find that hot?"

"Don't misunderstand. It's not hot on *everyone*. But it's hot on guys like you, who have that sexy V in their hips and defined abs."

"It sounds like you've done a lot of research on this."

"Oh yeah, I'm an expert," I reply and wish again that he were with me so I could drag my fingertip down that sexy V.

"Okay, now you tell me what you're wearing."

"Nothing."

"Excuse me?"

"I've gotten used to sleeping naked."

"Tell me you and Jax are *not* sharing a room."

"No."

"Send me some dirty pictures."

"No!"

"Come on."

"Hell no." I giggle uncontrollably, loving the playful side of Mark.

"Just send me your boobs. You don't have to include your face."

"Not on your life!"

"Okay, I'll take a pussy shot."

"You are so dirty." I try to make my voice sound stern, but fail miserably.

"Only when it comes to you, baby."

"I should hope so." I sigh and feel my eyelids grow heavy. "I miss you already."

"I missed you before you boarded that fucking plane."

I grin. "Sweet talker."

"Get some sleep, baby. I'll talk to you tomorrow."

"We should wrap up by about five, so I'll call you no later than five-thirty."

"Okay. Goodnight, M."

"Goodnight, M."

He ends the call and I switch my phone to camera mode, flip on the flash and take a selfie then text it to him. The sheet is tucked under my underarms and my hair is fanned out around me on the pillow. I don't have any makeup on and I look exhausted.

Several seconds later, he responds with a photo of himself, smiling softly at me through the lens. He's written one line: *Love you, beautiful.*

CHAPTER ELEVEN

~Mark~

"I was surprised to hear from you today," I say and take a bite of my cheeseburger.

"I escaped the lab. I left Colin to fend for himself," Lena replies and winks at me. "We haven't seen you in a while."

I shrug and pop a greasy fry in my mouth. "I've been busy."

"Who is she?" She smiles knowingly and takes a bite of her grilled chicken sandwich. "Why did I get this? I should have got a burger."

My phone beeps with an incoming text on the table next to me.

"Sorry, I have to check this."

This is Jax. I borrowed Mer's phone. Here's a photo of her working.

The photo is stunning. Mer is standing behind Starla and both are looking in the mirror before them. Mer is talking and pointing to Starla's stomach, clearly coaching the celebrity.

God, I fucking miss her like crazy.

I quickly type out a thank you and set my phone aside.

"Meredith," I finally answer Lena and smile widely.

"The Meredith who broke your heart after high school?" she asks in surprise. "The one that broke your heart so badly that you wouldn't give me the time of day?"

I chuckle and shake my head at the beautiful brunette. Lena is curvy, with long dark hair and big blue eyes, and a killer rack.

Not that I'd ever tell her that. Or her husband.

"You only had eyes for Colin," I remind her. "Maybe it was *you* who broke my heart."

"Whatever." She sips her diet soda and glares at me. "Tell me everything."

"Yes, the same Meredith from high school. We've reconnected with each other." I sit and tell her everything, from the minute I saw her at Addie's funeral to our conversation last night. "I've been nervous about this trip."

"You don't seriously think she'd leave you again for a dance job?"

"I don't think so," I concede and cringe when I think of the way I broke out into a cold sweat when Mer told me that she and Jax were going to LA for this job.

"Building trust in a new relationship is a process," she says and checks her own phone when it buzzes. "My turn to be rude. Colin's calling. Hey, babe."

I pull the photo back up of Mer and Starla and smile at my girl. God, she's so gorgeous. Her hair is up in a messy knot, as usual. She's in a tight tank and yoga shorts.

Her body makes me want to sit up and beg.

Just as Lena is finishing up her conversation my phone rings.

"Hey, baby, what are you wearing?" I grin, excited to hear Mer's voice.

"Uh, sorry, Hot Tamale, it's just Jax. But I'm in shorts and a Nike tank top. How about you?"

"Is she okay?" I ask as ice forms in my stomach.

"Oh yeah, she's still working."

"I'm stealing half your burger," Lena announces and snatches my burger away.

"Oh, I'm sorry," Jax says. "I didn't mean to interrupt anything."

"You didn't. I'm having dinner with an old friend."

"Anyway, Mer's still working, but she promised to call you no later than five-thirty, so I'm letting you know she'll be a little late."

"Thanks for that, man. Everything going okay?"

"You eat pickles on your burger?" Lena groans loudly. "Ew."

"Yeah, we're good. We'll be home tomorrow."

"Okay, great. I'll see you then." Jax clicks off. "She's working."

"I heard." Lena happily munches on my burger, now missing pickles, so I reach for her chicken burger.

"Do you steal Colin's food often?"

"His tastes better than mine." She shrugs and grins smugly. "When are you coming to work in the lab?"

"I'm not."

"I don't get it. You're a brilliant scientist. I've never known anyone who can do what you do, or as quickly. Your brain never shuts down."

"So?"

"So you'd rather waste all that brilliance on building houses? You could be doing so much more."

"There's nothing wrong with my career," I say and scowl down at the chicken. "This is disgusting."

"I know."

"I like my job, Lena. I'm glad you and Colin are happy in the lab. By the way, when are you going to start having babies?"

"Not you too!" She groans and hangs her head in her hands. "Between you and my mother you'd think my vagina is shriveling up by the day."

"I really don't want to think about your vagina doing anything."

She giggles and wipes her mouth off with a napkin. "Colin appreciates that. No kids for a while yet."

I nod and eat the rest of my fries.

"Are *you* thinking about kids?"

I scoff at my friend. "I'm not even married."

She simply raises a brow and watches me quietly.

"I'd marry her tomorrow and have a house full of kids with her if that's what she wants."

"What if that's not what she wants?"

"One day at a time," I mumble. "But I think she does. She's mentioned that she can see us having a family one day. In the meantime, we're good with taking things one day at a time. It's early days yet."

"I'm happy for you." She rests her chin in her hand and watches me with this goofy, dreamy look on her face. "It's kind of romantic."

"God, you're a girl."

"Hence the prior conversation about my vagina."

"There was no conversation. And stop saying vagina."

She laughs loudly then raises a brow when my phone pings again.

Thought you'd like a video of Mer doing what she does. Jax.

I tilt the phone so Lena can see and press play, and suddenly there's Mer, counting the rhythm for Starla and calling out moves. Finally she stops her and dances it herself, telling her where she's getting her feet wrong. The video stops right after Starla says, "Fucking A!"

"She's pretty," Lena says with a smile. "And did you see what she can do with her leg? Holy shit."

"It doesn't suck," I agree and smile at my friend.

"This was fun. I want to meet her soon."

"We're heading to Vegas this weekend, but maybe next week?" We stand and throw our garbage away and step out onto the street.

"Sounds good. I'll make my nerdy husband poke his head out of the lab long enough to interact with real people."

"Tell him I said hi, and thanks for sharing his nerdy but gorgeous wife with me today." I give her a quick hug and kiss her cheek, then watch to make sure she gets into her car safely and pulls away.

Just as I sit in the driver's seat of the Jeep, my phone rings.

"Hey."

"Who the fuck are you having dinner with?" Meredith demands. She's panting and I can hear Jax in the background say, "Not cool, KitKat."

"I'm sorry, is this my loving girlfriend?" I raise a brow and push the key in the ignition but sit and wait for her reaction. I don't think I should drive and have this conversation at the same time.

"Oh, you remember you *have* a girlfriend? Great. Answer my question."

"I was having dinner with Lena."

"Why haven't I ever heard her name before? I don't believe this, Mark. I leave for a few days and you can't keep it in your pants?"

"That's enough," I bark and clench my fist around the steering wheel. She goes quiet but I can hear her breathing hard and I know it's not from dancing. She's fucking pissed.

And so am I.

"I don't remember being on a leash, but I was having dinner with a very old friend, Meredith."

"Have you ever fucked her?" Her voice is small and quivering. I lean my head against my headrest and clench my eyes closed.

"No. And the fact that those words would even come out of your mouth hurts, Mer. She's a college friend. I worked in the same lab as her and *her husband*. Well, he was her boyfriend in college, but now they're married."

She doesn't reply but I can imagine her cheeks darkening in embarrassment, and I'd be lying if I said that her little fit of jealousy wasn't a balm to my ego. I've done my best to keep myself busy since she's been gone and remind myself that I trust her and she'll be home soon.

But apparently she doesn't trust me.

"I've made lots of friends over the years, most of whom you don't know. Just like I don't know all of your friends. Am I to assume that you've fucked every man you've met in the past ten years?"

"Of course not," she replies. "Is this where I say I'm sorry?"

"Yes."

"I'm sorry. Jax told me not to jump to conclusions, but when he said he heard a woman's voice in the background it pissed me off."

"Maybe it was my sister. Or one of the many Montgomery girls. Are you going to always be this jealous, M?"

"No, it was just a knee-jerk reaction because *I* miss you and *I* want to be the one there with you. Also, the thought of her with her hands on you made me want to commit murder. The bloody, violent kind, not the poison your food kind."

"She did talk about her vagina," I say and laugh when Mer growls. "Do you honestly think that I'd screw up what we have the second you leave town for a quick lay?"

"No."

"I love you so much it hurts to breathe, Meredith. You know me better than that."

"I know. Like I said, it was a knee-jerk reaction."

"I think we need to talk when you get home, sweetheart."

"I'm really sorry," she says. "Why haven't you ever talked about her before?"

"Because I don't see her often. She and her husband are workaholics."

"Oh."

"How was work?" I start the Jeep and pull into traffic now that the jealousy storm has passed.

"Long day." She sighs. "I miss you."

"I miss you too. I'll pick you up tomorrow. You land at two, right?"

"Yes, but you don't have to pick us up. We can grab a cab."

"I'll be there." I sigh and push my hand through my hair wishing I could hug her and reassure her that everything is okay. "No more jumping to conclusions, okay?"

"I'll work on that," she says. "Who knew I was this jealous?"

"Not me. You never even got like this in high school."

"Weird," she whispers.

"The video Jax sent me was amazing."

"Thanks."

"Mer?"

"Yeah?"

"You okay?"

"No. I feel like an idiot."

"You're a pretty idiot." She finally laughs and I smile in response. "Call me later when you're ready for bed."

"What if I call you naked again?"

"Will you send me pictures?"

"No."

"I'll talk you into it."

"Sure you will. I owe you big when I see you tomorrow."

"You don't owe me anything, but we'll be having that talk." I pull into my driveway, surprised to see my sister sitting on my front porch. "Sam's here. I'm gonna go see what she's up to. Love you, baby."

"I love you too."

I slam my door and pull my sunglasses off as Sam types furiously on her phone.

"Good to see you finally showed up," she says as she tucks her phone in her jeans and stands to hug me.

"Did we have plans?"

"No, I surprised you."

"You're weird. You can't be mad at me for not being here if you came over without calling." I pull her hair and dodge a punch to the shoulder then lead her inside and back toward the kitchen. "What can I do for you?"

"I just came over to see your adorable wittle face." She pinches my cheek then laughs when I chase her with a damp sponge out of the sink.

"Seriously, what's up?"

"I have issues."

"This is not a newsflash, sis."

"Bite me."

"Ew."

She crosses to the fridge and opens it wide, surveying the contents. "I'm hungry."

"There's some left over pizza in there," I reply and lean back on the counter, waiting for her to get to the point. "Where's Leo?"

"At the studio," she says and sniffs at the loaded pizza. "Why do you eat mushrooms?"

"Why is everyone questioning my choice of condiments today?"

"Because you eat gross things."

"What is going on, Sam?"

She takes a bite of the pizza, chews for a few seconds, then spits it out in the garbage. "How long have you had that in there?"

"About a week," I say with a smug grin.

"Ew. You're trying to kill me." She glares at me as she guzzles some water and then opens a bag of Fritos and shoves a handful of the salty corn chips into her mouth as she hops up onto a stool at the breakfast bar.

"Make yourself at home." Sam has always cracked me up. She can be such a hard ass, but she can be a mother hen too, especially to Luke and me.

"Talk about Meredith."

"What would you like to know?"

"What's going on with her?"

"She's my girlfriend, Sam. I think that was pretty obvious when you saw us at Will's house."

She nods and chews on more chips. "She looks good."

"Yeah, she does."

"She has balls."

I nod and grin at my sister. "She stood up to you."

"Like I said, she has balls." She shrugs and sips some water. "I have trust issues, though."

"You have trust issues with everyone."

"That's not true. I trust you. Leo. The family, even the crazy Montgomerys."

"Look, I know that you have your reservations, but I'm a grown man, Sam. I got this."

"She hurt you," she whispers and stares down at her bag of chips. "You were a mess for *years*."

"I'm not a mess now."

"I don't want that to happen again, Mark."

"I don't want you to get hurt by your rock star boyfriend either, you know. What are we supposed to do? Stay single forever so no one gets hurt? Maybe it'll work out."

She nods and then shrugs. "I wasn't a bitch to her."

"I appreciate that. I'd also appreciate it if you continued not being a bitch to her, especially this weekend in Vegas."

"You're bringing her?"

"Yes."

She nods again and blinks, thinking it over. "Okay. It could be fun."

"You'll probably like her."

"Let's not go crazy now."

I laugh and snatch my bag of chips out of her hands before she eats the whole damn bag. "You talk a big game, but you're just a big softie."

"I am not!" She gasps and glares at me. "How dare you call me that?"

"Because you are. You just want us all to think you're badass."

"I don't have to sit here and take this from you."

"Blah blah blah..." I roll my eyes and pull her off the stool. "Come on, let's watch a movie."

"Only if you order pizza." Her phone rings and she answers. "Hi, Mom. Yep, I'm actually with him right now. Okay."

She hands the phone to me and cackles like a witch as she passes me in the hallway and drops into my recliner.

"Hi, Mom." I've been on the phone more today than I have been in the last ten years combined.

"Hi, darling. I'm having dinner here tomorrow and I want you to bring Meredith."

"On a Wednesday?"

"You're all going on your little adventure in Vegas this weekend," she reminds me. "I want to see Meredith. Bring her over. Luke, Nat and the babies are coming along with Sam and Leo too."

"She gets home from LA tomorrow afternoon, so I'll ask her when I pick her up from the airport." Sam chooses a cheesy '80s movie on the on-demand menu, making me roll my eyes.

"Don't ask. Just bring her. I mean it. I always loved that girl."

"Okay. Do you want to harass Sam now?"

"Sure. Love you, sweet boy."

"Love you too, Mom."

I pass Sam her phone and steal the remote from her hands.

"Mom! Mark just stole the remote and I had it first!"

"Seriously? You're *tattling?*"

She sticks her tongue out at me and talks to Mom about dinner tomorrow while I give in and settle back to watch a bunch of kids in detention on a Saturday. At least the music's good.

"Molly Ringwald was kind of hot," I say when Sam ends the call with Mom.

"Judd Nelson was hot," she says and kicks her feet up.

"How late is Leo gonna be?"

She shrugs and doesn't meet my eyes.

"Sam?"

"He's been working late a lot," she says. "I don't know when he'll be done."

"Is everything okay there?"

"Sure." She offers me a fake smile but it falls from her face when I simply sit and watch her. "I think so. He's been quiet this week, and busy so I haven't had a chance to ask him what's going on."

"He loves you."

"I know. I'm just worried about him."

"Keep me updated."

"Okay. Now shush. This is the part where Judd Nelson pushes his face into Molly's crotch. It's hilarious."

"I didn't realize it was porn."

"You're gross."

CHATPER TWELVE

"Hey, man." Logan claps me on the shoulder and shakes my hand. We're standing in the airport, at the baggage claim carousel that has Mer's flight number listed for pick up. They landed five minutes ago, and I can't wait for her to get her sexy ass down here.

"How's it going?"

"Good, thanks." Logan nods and pushes his glasses up his nose. "I thought I was going to be late. Traffic was horrible."

"Came from work?" I gesture to his suit and tie.

"Yeah. I took off early today and I'm taking the rest of the week off."

"Good for you. Do you have plans?"

"Jax has been gone for a few days, and he's leaving again on Friday for Vegas, so I thought I'd take some vacation time to hang with him." He smiles shyly and loosens the top button of his dress shirt.

"Actually, I was going to talk to you about this weekend. How do you feel about meeting us down there? Jax and the girls would love it."

Logan smiles softly. "I was going to ask you if it would be inappropriate if I surprised him. I was thinking about coming down Saturday afternoon, if that's okay with you and your family."

I smile widely and shake my head. "If it were Mer, you couldn't keep me away.

Feel free to come down. I'll give you my cell number and I'll keep you updated on where we are on Saturday so you know where to find him."

"Thank you. Isn't the news of Starla asking Jax and Mer to go back on tour crazy?" He shakes his head and grins, but my heart stops. Meredith didn't mention this to me. She's going back on tour?

When? Is she planning to break things off again, or does she think we'll do the long-distance thing while she's gone for fucking months at a time?

"They're here!" I turn at the sound of Mer's voice just in time to catch her mid-air. "Oh my God, I missed you so much."

She wraps herself around me and kisses me hard before burying her face in my neck, right where she needs to be. My hands are full of lush woman as her scent floats around me, and my nerves settle some.

"Hi, baby. How was your flight?"

"Too long."

I glance over in time to see Jax and Logan with their foreheads together and a soft smile passing between them.

"I'm happy to see you," I whisper and kiss her cheek just as the carousel begins to spin.

"Me too." She kisses me again, her lips linger on mine for a long minute.

"Here's your bag, lollypop," Jax says as I lower Mer to the floor. "And we were only gone for three days. Not three months."

But you'll be gone for three months in the near future?

"Bite me," Mer says with a big smile.

"It was a long three days," Logan adds as he links his fingers with Jax's and raises them to his lips. "Let's go."

"Don't wait up," Jax says with a grin. "Not that you'll be at home anyway."

"No," I agree with a smile and take Mer's bag, leading her toward the parking garage. "She won't."

Jax winks at both of us and then the two of them set off in the other direction.

"It's so nice that Logan came to pick Jax up," Mer says.

"Mmm." I don't mention Logan surprising Jax in Vegas. It'll be a surprise for both of them.

"It was nice of you to pick me up too," she says and kisses my shoulder. "Thank you."

"Anytime, baby." I pay for our parking and toss her bag in the Jeep and soon we're on the freeway, heading toward Mer's apartment. "My mom is having dinner at her place tonight at around six. I believe she might have threatened to disown me if I didn't bring you with me."

"I'm a mess," Mer says and looks down at her yoga pants and loose T-shirt. "I'm dressed for a flight, not dinner with my boyfriend's family."

"You always look beautiful, but we have time to swing by your place for a while."

"Okay." She takes my hand in hers and holds it tightly, and just that small touch has my cock on full alert. "How is your week going?"

"Not bad," I reply. "Work is busy, as usual. I've done a little more work on your house."

"Your house," she replies immediately, making me grin. She can pretend all she wants that the house isn't hers, but since the other night, there's no question in my mind.

It's Meredith's house. And I'm going to live in it with her for the next sixty years.

That is, if she doesn't dump me on my ass to go back on tour with a pop star.

Fuck me.

"Our house?" I shoot her the smile that always makes her melt and she bites her lip. I'm going to bite that lip when I get her back to her apartment.

"Your house," she whispers.

She's not fooling anyone.

"I'm going to take a shower," she says when we get up to her apartment. "I have airplane grossness all over me."

"I'll help." I pull her behind me to her bathroom and start the shower to let the water heat up, but instead of immediately ripping her clothes off her, I take my time. I pull her shirt and bra off and spend a few minutes kissing and nibbling her shoulders, around her breasts and down to her navel. She tugs my shirt over my head and gently sweeps her fingertips over my skin, sending goose bumps over me, making my cock even harder for her.

Jesus, I'm fucking addicted to her.

My lips trail down her stomach to her smooth pubic bone as I peel her leggings down her hips and thighs, and then hold her hand as she steps out of them.

"Two nights without you is too long," I murmur and kiss her inner thighs, cup her bare ass in my hands and squeeze as she plunges her fingers in my hair and holds on tight.

"Definitely too long. You still have your pants on," she says.

"I don't give a shit about my pants," I reply and prop her leg over my shoulder, opening her up to me. I brush a fingertip gently over her swollen clit and through her pussy lips, making her gasp.

"I do." She's panting now and has my hair clenched in a death grip. "I want you out of them."

"I will be," I murmur and lean in to kiss her swollen flesh. "Fuck me, you smell like sex."

"Not yet," she says and lets out a small chuckle. "But I'm hoping to very soon."

I look up into her ice blue eyes as I lick her from her wet opening to her clit and back down again, then sink in and go to town on her, making her cry out as her legs begin to shake.

"I'm going to fall!"

I shake my head no and brace her ass in my hands, not letting up until she comes long and loud on my mouth. Her juices are dripping down my chin. She's the sweetest thing I've ever tasted and the noises coming from her make my cock throb.

I stand slowly, peppering kisses up her tight body, then quickly strip out of my jeans and boxer briefs and lead her into the shower. Mer immediately reaches for my wash-cloth and shower gel and busies herself washing me, dragging the soapy cloth over my body, around my pulsing, hard cock, slower than fuck just to make me crazy, I'm sure.

When she's finally done, I turn the tables on her, slowly washing every inch of her perfect skin.

"If I say I'm sorry for torturing you, will you go faster?" she asks breathlessly.

"No."

She chuckles and then moans when I drag her shower puff between her legs, washing her pussy.

"You're extra dirty here."

"That's your fault." She gasps and grips my biceps to keep from losing her balance as I press just a little harder. "God, that feels good."

I kiss her cheek and down to her neck, biting softly but not hard enough to mark her. Her fingertips dig into my arms when I drag the soapy puff through her folds one last time before dropping it to the floor so I can rinse her off.

"How is it possible that you feel more toned than you did just last week?"

"I probably am," she replies before kissing my chest. "The routine for Starla was more rigorous than anything I've done in the year I've been home. It toned me back up. Does it bother you?"

"Nothing about you bothers me. I love it when you're curvy and I love it when you're leaner. Fuck, M, I'm addicted to you any way I can get you." I turn off the water and dry us both off then lead her to her bed.

"I thought we were going to talk," she murmurs as I lower her to her bed and cover her body with mine.

"Later." I slide my hand over her breast and down her ribcage to her hip. "The thing you need to remember, sweetheart, is you're *mine*. Only you." I kiss her neck and collarbone. "This is the only body I fantasize about." I leave open-mouthed kisses over her breasts, pull on her tight nipples, then leave a mark right over her heart, where no one but me can see it.

Suddenly, she pushes on my shoulders, reversing our positions and braces herself on my chest. "That's good to hear," she says breathlessly as she raises up on her knees and lowers herself onto my cock. "Because I feel the same way. It's only you, M." She guides my hands over her breasts and down to her hips where I grip her tightly and lead her into a steady rhythm, watching with fascination as she rides me. She runs one tiny hand of hers down her stomach to her clit while the other hand cups her breast, pinching her nipple as she rides me with abandon. Just when I think she can't get any more beautiful she completely beguiles me, throws me for a loop and knocks me off balance.

She bites her lip and tips her head back as she increases her pace, her hips rolling over mine quickly now.

My fingers dig into her hips, pulling her down onto me harder with every thrust.

"Jesus Christ, M." I groan. She opens her eyes and pins me with her gaze as she bears down, clenches around me harder than she ever has and comes hard, shivering and bucking against me.

"Oh God!"

"Holy fuck!" I cry and sit up straight, wrapping my arms around Mer's waist and hold her close as I come with her. My cock explodes inside her as her pussy contracts around me, milking every last drop from me.

"I think you missed me," she whispers and lays her head on my chest.

"I think you're right." I lie back and cuddle her against me. She was right, we do have to talk, but it'll wait. For now, I just want to hold her close and breathe her in and not worry about her being jealous or the possibility of her leaving me.

"Sex with you is more exhausting than eight hours of dance with Jax," she mumbles. I grin and kiss her hair softly. "And did I see you leave a love bite on my boob?"

"You did."

"Aren't we too old for that?"

"No one can see it but me." I tilt her head back so I can look in those baby blues. "I enjoy marking you."

"You *are* a caveman, you know that, right?"

"With you, yes I am. And I won't apologize for it."

"I wasn't asking you to." She wiggles closer to me and sighs contentedly. "Do we have time for a nap?"

"Sure, baby."

"We'll talk when we wake up?"

"It's a date." I kiss her forehead and smile when she moans softly and I feel her body melt against me, limp in sleep. Before long I feel my own body relaxing and my eyes drift shut as Mer's rhythmic breathing pulls me into sleep with her.

***

"Shit, we're going to be late!"

I jerk awake to find Mer jumping out of the bed.

"Wake up, Mark! We overslept. We have to be at your mom and dad's in twenty minutes."

"Damn," I mutter and scrub my hands over my face. "Well, at least we already showered."

"And got dirty again." She laughs.

"Can I persuade you to take another shower with me?"

"No. Get dressed, horny man."

"I'm sorry, I couldn't hear you over the sound of us having loud, crazy sex in my head."

She laughs and throws my shirt at me. "You're insatiable."

"With you, yes." I tug on her waist, pulling her into my lap so I can kiss her neck. "I'll never get enough of you."

"Well you'll have to wait," she whispers and kisses my cheek. "Because we're going to be late."

She bounces out of my lap and finishes dressing. I don't move, I just sit with my shirt in my hand and watch her pull on a long black skirt and black and white top, then step into black sandals. She brushes her hair out and leaves it loose around her face, then applies the smallest amount of makeup, but it makes her eyes even bluer and her lips shine.

"You're not dressed." She props her hands on her hips and watches me with amused eyes. "Mark?"

"Yeah."

"You're not dressed."

"You're so fucking beautiful it hurts to breathe."

She blinks in surprise and crosses to me. "Are you okay?"

I take her hands in mine and kiss her knuckles softly, then stand and hug her close. "So fucking beautiful," I whisper and tilt her head back and place an easy kiss on her lips, before I pull away to dress.

She looks shell-shocked as I quickly dress and lace up my shoes, then take her hand in mine and lead her to the car.

"What was all that for?" she asks.

"It wasn't for anything. It's how I feel." I shrug and lace our fingers as I drive us to my mom and dad's house.

***

As we pull up to the house that I grew up in, Sam and Leo pull in behind us in Leo's black Camero.

"You're late," Sam says and glares at me.

"What does that make you?" I ask and clap Leo on the shoulder as he laughs at Sam.

"Fashionably late."

She offers Mer a real smile, and Mer returns it happily.

"It's good to see you, Sam."

"Don't let Mark make you late for everything. It's a bad habit of his." Sam links her arm through Mer's and leads her into the house with Leo and me bringing up the rear. "How did it go with Starla?"

Meredith glances at Sam in surprise. "How did you know Jax and I were working with Starla?"

"Mark told me," Sam replies.

"It was fun, but I'm happy to be home."

But for how long are you going to be home?

"Hello, everyone!" Mom is holding a sleeping Keaton on her shoulder, swaying her hips back and forth, rocking him soothingly as Livie and Luke sit on the floor playing with a toy kitchen.

"Hi, Mom," I say and kiss her cheek, then gesture to Meredith. "You remember Mer."

"Of course. Hello, darling. I'm so glad you came."

"Thank you for inviting me." Mer grins and kisses Keaton's head, then Mom's cheek.

"My turn," Dad announces as he joins us from the kitchen. He collects hugs from Sam and me and then lifts Mer off her feet in a big bear hug. "It's so good to see you, Meredith."

She grins and blinks back tears as he sets her on the ground, then moves on to shake Leo's hand.

"You okay?" I whisper down to her. She replies with a quick nod and a brave smile.

"Hi, guys," Nat says and waves from the dining table off the kitchen. She's drinking a glass of wine and smiling happily.

"You must be done breastfeeding," Sam guesses and joins her.

"Yes, ma'am. I figured it was for the best, especially with the Vegas trip this weekend."

Liv stands and walks over to the bookshelves by the television in the family room that opens up to the kitchen.

"No, baby, you can't have those," Luke says and catches her before she can pull Mom's glass bells off the shelf. "Mom, you have to babyproof this room. She'll break these."

"She's never paid any attention to them before. I guess it's time to pack them away for a while," Mom says and kisses Keaton's cheek. I hold a chair out for Mer then sit next to her and pour her a glass of wine. My phone buzzes in my pocket, so I pull it out to find a text from Isaac.

Take the rest of the week off. See you Friday at the airport.

"Everything okay?" Mer asks as I set my phone on the table.

"Yep. Isaac just gave me the rest of the week off."

"I like him so much," Mer says with a grin. I can't help myself, I lean in and kiss those lips before taking a sip of my wine. "Me too."

"Okay, men, I need you in the kitchen," Dad announces as he starts pulling stuff out of the fridge.

"That's my cue," I whisper and kiss Mer's cheek before joining Dad and Luke in the kitchen. To my surprise, Leo joins us too and smirks when I raise a brow at him.

"What? I can cook."

"Really?"

"Yes, really."

"Want to wear one of Mom's aprons?" Luke asks and then laughs when Leo flips him off.

"Livie!" Nat jumps up and runs after her daughter who has gone straight for Mom's bells again.

"Okay, troublemaker," I say and scoop Livie into my arms. "You've wrecked enough havoc today. You can come cook with me."

"Unca Mawk," she says and grins. "Cook wif you."

"That's right." I plant her on my hip and set about getting the rice ready and glance over to see Mer laughing with Nat, Sam and Mom.

She fits perfect here.

And then I remember Logan's remark at the airport and all of the air leaves my lungs.

Leo blows a raspberry on Liv's cheek as he walks by, making her giggle and pulling me out of my depressing as fuck thoughts.

"Daddy's cookin'," she says and points at Luke.

"He thinks he is," I reply and whisper in her ear, "but he's not as good as Uncle Mark."

Liv giggles and Luke flips me off behind her back.

"So, Nat," I begin and watch Luke with a smug smile. "When are you going to run away with me?" I cross to where she's sitting at the table and rest my hand on her shoulder. Mer's pursing her lips, but her eyes are laughing at me.

"I have to check my calendar," she says and leans her face on my arm.

"Dude, get your hands off my wife. You have your own girl."

"I don't know," Mer says, playing along. "I think they make a cute couple."

"You're not supposed to encourage him," Luke says, glaring at Mer.

"You know you prefer me," I continue. Livie is watching us avidly, turning her gaze from her mom at my side to her dad, who is now leaning on the kitchen counter glaring at me.

"Mmm…" Natalie acts like she's thinking it over, then shakes her head. "No, I'm still gonna stick with him." She points to Luke and then pats my arm consolingly. "You have a better option over there anyway."

"I guess our love was never meant to be," I say, my voice full of drama.

"I guess not."

"You're all sickening." Sam rolls her eyes. "Seriously, run while you still can, Mer. They're all a bunch of crazies."

"I think I'll stay," Mer says with a laugh. "I kind of like it."

Yes, for the love of all that's holy, stay.

"My kind of girl." I kiss Mer's cheek and lower Liv into her lap on my way back to the kitchen. I busy myself chopping vegetables for the salad, listening to the girls chatter and laugh. Luke and Leo are talking about a mutual friend in LA. Dad is seasoning the steaks for the grill.

I glance over at Mer to find her watching me with sober eyes, her lips tight. What is she pissed about?

Before I can ask her, Mom stands, lowers Keaton into his portable crib and gestures to the girls. "I want to show you girls my garden."

"Will you guys listen for Keaton? We'll take Liv with us," Nat says.

"Sure, baby. Enjoy." Luke smiles at his beautiful wife as the girls file out the patio door to the back yard.

Meredith won't meet my eyes.

What the fuck just happened?

CHAPTER THIRTEEN

-Meredith-

"My kind of girl." Mark kisses my cheek and lowers Liv gently onto my lap before joining the others in the kitchen. Liv looks up at me with wide eyes.

"Your name?" she asks with her sweet little voice.

"Meredith," I reply.

"Meme," she replies and smiles widely, then slaps her hands on the table and glances over at her mama. "Hi, Mama!"

"Hi, baby," Nat says and smiles at her daughter.

"What are you packing for this weekend in Vegas?" Sam asks us.

"Are we doing formal stuff?" I ask and brush my fingers through Liv's fine brown hair.

"Maybe. I don't really know what the plan is," Nat says with a shrug. "I'll probably bring a cocktail dress and heels, just in case. I'm definitely taking my bathing suit so we can lounge by the pool."

"I hate you for just having a baby a few months ago and you already have your pre-baby body back." Sam glares at Natalie.

"I'm telling you," Nat says with a grin. "It's the yoga."

"You do yoga?" I ask eagerly. "I've been trying to find a class since I moved back."

"I teach a class," Nat says. "You should come."

"Awesome."

"Well, I'm not taking yoga," Sam says.

"You don't need it," Leo calls from the kitchen. Sam blows him a kiss.

"Okay, so something nice and a bathing suit," I say and mentally thumb through my closet. "I guess I'll take some jeans and tops too."

"Yeah, bring a little of everything," Sam says with a nod.

"How are you doing, Meredith?" Lucy covers my hand with her own and offers me a kind smile. She was always so nice to me, and the feel of her hand on mine reminds me of my mom and I'm caught in the grip of grief so quickly, I didn't see it coming. My chest aches with a longing I've become used to feeling, but I keep the tears at bay and offer Lucy a smile.

"I'm doing well. The studio is doing great."

"It's such a joy to be able the spend time with you again," Lucy says and pats my hand before turning her attention to Liv, who's trying to squirm out of my lap so she can climb into Lucy's.

Before I can respond, I see the screen on Mark's phone light up at my elbow. I glance down to see a message from someone named Tami.

It's been a while, sexy. Tonight work for you?

Seriously? He has women still calling him for booty calls?

I want to confront Mark right now, but now is not the time. We're with his family, for crying out loud.

It'll have to wait for later. We need to have that talk anyway.

Sam catches my eye and offers me a supportive smile. She obviously saw the text too. I just shrug, smile bravely and do my best not to stab Mark in the arm with the knife he's currently using to chop the salad.

Just as I lift my glass to take a sip of my wine, Mark's screen lights up again, but this time it's from someone named Marcy, and it's a photo.

Of her motherfucking tits.

Are you fucking kidding me?

"Man whore," Sam mumbles and shakes her head. I don't think I could confront him right now without killing him if I tried.

My skin suddenly feels clammy and I'm seeing red.

"I want to show you girls my garden."

"I could use some fresh air," I respond immediately. Maybe I'll be able to breathe through the fury so I can talk with Mark calmly. But just then, the screen comes to life again, the way they do when you haven't checked the last message that came in, reminding you it's there, and I get a second look at Marcy's double-D's.

Lucy announces that we're going outside just as Mark catches my eye. His brows rise in surprise when he sees my face, but I turn away, unable to look him in the eye. Luke agrees to listen for the baby as we shuffle outside.

"I planted some new rose bushes," Lucy begins as she leads us to the back corner of the large yard. I smile and nod and follow along, but don't really hear what she's talking about as she gives us the grand tour on the pretty light-lined paths that meander through the yard.

"It doesn't mean anything, you know," Sam says quietly beside me. She and I slow down, falling behind Lucy and Nat, who continue to happily chat about Lucy's plants. Nat is carrying Livie, who happily points to butterflies and birds flying nearby.

"Doesn't it?"

"No." She shakes her head and loops her arm through mine. "You have to know he wasn't celibate for ten years."

I toss my head back and laugh. "Of course not. Have you *seen* him?"

"I have. He's not gross."

"No, he's not." I sigh and shove my hair behind my ears. "We need to talk."

"I think I might bust Leo's balls if it were me. But then, I'm not a terribly jealous person, I would just want to mess with him a bit."

"I'm not typically jealous either, but seriously? That chick sent him a picture of her boobs."

Sam shudders and then laughs. "Girls strip their shirts off and shove their tits in Leo's face. It's delightful."

"Ugh." I sigh and bite my lip. "Girls suck."

"Yes, they do. She probably doesn't know he's with you now."

"A lot of girls don't care," I remind her.

"True. He'll tell them. He'll be embarrassed when he sees what you saw."

"I don't want him to be embarrassed."

"What do you want?" she asks.

"I don't know." I jerk one shoulder up in a shrug and then smile at her. "To unsee it. Thanks for talking me down from the ledge."

"You're welcome. Now when you talk to him, you can do it in a productive way."

"I was daydreaming of stabbing him with that knife he was using," I confess, making Sam laugh.

"Well, I guess that means you love him, because if you didn't, you wouldn't care who texted him."

"I love him," I say. "But I'm still pissed."

She nods just as Lucy and Nat join us.

"Your yard is beautiful, Lucy," I say and smile.

"Thank you, dear. I think dinner should be ready by now."

When we step inside, the house smells amazing. The guys are just setting steaming plates on the table and Luke is feeding Keaton a bottle.

"He woke up?" Nat asks Luke.

"Yeah, he's hungry," he replies with a grin. Seeing Mark's handsome older brother with the baby is a sight to behold. There's a reason that Luke graced magazine covers and teenagers' walls for so long. The man is hot.

"Are you okay?" Mark asks as he slips beside me and wraps his arm around my waist.

I could lie.

But I won't.

"No. You missed some texts." I point to his phone and walk away from him, sit at the table and decide to enjoy the rest of my evening with these nice people. Mark retrieves his phone as he sits next to me and checks the messages and then cringes and shakes his head in disgust.

Dinner is a flurry of good food and even better conversation. I forget about those stupid women on Mark's phone for a little while and enjoy the people around me. When we've finished eating, the girls jump up to clean while the guys take the babies into the family room.

When the last dish is placed in the dishwasher and the kitchen is clean, we join the guys.

"Can I hold him?" I ask Luke, who is holding a sleepy Keaton.

"Of course you can," he replies and gently passes the baby into my arms.

"I'm getting braver with the little ones," I say with a smile. "How do you hold them all the time and not worry about hurting them?"

"They're stronger than they look," Neil replies and wraps his arm around Lucy's shoulders, tugging her close to his side. No wonder the Williams men are affectionate. They've learned it from their father. "You won't hurt them, sweet girl."

I brush my finger down Keaton's nose and kiss his little round cheek. He makes little sucky motions with his lips.

Suddenly, there's a very foul smell coming from the little bundle of joy.

"Um, I think he needs to be changed," I say and glance around the room in a panic.

"Come on." Nat stands and motions for me to follow her. "I'll help you."

"Oh God. I don't want to break him," I whisper and follow Nat down the hallway to a small nursery. "Lucy and Neil put in a nursery?"

"They did. They love keeping the kids." Nat helps me lay Keaton on the changing table and walks me through changing his very dirty diaper.

"Dear God, Keaton!" I exclaim when I open the diaper. "What are they feeding you?"

Nat laughs and hands me baby wipes.

"I should be wearing a hazmat suit," I mumble and clean the baby's butt, powder it and under Nat's supervision, wrap him back up again.

"You're a natural," she says with a smile.

"I might need therapy now."

When we return to the family room, everyone is laughing and watching us walk down the hallway.

"What's so funny?" I ask and settle back on the couch with the baby in my arms.

"You are," Mark replies and kisses my temple. "We could hear you through the baby monitor."

"Yeah, well, Keaton's parents should reconsider his diet." Keaton, wide awake now, is chewing on his fist, watching me talk. He grins a wide, toothless grin, and I fall even more in love with him. "You're too handsome to smell like that. Yes you are."

"Sam, tell Meredith the story of you and Leo babysitting Liv when she was a baby and you had to call Meg to come change her diaper for you." Luke is laughing now, holding his stomach. "It was so classic."

"It was the first time we babysat her by ourselves," Sam begins.

"First and only time," Mark adds, earning a glare from Sam.

"And she filled her diaper. I had never changed a diaper before, and neither had Leo."

"I still say it's unethical for a man to change a little girl's diaper," Leo says, holding his hands up in surrender. "It's not appropriate."

I giggle and watch Sam and Leo take turns telling the story of waiting forever for Meg to show up and change the screaming baby's diaper. They're so great together, finishing each other's sentences and looking at each other with so much love in their faces it's blinding.

"It worked out in the end," Leo says as the story comes to a close.

"That's hilarious," I reply and gaze down at the baby blowing bubbles in my arms.

"We should go put the kids to bed," Luke says and kisses Nat's cheek. "I'm ready for some alone time with my wife."

"Ew," Sam says and wrinkles her nose. "We don't need that announcement."

Luke just smiles smugly and kisses his wife again, making Sam gag.

"You guys are funny," I say, not realizing I said it out loud until Sam laughs and shrugs.

I lay Keaton in his car seat and step aside as Luke buckles him in and lifts him off the floor. Nat is carrying Liv and we all walk outside to say goodbye.

"We should go too," Mark says.

"I have some work to do," Sam says and smiles up at Leo. "Ready?"

"I'm ready."

There are many hugs and promises of calling soon as we all climb into our vehicles and wave at Lucy and Neil before pulling away from the house.

"I'd like to go home, please," I say and stare out my window.

"I was going to take you to my house."

"I'd rather just go home."

Mark sighs next to me and drags his hand down his face. Now that we're alone, the anger is back. I'm tired and honestly, my feelings are hurt.

And I don't really care if that's irrational.

"Mer—"

"We'll talk when we get there, Mark."

I close my eyes and settle back in the seat and let him drive to my apartment in silence.

***

"I'm going to change," I announce as soon as I get inside my apartment, but Mark stops me.

"No. You're going to sit and we're going to talk."

I turn on him and cross my arms over my chest. "Really? This is the moment you're going to choose to be bossy?"

"Sit down, Meredith."

"Fuck you, Mark."

"Are we going to do this again? Do you honestly believe I'm fucking those women?"

I pace away and fling my arms out at my sides.

"No, I don't believe that, Mark! That's ridiculous."

"Then why are you so angry?"

I stop and stare at him as if he's just grown a second head.

"Because," I begin and take a deep breath, "two women obviously think they can text you, crook their finger, and you'll come fuck them at a moment's notice."

"But they can't. You know that."

"*I* do. *They* don't."

He frowns and scratches his fingers over his scalp in agitation. "So?"

"We've been together long enough for you to let your fuck buddies know that you're no longer available, Mark."

"I haven't even thought about them since you and I have been together, Meredith. Why would it occur to me to text and tell them I'm in a relationship when *you're* all I fucking think about?"

I shake my head and pace away.

"Look. Clearly you had a healthy sex life before I came back into your world. But I didn't need it to blindside me while I was sitting at your mother's dining room table. Your *sister* saw it. It was humiliating."

"Meredith, listen to yourself. *You* were at my mother's table. None of those women ever met my family. I don't give a flying fuck about those women and you know it. How many times do I have to tell you that I love you?"

"I don't question your love for me, damn it!"

"I'll make it clear to them and anyone else that contacts me that I'm happily unavailable, Meredith. I don't have a problem with that. I do have a problem with this jealous streak you've developed in the past ten years."

I open my mouth to respond, but he holds up a hand, shutting me up.

"Lena," he begins, "and I have been friends since our freshman year in college. She and Colin, her now husband, were the closest friends I had for a long time. They knew about you."

I cringe when he raises a brow.

"For years we helped each other through classes and labs. I was the best man in their wedding, Mer. Lena is a very good friend, and she's looking forward to meeting you."

"Okay."

"If you have a question, ask me. Want to go through my phone?" He tosses his phone at me, but I toss it right back. "I don't care if you go through it. I haven't done anything wrong."

I sigh and deflate onto the couch. "I don't think you've done anything wrong, Mark. I'm not accusing you of anything."

"But you don't trust me."

"I don't trust women." My head jerks up as I stand again, passionate about making him understand. "I don't trust women."

"Why?"

"Because women can be catty, and many don't seem to care if a man is taken. But the bottom line for me is this: those women shouldn't be sending you messages like that. I know you didn't do anything wrong, but it doesn't make me feel any better."

"Well, then let's move on to the next issue. When were you going to tell me that you're going back on tour with Starla?" His hands are propped on his hips and he's glaring at me accusingly.

"I'm not."

"Don't fucking lie to me." His voice is low and rough and thoroughly pissed.

"I'm not lying to you. She offered us our old jobs back." I hold my breath as he closes his eyes on a long sigh. "But we turned her down."

No answer.

"Mark?"

Nothing.

"Mark, we turned her *down*."

He clears his throat. "Go on."

"She said that she misses having us with her, and now that Mom's gone and life has settled a bit, she was hoping we'd choreograph her next tour and go back out on the road with her next year. But you know what?"

"What?" he whispers. I hate the slight tremble in his voice. I move to walk to him, but he holds a hand up, stopping me.

"For about ten seconds, while she was stating her case, I thought it over. I thought about the long days of travel, not knowing where I am, not having a real home. Not to mention, I'm not super young anymore and I could get hurt with as rigorous as Starla likes the routines to be."

I pace away and shove my hands through my hair.

"And I told her, it's just not for me anymore. I love my studio and my students, and I love you. I'm happy in Seattle. That world doesn't fit me anymore."

"Are you sure?" he asks softly.

"It was never going to be a yes, M. Even if I didn't have you, which I'm *so glad* that I do, I still would have turned her down. That time in my life is done, and I like where my life is now."

"What did Jax say?"

"He said no as well. For pretty much the same reasons."

"He's in love with me too?"

And there's my funny man. I exhale deeply and smile at him.

"Hopelessly, yes." I laugh and hook my hair behind my ear. "I think he's in love with Logan."

"Are you just now realizing that?"

"It's complicated with Jax."

"I can imagine."

"Did he tell you about his past?" Mark nods and shoves his hands in his pockets.

"So, what we have here is a lack of trust on both parts," he murmurs. He still isn't pulling me into his arms. "You think I'll fuck anyone who smiles my way…"

"I never said that…"

"And I'm still scared shitless that you'll end up choosing dance over me and leave me high and dry."

He seriously thinks that? That I would do that again? I sigh and I'm suddenly exhausted. The long days of physical work and being put through the emotional wringer with Mark have caught up with me.

I walk toward my bedroom. "You know what, I'm going to change out of these clothes, and I think I want to be alone tonight."

"No."

"What did you say?" I spin around to look at him. His hands are balled into fists at his sides and a muscle ticks in his jaw from clenching it so hard.

"I said no. I just spent two nights without you, Meredith. I'm not doing it again."

"Well, I don't want to sleep with you tonight."

God, I'm being a complete bitch! Stop it!

But I can't.

"I'll sleep on the couch then," he replies.

"Do what you want." I turn and walk to my room, slam the door and wonder what in the hell is wrong with me.

I pull my phone out of my pocket and text Jax.

I'm an idiot. Tell me to get over myself.

I strip out of my clothes and climb into my bed, not paying attention to the tears rolling down my cheeks.

Finally my phone beeps with an incoming text from Jax.

Get over yourself. Why did I just say that?

I wipe my cheeks with the back of my hand and respond.

Because I'm mad at Mark for something he didn't really do. Girls texted him for booty calls today. He didn't reply to them. But one sent her tits!

I hit send and less than ten seconds later, my phone rings.

"You didn't have to call me."

"Do I need to come home?" Jax's voice is full of worry and it makes me love him even more.

"No. I'm being dumb. But I'm still mad at him."

"Not all men are cheating bastards like Scott was," Jax reminds me.

"Scott and I weren't even officially a couple."

"No, but he still fucked anything that looked at him sideways while he was fucking you, and it screwed you up, tootsie roll. Mark isn't Scott, and just because a couple trollops sent him messages today doesn't mean he did anything wrong. So yeah, get over yourself."

"Damn. Tough love sucks ass."

Jax chuckles. "Did he leave?"

"No, he..." The front door slams, making the tears come again. "Yeah. He just left."

"Sleep off your shitty mood and then go apologize. With a blow job."

"Thanks, Dr. Ruth."

"My pleasure. See you on Friday."

***

My head is pounding when I wake up. It's not quite light out yet. Gray shadows are cast across the room as the first rays from the sun are just starting to surface.

I climb out of bed and shuffle into the kitchen to take some painkillers, toss the left over water in the sink, and turn to go back to bed, but a dark figure on the couch catches my eye.

Mark.

He didn't leave.

He's stretched out on his back, a quilt I recognize from the night we sat on the pier draped over him. As I step closer, I can see he's asleep.

And suddenly, I just can't stay away from him anymore.

I climb on top of him, curling up in a ball on his chest and suddenly his arms come around me, holding me tightly.

"I was such a bitch," I whisper as the tears start again. "But I can't apologize for my reaction, Mark, because you're *mine* and those text messages just pissed me the fuck off."

"I got that," he replies softly and kisses my head. "When I thought about it from your point of view, I got it. If the roles were reversed, I'd be in jail for assault."

"I'm not usually super jealous, but honestly, Mark, her *tits*?"

"I know. I'm sorry about that too. I texted every woman in my phone last night, those I remember and those I don't, and told them that I'm off the market for good and not to text me again."

"You did?"

"Yes. My sister and mom weren't impressed."

I chuckle and slap his arm without any real malice behind it. "I had a brief relationship with a guy a few years ago and when I say brief, that's no lie. Super brief. Mostly because he didn't think it was necessary to stop sleeping with everyone else he knew while he was sleeping with me."

"I'm not like that and you know it."

"I know. And I feel more than a little foolish this morning. If it helps, I cried myself to sleep last night."

"No that doesn't help," he says as he caresses my back and kisses my head. "I hate it when you cry."

"I hate it when I'm stupid."

"You're not stupid. We're learning each other again, remember?"

"Yeah."

"I'm learning that you have a helluva possessive side."

"I do."

His hand travels down my back to cup my ass firmly.

"I do too. There won't be a repeat of last night, M. I promise. And this is the last time I'll ever sleep on the couch. You can't blame me for things that aren't my fault."

I grin and kiss his chest. "I'll try to rein in the jealous bitch."

"Do that. You don't have anyone to be jealous of, baby. You're all I see. You know that."

I raise up to gaze into his face in the gray glow of the living room. He brushes his thumbs under my eyes, wiping the tears away. "You're all I see," he whispers.

"About the other thing, Mark. I don't ever want you to think that I would choose dance over you again. I wouldn't. I said no *because* of you, because I couldn't be away from you for so long. I made it clear that I've moved on from that life."

He kisses my cheek and pulls me back down against his chest.

"I believe you," he whispers. "And I'm sorry for jumping to conclusions of my own."

Chapter Fourteen

"Where are we going?" I ask and push my hair out of my face. Mark took the top off his Jeep, and we're speeding down the freeway on this gorgeous spring day. The sky is bright blue, not a cloud in it, and the chill from early spring is finally being burned off by the sun.

"We have work to do today."

"Um, no, we have the week off." I glance over at Mark and feel the breath leave my lungs. Will I always lose my breath when I look at him? He's wearing dark Oakley sunglasses. His blond hair is messy from the wind and my fingers. His white T-shirt molds against his chest and arm muscles like a dream and his forearms flex as he grips the steering wheel.

I can't even think about the way those faded blue jeans hug his ass and thighs without breaking out into a sweat.

I could easily just sit here and watch him all day.

"Mer?"

"Yeah?"

"You're not listening to me."

"Sorry, it's hard to concentrate when you're over there looking like that."

He laughs and lifts my hand to his lips to kiss my knuckles. "You're funny."

"You're sexy."

He tosses me a hot look before pulling into a home improvement store, parks and cuts the engine.

"What are we doing here?"

"I want you to come help me figure out how to remodel your kitchen."

"I don't have permission from my landlord to remodel my kitchen."

He tilts his head to the side and cocks a brow at me. "Don't be difficult."

"Why do you need my help?"

"Because, you'll be living with it for a long time, so you should be the one to tell me what you like."

He climbs out of the Jeep, but all I can do is sit here and stare after him, not sure what to say. He opens my door and helps me out of the Jeep, takes my hand in his and leads me inside the cavernous store. It smells of sawdust and grass.

"I don't think girls are supposed to be in here," I say and bite my lip. Mark laughs and props his sunglasses on his head.

"It's an equal opportunity store, M."

"I'll like anything you do to your kitchen, Mark. You don't need me to tell you what to do." He leads me back to the appliance and kitchen area, where they have kitchen displays set up so you can see what the appliances and countertops look like together.

"Just humor me." He kisses my temple before dropping my hand and gesturing to a kitchen nearby. "I'm going to leave the existing cabinets, but I was thinking about painting them."

I tilt my head and look about the space, thinking about the kitchen as it is now.

"White would brighten it up a lot."

"Exactly." He grins and nods. "I was also thinking about replacing the doors with some that have glass in them."

"No way." I shake my head adamantly. "If they have glass fronts, you can see the mess inside. Maybe just some glass ones where the plates and bowls go. I like colorful dinnerware, so that would be pretty, but the rest shouldn't have glass."

He's nodding as I talk, thinking. "I can do that. Okay, white cabinets with just a couple glass-front doors. Now, let's talk countertops. I want granite, but let's look at colors." He leads me to a wall covered in granite samples. "I'm going to make the island bigger to give us more work space."

"What about a small sink in the island?" I ask. "It would be handy to have a small sink to wash vegetables and stuff so I don't have to constantly walk back and forth to the big sink."

"We can do that," Mark says with a wide grin. "See? This isn't so hard."

I bite my lip and look away. Holy shit, I've jumped right into the spirit of this. I need to rein it in just a smidge.

"Since the cabinets will be white, how do you feel about a dark countertop?" He points to smooth, shiny black granite that has little silver flecks in it.

"That's pretty."

He moves behind me and wraps his arms around my waist, leaning in to whisper in my ear. "I can just picture you spread out on that black countertop, your white skin glowing with sweat as I eat you out and make you scream."

I gasp and then giggle breathlessly as I toss a smile over my shoulder at him. "You're naughty today."

"I'm naughty every day, baby. You'd look hot against that black granite. If you prefer, I'll bend you over it. I'm flexible like that."

"Well, when you put it like that, I think I love the black too."

He chuckles and kisses my cheek, then leads me away to choose a backsplash and hardware for the cupboard doors.

"Okay, let's talk appliances."

"You're replacing the appliances too?"

"Yep. All new stuff. Of course, now that I think about it, it'll be easier if you don't move in with me until the kitchen is done. We can live at your place while I work on it."

"I don't remember agreeing to move into your house."

"Our house."

"Your house." Now it's just fun to be stubborn and disagree with him. I'm totally moving in with him. I'm not sure when, but it's going to happen.

"You've become quite stubborn in your old age," he says. "I'm going to talk you into it, you know."

"If you say so. What kind of stove do you want for your kitchen?"

"*Our* kitchen needs a gas stove."

We wander through the appliances, looking at all the different stoves, refrigerators, and all of the other appliances a person could ever need. And many they won't ever need, but are cool anyway.

A beautiful wine cooler catches my eye. I squat next to it and check it out. White wine is my favorite, and I prefer it very cold. This would be awesome built into the bigger and better island Mark plans to build.

"Do you like that?" he asks.

"It's nice. Would free up space in the fridge. Not that I drink a lot of wine."

He just nods and walks away, but I have a feeling this will end up in the new kitchen.

"What do you think of a double oven?" he asks and points to two ovens mounted in a wall.

"I barely cook with one oven," I reply dryly. "Let's not go too crazy. I do like that fridge with the French doors."

"Is that the one you want?"

"It's not my kitchen. But if it were me, I'd probably go with that one."

"Now you're just mocking me," he says with mock despair. "I kind of like this other fridge over here." Before he can walk away, I grip his arm and pull him back to the other one.

"*If it were me,* I'd go with this one."

"I have news for you, M." He leans in with a half smile and presses his lips to my ear. "It's always going to *be* you." He winks and walks away and I'm left in a puddle of mush. God, he says the sweetest things at just the right time. I can't even remember why I was so pissed last night. He's *mine.*

He stops at the end of the aisle and turns back to me with that naughty smile still in place. "Let's pick out a dishwasher and we might as well grab a washer and dryer while we're here."

"You're spoiling the house rotten." I walk toward him and bite my lip when his eyes roam up and down my body, then smile when he reaches my face.

You're spoiling me rotten.

"It's for you," he says simply with a shrug, as if men say things like that every day, threads his fingers through mine and leads me to finish choosing the appliances for our house.

***

"I didn't realize we'd be painting the cabinets today," I say and load my brush with more white paint and spread it over the sanded wood. "You must have cleared this all out while I was gone."

"I did. I finished sanding them down the night before you got home."

I'm standing on the old Formica countertop, painting the tops of the cabinets bright white. We've been working on them all afternoon and are almost finished.

Mark's phone vibrates on the countertop by my feet and I glance down at it to see Lena's name flashing with the incoming call.

"Lena's calling," I say and hand Mark his phone.

"Hello?" He winks at me and smiles when the other woman begins talking. "Wow, he's willingly coming out? Sounds fun, but let me check with Mer." He lowers the phone from his face. "Lena and Colin would like to take us out for dinner tonight. I'm warning you, Colin is pasty white, like Luke in *Nightwalker*. The man never goes outside."

I chuckle and finish painting my end of the cabinets. "Sounds good to me."

"We're in," he says into the phone. "Great. We'll see you then." He hangs up and helps me off the counter, lifting me into his arms. I plant my hands on his shoulders and kiss him quickly, then rub at a spot of paint on his cheek.

"How much time do we have?"

"About an hour."

"Good." I help him gather our dirty brushes and clean up our mess then take his hand in mine and lead him to the stairs. "You need to finish what you started in that store today."

"What did I start?"

"Horniness."

"Oh, I can definitely finish that, baby."

***

"So then, he told the professor to kiss his ass and flipped him off on the way out of the lab!" Lena exclaims, laughing hard.

"You did?" I stare at Mark, who is blushing bright red.

"Yeah. He pissed me off. I was right."

"You were right, but you also got yourself thrown out of that class and had to repeat it the next semester." Colin shakes his head and takes a drink of his beer. Colin is *not* pasty white. In fact, his skin is a dark, rich mocha and he has the kindest brown eyes I've ever seen. He's very tall, at least six foot five, and lean. He shaves his head bald.

Colin and Lena make a very unlikely couple, but they clearly couldn't be more in love with each other.

They're also all incredibly smart. When they start talking about work, I can't keep up.

"English," I beg and hit my forehead with the palm of my hand. "Speak English, not Super-Smart-Genius. I can't understand you."

"It's all boring anyway," Mark says and pulls me against his side.

"It does sound kind of sexy when you pull out the genius-speak," I say and kiss his cheek. "Kind of like a foreign language."

"You like that do you?" He smiles that naughty smile. "I'll tell you all kinds of things later."

"Awesome."

"Does my vast rocket science knowledge turn you on?" Colin asks Lena while wiggling his eyebrows.

"Oh, yes, definitely." She snorts and sips her sparkling water.

He leans down to whisper in her ear and to my surprise, she blushes bright red. "Now that turns me on," she says.

"Why do I feel like we just witnessed something we shouldn't have?" Mark asks with a frown. "Should we leave you alone?"

"Nah, I just gave her something to think about for a while," Colin replies and winks down at his wife.

Lena clears her throat and sips her drink again.

"I need more dirt on Mark's college years," I inform them. "Tell me everything."

"There isn't any dirt," Mark insists.

"Come on. Frat parties? Girls lined up at his door? Spring Break trips to Daytona?"

"Not really," Colin replies. "He was too focused on graduating early. Which he did. A full year early."

"I've never known anyone to get both a bachelor's and master's in five years," Lena says and shakes her head. "He was like a man possessed."

"I told you," Mark says with a shrug. "If I worked my ass off, I wasn't thinking about you."

The table grows quiet at that admission until Lena finally says, "We did have fun together. We worked hard, but vacation breaks were fun. Mark usually invited us to come stay with his parents and they were cool."

"His parents are the best," I reply and hold Mark's hand as he leans in to press his lips to my hair.

"You two are adorable," Lena says as she leans on Colin's arm and watches us with a soft smile.

"So are you guys," I reply. "This was fun."

"We'll do it more often. Colin needs to learn to work less, especially now." Lena grins at him then announces, "We're going to have a baby."

"No way!" Mark exclaims. "You said you weren't planning to for a while."

"I didn't know I was pregnant when I saw you." She shrugs and tosses her long dark hair over her shoulder. "I just found out this morning. Peed on a stick."

"That's awesome," I say and squeeze the other woman's hand. "Let us know if you need anything."

"Our parents are going to freak and buy this kid way more than it'll ever need, but I'll keep you posted."

"I'm excited for you," Mark says. "It's about time."

"We might need you to remodel the bedroom we've been using for storage into a nursery suite," Colin says.

"I'm happy to. I'll come look at it next week."

"He's crazy good at the remodel thing," I say, so proud of him. "We'll invite you over to see the house. He's made it incredible."

Lena's eyebrows raise as she glances at Mark then back at me. "We'd love to see it."

"We picked out kitchen stuff today, so when it's all done, we'll have you over for dinner."

"Sounds like a date."

I glance up to see Mark staring down at me with deep blue eyes and a happy smile.

"What?"

"I just love you."

"I love you too."

"And now, ladies and gentleman, I'm going to escort my knocked-up wife home so I can do all the things I whispered in her ear earlier." Colin claps his hands and leads us out into the mild evening air. "It's been great to meet you, Meredith," he says and kisses my cheek.

"You too," I say and am surprised to be swept up into a hug from Lena.

"I'm glad he found you again," she whispers in my ear. "I've never seen him this happy."

She pulls away and smiles at me before hugging Mark and walking away with her husband.

"What did she say?" Mark asks.

"Just that she's happy for us."

"Aside from my family, those are two of the best people I know." He takes my hand in his but instead of leading me back to his Jeep, we set off in the opposite direction toward a nearby park. "I'm glad you finally met them."

"Me too. I'm also very glad that you've had them in your life all these years. They're kind of your Jax."

He nods and purses his lips. "Yeah, I guess they are."

This park is in full spring bloom, a riot of color in pink, purple and red. Kids are running and playing, dogs on leashes are walking on the paved paths with their masters. There's a fishing pond with benches on the shoreline. Mark leads me to one and sits down, then tumbles me onto his lap.

"It's beautiful out here," I murmur and push my fingers through his hair. His arms are wrapped tightly around my middle, his face buried between my breasts as he hugs me close.

"You feel good."

"You okay?"

"Mm… just enjoying the way your boobs feel against my face. I need a moment of silence."

I chuckle and kiss the top of his head then pull back so I can look down at him. "There are children around."

"They can find their own boobs."

We laugh together for a long moment until I take a deep breath and tilt my forehead down on his. "Are you excited for Vegas?"

"I am. It'll be fun. There are some surprises planned."

"Tell me."

"I can't. Then it won't be a surprise."

"Spoil sport." I kiss his forehead then stand and hold my hand out for him. "Come on. Let's go pack for our trip."

"You do know we're getting very dirty in Vegas, right?"

"I was counting on it."

Chapter Fifteen

"I wanna double-down, bitches!" Meg exclaims and sips her drink.

"No, you don't," Nate informs her with a shake of his head and stares at Will in exasperation. "Dude, control your woman."

"Yes, I do," she insists. "I like the way it sounds when you say it. Double-down, bitches!" The dealer laughs and follows Meg's instructions as I lean back against Mark's hard chest and laugh my ass off.

"It sounds like a sexual position," Sam says and motions for the dealer to give her another card.

"Ooooh," Jules murmurs and glances up at her handsome husband. "Maybe we should try the double-down later."

"I believe we tried it this morning," he says and kisses her head.

"Seriously? I do not need to hear about you banging my sister," Will says with a glare. We are at the Blackjack table with Nate, Jules, Sam, Meg and Will. The others are scattered through the casino, playing slots or sitting at the bar.

"We have a baby," Jules reminds her brother. "We clearly bang."

"Shut up."

"A lot," she continues.

"Stop talking, Jules."

"He's really good at it." Jules sips her drink smugly when Will glares at her, not bothering to continue to tell her to shut up.

"Thank you, baby," Nate says and kisses Jules' cheek.

Meg pouts when she loses her twenty dollars then swings around in the seat and wraps her arms around Will's middle, pressing her cheek to his broad chest. "I lost my money."

"That's what happens when you double-down when you have a total of six," Nate informs her. "Have you ever played this game before?"

"No."

"Oh my God!" We all whip around at the sound of Natalie's exclamation to find her sitting at a slot machine, grinning and jumping up and down in her seat. Luke comes running up behind her from the bar.

"What's wrong?" he demands, his eyes worried.

"Nothing! I just won like fifty thousand points!" She claps her hands, then grips Luke's collar in her fists and kisses him soundly.

"How much is that worth?" I call out. She studies the machine and tallies the math.

"Fifty bucks," Mark whispers in my ear, chuckling.

"Fifty dollars!" Natalie exclaims, as if it's fifty million dollars. She looks so pleased with herself as Luke kisses her cheek and helps her cash it out.

"Drinks on Natalie!" Jules says.

"We're drinking for free already," Mark reminds her.

"Drinks on Natalie later!" she says, then flags down a waitress to order another drink.

Jax is at the bar with Stacy, Brynna and Nic, telling them all kinds of elaborate stories, I'm sure. They're hanging on his every word. It doesn't hurt that he's hot as hell and funny too.

And he's a horrible flirt.

"Jax is in his element," I say to Mark and gesture to my friend as he's making the girls laugh.

"I knew they'd love him," Mark says. "They can flirt with him without their men losing their shit."

"Isaac's watching," I whisper and point to the oldest Montgomery who is at a roulette table with Leo, Matt, Dom and Caleb. Isaac's eyes are trained on his wife, who is laughing hysterically at something Jax just said.

"They'll all keep their eyes peeled. That's what we do." Mark shrugs and points to the blackjack table. "Do you want to play?"

"Nah. I'm a horrible gambler."

"You don't have a poker face." Mark kisses my head. "And you look delicious in this little dress." He gestures to my simple black tank dress that shows off my curves and legs. When I put it on before leaving the hotel room, it was with the intention of making Mark suffer for the night.

"You don't look too bad yourself," I say and sip my sex on the beach. He's in dark jeans and a tight American Fighter T-shirt that is just begging for me to rip it off his hard body.

"Are you wearing panties under there?" he whispers in my ear.

I shake my head no and grin to myself when he growls deep in his throat.

"You're killing me."

"I'm not doing anything."

"You two need to get a room," Jules says as she wrinkles her nose. "What is it with the Williams men? You're all so freaking mushy." She points to where Luke and Natalie are snuggled up at the roulette table now, watching the guys play.

"We're romantic," Mark corrects her.

"It's disgusting."

Leo saunters up behind Sam and rests his hand on her hip as he watches her play cards. "You're good at this, sunshine."

"Thanks. It's just math."

"No it's not," Mark says. "If it was just math, everyone would win. It's strategy."

Sam shrugs but smiles softly as Leo kisses her cheek. "My chick is hot *and* smart."

"There's so few of us around," Jules says with a sassy sigh.

"I'm done doubling down," Meg says and smiles up at Will. "What are we doing next?"

"You and I have a date," Will says and turns to the rest of us. "We're going to peel away for the night, guys. I have some plans for Meg, so we'll see you all tomorrow."

"I'll be at the pool most of the afternoon," Sam says.

"Have fun tonight," I say as they walk toward the bar to fill everyone else in.

"What's everyone else doing?" Mark asks.

"We're going to a Cirque du Soleil show with Nat and Luke," Jules says.

"Leo and I are meeting with some of the guys from his band who came over from LA to hang out tonight," Sam says. "It'll be good to see them."

"We saw them a month ago," Leo reminds her with a grin.

"You miss them too. You don't fool me."

We all walk toward the bar, meeting the others from the roulette table.

"A bunch of us are going to go up to the club here in the hotel for dinner and dancing," Brynna says and lays her hand on Jax's arm. "You have to come with us."

"Only if I can dance with you," he says and winks at her.

"Do I have to kill him?" Caleb asks Mark.

"Nah, he's cool." Mark laughs when Jax glances at Caleb and looks him up and down.

"You might not be safe from me," Jax says.

"By all means, dance with my wife," Caleb replies and shakes his head. "You guys in?"

"Sure," I say and grin up at Mark. "I haven't danced with you in years."

"I'm not very good."

"I'll help. I do that for a living, you know."

"Sounds good. Let's go."

We break into groups, Sam and Leo leaving to meet his band, Nat and Jules giggling as their men follow them out to catch their Cirque du Soleil show and the rest of us taking the escalators up to the fourth floor of the Cosmopolitan here in Vegas to wreck havoc on the dance club.

We've been in Vegas for all of six hours, and I have never had so much fun. I have a feeling things are just getting started.

We find two tables and push them together, then sit back and watch the few couples on the dance floor as we wait for our drinks.

"Are we ordering food?" Matt asks and surveys the menu. "At least some appetizers to soak up all the alcohol you're all consuming."

"Good idea," Caleb says. "Let's just order two of everything."

"Three orders of potato skins," Stacy says. "This music is great, but the dancers are lame. Not fun to watch at all."

"Yeah," Brynna agrees and winks at her. "It's really boring."

"I think they're hinting at something," Dominic adds. "They're so subtle."

"They need someone to show them how it's done," Nic says and smiles smugly at me. "You and Jax should go show off."

"Subtle as a heart attack," Matt agrees and brushes his hand down the back of Nic's head. "But beautiful."

"Just Dance" by Lady Gaga begins to play and Jax laughs as he looks over at me and raises a brow. "That feels a little too coincidental."

"Go have fun, baby," Mark urges. "But watch yourself. That dress is short." His eyes finish his sentence. *And you're not wearing underwear.*

"Go dance!" Brynna says and claps her hands.

Jax takes my hand and leads me out onto the floor.

"I'm in heels with no underwear, so no horizontal lifts, okay?"

"Got it, marshmallow."

And off we go, Jax leading us around the floor. He spins me out and in and within five steps, it's just me and Jax, feeling the music and dancing the way we always do.

I love it when he improvises. He's just genius, and he challenges me. He's mindful of my heels, and does lift me, but keeps his arm on my thighs, holding my skirt down.

When I land on my feet, he rolls his hips and backs away, singing to me, making me laugh. The girls at the table are cat calling, egging him on.

Everyone in the room applauds when the song ends and we return to the table and collapse in our seats, drinking the water that was delivered while we were dancing.

"You guys are fantastic," Stacy says. "I never could move like that. My hips don't do that."

"Your hips do just fine, baby," Isaac says and winks at her, making her blush.

"My turn!" Brynna exclaims and pulls Jax from his chair. "I want to dance."

"I had no idea she liked to dance so much," Isaac says as he watches Brynna and Jax walk to the dance floor.

"She always loved to dance in college," Stacy says and laughs when Brynna starts to move her hips, mirroring Jax. "You should go out there and surprise her," she says to Caleb.

"I'll dance with her in a bit. She's having fun with him."

"You're not usually so willing to share," Matt says mildly and sips his water. His hand has stayed on Nic's neck the whole time they've been sitting here.

"He's no threat," Caleb says with a grin. "You and I both know that."

"He's charming, and the girls like him," Dominic adds.

"Plus, he's fun," I say and watch my friend with the pretty brunette. They're laughing together as he shows her some more intricate steps.

I uncross and recross my legs. Mark lays his hand high on my thigh.

"Don't do that," he whispers in my ear.

"No one can see anything," I reply and turn back to watch the show on the floor. Mark loops his arm around me and gently caresses my shoulder, my neck, my naked back, thanks to this barely-there dress, with his fingertips. My breath catches and goose bumps break out on my skin when he drags his nails down my spine.

"Look at me," he whispers.

His eyes are on fire as he stares down at me for a long minute, then he stands and without a word, tugs me to my feet and leads me past the dance floor and out the front door. Instead of walking toward the escalator, he turns the other way where the buffet is. It's closed now, and the hallway is dark. He pulls me into a secluded doorway, away from anyone's line of vision.

"What's wrong with you?" I ask with a laugh. He pins me against the wall and leans his forehead against mine.

"Nothing at all is wrong," he says and kisses my nose then drags those magical lips down my cheek to my ear. "You've been turning me on all night."

"I haven't done anything." I brace my hands on his shoulders as he kisses his way down my neck, making my center clench and immediately go damp.

"You don't have to do it on purpose. You breathe and I'm hard," he says as his hands drift down my ribcage to my hips then slips one hand under my skirt and between my legs. "I'm going to taste you, right here."

"There are probably cameras here," I say then gasp when he tweaks a hard nipple through my dress.

"I don't give a fuck." He squats before me, pushes my dress up high on my thighs so only he can see what's under it. "Fuck, you're sexy."

I brace one hand on the wall to my left and push my fingers into his hair as he leans in and barely brushes the tip of his tongue over my already swollen clit. "Oh God, M."

"You're already so wet." His voice is hushed. His fingers glide through my lips then he pushes one finger inside me, he presses his thumb on my clit and I have to bite down on my lip to keep from crying out. He lifts my right leg over his shoulder, hiding me and his face from any camera that might be pointed our way and wraps his lips around my clit, sucking hard.

"Mark, holy shit."

"Mm," he hums, pulls his finger out, then plunges his tongue inside me, kissing me in the most intimate way possible, making me see stars. He's simply amazing. His hands are holding me firmly, making sure I don't fall, as he laps at my core, sucking, licking and kissing me until I couldn't even tell you my name. Even my fingertips are vibrating from the amazing sensations rolling through me and suddenly, my stomach clenches as I fist my hand in his hair and come hard against his mouth. His eyes are turned up to mine, watching me come undone, and when I'm done, he doesn't stop. He continues to nibble and make love to my folds, then kisses my inner thighs, lowers my leg off his shoulder and stands, fists my hair in his hands and kisses me hard. I can taste myself on him and it turns me on even more.

I wrap one leg around his waist and have half a mind to simply climb him when he lifts me against the wall, reaches between us to unzip his jeans, frees himself and pushes inside me in one swift thrust.

"Jesus fucking Christ, Meredith," he whispers against my neck. "I shouldn't be doing this here, but you'd tempt the Pope himself." He begins to fuck me fast and hard, and within five strokes, he stills and comes, his hips jerk against mine as he empties himself inside me, grinding against my clit and sending me into another amazing orgasm.

"Are you fucking trying to kill me?" he murmurs as he slips out, tucks himself away and helps me right my dress. His semen rolls out of me and down my leg.

"Well, that's not obvious at all," I say sarcastically.

"Here." He pulls his T-shirt off, and the white undershirt beneath it, squats again and uses his undershirt to clean me up as much as possible before tugging his T-shirt back on.

"I hope that doesn't end up on the internet," I say playfully. Mark's face goes white as he stares down at me.

"Oh my God, I'm so sorry. I didn't even think—"

"I'm just kidding. It's fine. I'm sure this happens all the time in Vegas."

He pushes his fingers through his hair and shakes his head. "I've never lost it like this with anyone. It's you. You've put some kind of spell on me."

"Yes, I call it the sexy spell," I reply and kiss his chin. "I'm going to cast it all night, so get ready."

"Come on, sassy witch." He spanks my ass playfully as we walk back toward the door to the club. He tosses the ruined tank into a garbage can. "I can't guarantee that I won't do that again if you keep shaking your ass on the dance floor."

"Well, we'll be disappearing a lot then because I plan to dance as much as possible."

"You *are* trying to kill me."

As we walk past the dance floor, Jax waves at me, grinning over Nic, Stacy and Brynna's heads as they all dance with him.

"He stole all your women," Mark says with a laugh as we sit at the table. My pussy is still throbbing from two orgasms and Mark's big cock. I squirm in my seat as Dominic catches my gaze. He winks and shakes his head, takes a sip of his drink and checks his phone when it vibrates on the table at his elbow. It's amazing how different Dominic looks from his brothers. He has the same blue eyes, but he's so dark. Inky hair and olive skin. He's big like them, though. Tall and broad and delicious. He's quiet. I haven't really had much of a chance to talk with him since that day at Will's house.

"Okay, who's next? I want to dance. I think all of you should get off your asses and dance." I point at all of the guys, making them smile.

"I'll dance with you," Mark says.

"Didn't you just do that?" Isaac asks with a laugh.

"I don't call that dancing," Mark replies with a smug smile and leads me out to the dance floor. The music is fast, but he pulls me into his arms and sways back and forth as if it's a ballad.

"This isn't what I had in mind," I murmur as I bury my face in his neck and hold on tight.

"It's what I had in my mind," he says and kisses my hair. "I just want to stand here for a few minutes and enjoy the way you feel in my arms."

"Jules was right, you are mushy."

"I don't care."

"I don't either."

When the song is over, Caleb, Matt and Isaac walk onto the floor and claim their women, pulling them into their arms and spinning them around the floor. Jax grins and takes advantage of the break. He returns to the table, but as soon as he sits down, a woman approaches him and asks him to dance. He shakes his head, sending her away and begins chatting with Dominic.

"I'm so glad you invited me to come here." I grin up at Mark.

"Me too."

"What are we doing tomorrow?"

"You're going to keep me permanently hard while you lay in a bathing suit by the pool," he replies with a grin.

"That sounds like fun. Will you put sunblock on me?"

"Of course."

"Will you bring me fruity drinks with umbrellas in them?"

"If you ask nicely."

"Will you keep your shirt off all day, also keeping me in a perpetual state of horniness?"

"If that's what it takes, yes." He laughs and tucks my hair behind my ear. "You make me laugh."

"I'm glad."

His face sobers as he drags his fingertips down my cheek. We're still swaying back and forth, dancing to our own rhythm.

"I crave you, you know."

"There's no shame in that," I reply as I smooth my finger over his lower lip. He puckers his lips and kisses me gently. "There are times I want you so badly my body feels like it's on fire."

"It's not just that. It's *everything*. I crave everything about you. Your body, your laughter, the way you make me feel when I'm with you. You're my drug, Meredith."

"I'm addicted in the same way, and I don't plan to ever have to recover from you again, Mark."

He stills for a moment and pins me with his blue gaze, sending shivers down my spine, as if he's reached in and touched my soul.

"There's no recovering from this."

CHAPTER SIXTEEN

"We've walked so much tonight, my feet are numb," Stacy grumbles as we stand on the escalator leading up to the club in our hotel, the Cosmopolitan.

"I think that's from the liquor," Nat replies.

"These chandeliers are crazy," Jules says and squints her eyes as she stares at the glittering glass surrounding us. "It really fucks with your head when you've had a lot to drink."

"I wonder if the bastards did that on purpose?" Sam wonders.

"We're definitely in the prettiest hotel on the strip," Brynna says with a grin. "I'm surprised you talked Will into this place, Meg."

"I don't think he cared where we stayed as long as it had a buffet and a bar," Meg replies with a giggle and sips her pink drink. "The buffet here is killer. I think Will would have been happy sleeping with the crab legs."

"The man can eat," Jules says with a sigh. "This fifteen minute break from Vegas shenanigans was not good. I'm feeling droopy."

We reach the top of the escalator and Sam steps between Jules and Nat, loops her arms through theirs and says, "Perk up, girls, the shenanigans are just beginning!"

"These women are hilarious," Jax murmurs to me and leads me into the club. "I haven't been flirted with this much since we were at that club in New York after the New Year's Eve show three years ago."

"That was a gay club," I remind him with a roll of the eyes. "Needless to say, I didn't see any action that night."

"Trust me, snickerdoodle, I saw enough action for both of us that night." He wiggles his eyebrows suggestively as the girls around us burst out in laughter.

"You're disgusting."

"You're hilarious," Nic says as we commandeer two tables, pushing them together again. The same bartender from last night is behind the bar and rolls his eyes at us as we sit down.

"I haven't recovered from you guys from last night yet!" he yells to us.

"You haven't seen anything yet, sugar," Stacy says with a wink. "We shook off our men and left our filters in Seattle."

"Great." He laughs and shakes his head as he walks down the bar to help a customer.

"I wonder if the guys are having fun?" Brynna asks and types away on her phone.

"You better not be texting the enemy," Jules says with a glare. "This is Meg's bitchelorette party."

"I'm just texting my mom to see how the kids are."

"Oh, good idea," Nat says and begins typing on her phone too.

"Okay, all the moms get their check ins with the babysitters now, because you won't be sober enough for it in a little while," Jax says and flags down a waitress.

"What are the guys doing again?" I ask and raise a brow when Jax starts typing on his phone. "I didn't realize you were a baby daddy."

"I'm not, smart ass. Logan hasn't been answering his phone today."

"Trouble in paradise?" My grin fades when his worried, dark eyes meet mine. "I'm sure he's fine. He's probably making up time at work from the days he took off this week with you."

He nods, but the frown on his face says he doesn't buy it.

"Remember? Not all guys are cheating bastards."

"I didn't say I thought he was fucking cheating." He scowls and slams back the shot of tequila the waitress just set before him. "But now I am."

"Trust me," Stacy says and leans across both Brynna and Meg to lay her hand over Jax's arm. "No one is going to cheat on a hot piece of ass like you."

"Oh God," Nat says and begins giggling. "And so it begins."

"You think I'm a hot piece of ass?" Jax asks with a delighted smile.

"Oh yeah," Brynna says with a decisive nod as the others smile and agree.

"I don't." I curl my lip and eye Jax then dissolve into giggles and admit, "Okay, yeah, you're a hot piece of ass. But stop feeding his ego! We'll never get his head through the door on the way out."

"That's what *he* said," Jax says, making us all laugh again.

"I'm so glad we have a gay friend now," Jules announces and raises her drink in a toast. "To Jax, the missing link in our circle!"

"To Jax!" We all slam back another shot and clap, some of us dancing in our seats to the pulsing music around us.

"Okay, no more alcohol for me," Nic announces and orders a diet soda.

"Why?" Meg pouts. "It's my party. We have to get stupid drunk."

"Liquor and diabetes don't mix well," Nic says with a grimace. "But don't worry. I can be stupid without it."

"Oh good," Meg says and kisses Nic's cheek. "I'm so glad you're all here. I'm so glad I'm finally marrying that big, sweet football star."

"We are too. You waited long enough," Nat says.

"There's always something that comes up. Football and family stuff and my promotion at the hospital."

"We knew you'd get around to it," Jules says. "God, these lemon drops are insanely delicious."

"You know what's insanely delicious?" Sam asks.

"What?" We all ask in unison then high five each other because, clearly, that was hilarious.

"When Leo slaps my ass." She bites on the straw of her vodka and cranberry juice.

"I bet Leo is insane in bed," Jules says with a sigh.

"Jules!" Nat cries as we all giggle.

"What? He's one of the few around here that I'm not related to! Let me lust after him."

"That's fair," Brynna says. "We get to lust after five hot Montgomerys, two hot Williams and a McKenna. Jules can have Leo."

In our fuzzy alcohol minds, this sounds perfectly logical.

"I want to know more about these apagasms I've heard so much about," Nic says, leaning forward in excitement. "Spill it, McKenna."

"Wait, what's an apagasm?" Jax asks.

"Nate has an apa," Meg informs him, as if these things happen every day.

"A what-a?" I ask and Jules breaks out in laughter.

"That's what I said the first time I saw it!"

"What is it?" I sip my sweet drink and lean in with Nic, ready to hear what this magical thing is.

"He has his dick pierced," Nat says, but cups her hand around her mouth and says it like it's a big secret, but the dude sitting at the table next to us whips his head around when he hears her and then laughs.

"Dude!" Jax exclaims and cups his hand protectively over his own junk.

"It's just… fantastic," Jules says with a dreamy sigh.

"I hate you," Brynna says with a glare.

"Are you saying Caleb is slacking in the sex department?" I ask.

"Hell no. The man can make me come just by looking at me. And he does this sixty-nine thing that I swear to Jesus is illegal in all fifty states." She covers her heart with her hand and bites her lip as the waitress magically reappears with more drinks.

God bless her.

"Did having babies change stuff?" I ask. "Like, how it feels?"

"For a little while, but it's still good, and then your body figures it all out again and you get back to normal," Natalie says.

"I don't want to hear about this part." Jax cringes. "Sorry, girls, but your bits and pieces don't interest me."

"Oh!" A very drunk Meg jumps up and down in her seat. "I have a question for *you*." She points her hand at Jax and then throws him a naughty grin.

"Yes! We can ask boy sex questions," Stacy agrees.

Jax clears his throat and then sits back in his chair and offers all the girls a fake serious look. "Yes, I am at your service, ladies. The doctor is in."

"Me first," Meg says. "What does an orgasm feel like?"

Jax blinks rapidly and we all snicker at him.

"What does it feel like for a girl?" he asks.

"Tingly, melty, explosive, tingly goodness," Nat says with a sigh. "Fuck, my husband's good at the orgasms."

We all nod in agreement. It must be genetic because Mark's fucking brilliant at them as well.

I believe I've had about thirty-seven of them since we've been in Vegas. It's like it's his life's mission to keep me permanently aroused.

It's awesome.

"Wait," Sam says and holds up a hand just as Jax begins to answer the question. "Let's get more specific than that. Where does the orgasm *start*?"

"Start?" Now Jax just looks confused. "Sugar, who gives a fuck where it starts? The end result is the most important part."

"God, I love the way he says *sugar*." Stacy smiles dreamily at Jax. "I'm so glad you're gay. I can flirt with you without my husband killing you."

"That's convenient," Jax sputters and then just covers his face with his hands and dissolves into laughter. "I love you ladies."

"What's not to love?" Nic says with a wink. "So, talk more about the boy orgasm."

"Boys don't have orgasms, sugar." Jax winks back at her and we all laugh some more, pounding the table with our palms and high fiving Jax.

"Well, obviously your balls tighten up," Sam says while tapping her lips with her finger in thought. "Is that when it starts?"

"I've never really thought about it." He scratches his dark head and looks toward the ceiling, also thinking about it. "No, that's just before you come, but it really starts in the spine. At least, for me. I'm sure it's different for everyone."

"In your *spine*?" Meg exclaims with wide eyes. "What the fuck happens to your spine?"

"It tingles."

"So, it's tingly for you too," Nat says, pleased that she was right.

"Yeah, I guess so."

"And then your balls tighten?" Brynna asks and sips her drink. We're all leaning in now, watching Jax with wide eyes, as if he's telling us the secrets of NASA and Area 51 all at the same time.

"Yes. I think so."

"Does that feel weird?" Jules asks. "I mean, the skin gets all tight and stuff too. I would think it would hurt."

"It doesn't hurt." Now Jax is blushing and laughing, his arms are crossed over his chest. "I don't know if I'm supposed to be telling you guys this stuff. It's man stuff."

"But you're our *gay guy*!" Brynna slams her hand on the table for emphasis. "You're the only one we can ask!"

"Ask your men," he says rationally then slams back another shot.

"If I ask Luke about orgasms, he just jumps right into giving them to me and then I forget what I was asking in the first place," Nat says with a frown. "He makes me lose my words."

"I lose my words all the time!" Meg exclaims. "It's the 'nesia."

"Orgasm 'nesia!" I high-five Jax and then giggle. "Mark is good at making me lose my words. He makes me lose everything."

"What do you mean?" Nic asks and just like that, all of the focus shifts to me. I blink at my new friends and try to find a way to clear my head enough to explain.

"He makes me lose my clothes, my words, my heart."

"Awww!" Sam exclaims. "I mean, ew about the sex with my brother, but aww!"

"He made me lose my virginity." My mouth is running now and I'm ticking off each item with my fingers. I'm pretty sure I'm miscounting.

"He was your first?" Nic asks.

"Yeah." I nod dreamily. "He was good even then. Of course, it took a while before I started having orgasms just because I was nervous and stuff, but holy shit the man has a cock on him!"

"Oh my god, okay you can stop now," Sam says and wrinkles her nose. "Ew."

"No, keep going," Brynna says and claps her hands. "Are we talking *meh* or *holy fucking shit*?"

"Holy fucking shit," I reply with a wise nod. "Since he was my first, I didn't know that wasn't normal, but then I fucked a couple losers after him, and they were sooooo tiny." I hold up my pinky finger to show them and they all laugh.

"Okay, my turn to say ew," Jax says with a shudder.

"What are you packin'?" Stacy boldly asks.

"Oh, sweetheart, I'm not even on a scale."

"Prove it." Meg stands and circles the table, straddles Jax's lap and dives for the button on his jeans.

"Uh, Meg, you're a beautiful woman, but I'm gay and you're getting married." Jax's face is almost panicked, making us all laugh.

"Are you scared?" she asks him with narrowed eyes.

"Yes." He nods as he lifts her off his lap.

"I just wanted to *see it*." She pouts and plops down in her chair.

"We need more drinks." I signal for the waitress.

"I want to text my man," Nic says and begins typing on her phone.

"No! We said we weren't going to." Stacy shakes her head adamantly then seems to rethink her stance. "Wait. I wonder if they miss us."

"Where are they again?" Jax asks.

"Probably a strip club," Meg pouts again.

"No, I doubt that. I think they're gambling." Nat pats Meg's shoulder and smiles widely.

"Do you guys have any idea how many women are probably flirting with our men?" Sam asks suddenly. "They're hot. And about half of them are famous. Oh God, what have we done?"

"So, let's remind them what they already have." Brynna's grin spreads and she stands quickly. "Everyone to the bathroom! You too, Jax."

"I'm not going in the ladies room," Jax says. "No way."

"Jax! How can I take a photo of your dick for Logan from out here?"

Jax chokes on his tequila and sputters, "I didn't realize that was in the plans for this evening."

"When did you become such a prude?" I stand and drag Jax up with me. "This is a man who used to have a whole folder of dick shots in his phone."

"How the fuck do you know that?"

"We know each other's passcodes on our phones, Einstein."

"That's not so we can snoop. That's so we can destroy any evidence if the other is incapacitated."

"Oh, that's a good idea! Here, Nat, here's my passcode," Jules says as she stumbles on her mile-high heels toward the restroom.

"Save our table! We'll be right back," Sam calls to the bartender who waves us off as we stumble away and file into the bathroom.

Thankfully, it's empty.

"Lock that door, Nic." Meg grins and stares at all of us. "Okay, what are we doing?"

"Boob shots," Brynna says. "We're going to send our guys photos of our boobs."

"Can we send them all *your* boobs?" Jules asks. "You have the best boobs."

"No," Bryn laughs as she strips out of her shirt. "They'll know they're not yours."

"Why do I have to be here for this?" Jax asks.

"Because you're taking the photos," Sam says with a grin. "You're the luckiest man in this hotel."

"And it's completely lost on me. Okay." He shrugs and takes a photo of our naked chests with each of our phones. "That's all of you."

"Now you," Nat says and tosses her long dark hair over her shoulder.

"No way. No dick pics for Logan." Jax shakes his head adamantly and then pins me in a stare. "No, Meredith."

"You *do* know her name!" Nic exclaims and then snorts. "Oh God, I'm not even drunk and I just snorted."

"Atta girl," Meg says, pleased.

"Okay, no dick pic," I say and pat Jax's shoulder. "But we have to send him something."

"Why? He's not answering me."

"Is he mad?" Jules asks and blinks her eyes, alternating between looking at Jax through her left eye, then her right. "Fuck, you're hotter through my left eye."

"What's wrong with your right eye?" Nat asks.

"It's getting drunker than the other."

"Is he mad?" Brynna asks, concerned. "Did we make him mad? Is it because Meg crawled on your lap? She'll 'pologize." She turns to Meg and props her hands on her hips. "'Pologize to Logan."

"I'm sorry, Logan. It's just, Jax is hot and he said his dick is really big, but you would already know that."

"Logan isn't here." Jax laughs out loud. "So he didn't see Meg on my lap. I don't know if he's mad. I can't reach him."

"Does he suck your dick?" Jules asks, peering at Jax through just her left eye.

"Oh God. That's too personal," Nat says and shakes her head.

"Do you suck Nate's dick?" Jax asks.

"Every chance I get."

Jax raises a brow and watches as Jules catches up.

"Ha! I knew it!"

"Okay, let's focus." I turn and look at all three of the Jaxes in front of me. That alcohol is kicking in nicely.

Meg smirks at that and primps in the mirror.

"Let's just send him a cute photo of you," I suggest and snatch his phone out of his hand so I can take the picture.

"Wait! Let's all crowd around him," Nic says and the girls all climb around him. Nat jumps up in his arms and before I know it, Jax is draped in women.

"Ha! This is awesome." I snap a few photos with everyone's phones then we make our way back to our table and order a fresh round of drinks.

"Okay, let's send our pics to our men," Sam says and pushes her face into her phone, concentrating.

"How do you spell tits?" Jules asks.

"'Nesia," Meg reminds her.

I bring up the text window for Mark and plug in the shot of my boobs and text under it: *here's your boob shot, perv.*

"How do you spell cock again?" Stacy asks the room at large. "As in, 'I want your cock between my tits'?"

Jax spits out the tequila he'd just swigged and chokes. "Jesus Christ, you're all a bunch of dirty women."

"Oh, honey, you have no idea," Sam says with a shake of the head. "Thankfully, our men like it."

With the text messages sent, we grin at each other and then explode into laughter.

"That's going to shock the fuck out of my husband," Stacy says, wiping her eyes.

"Okay, enough sitting around. Meg, I think you should sing," Jules says.

"There isn't a band, Jules. The music is piped in."

"There's a karaoke machine over there," Brynna points to the corner of the room. "I bet Hottie McHotterson over there will turn it on."

"Who?" Nic asks.

"The bartender."

"I got this." I stand and plump up my breasts, as though I'm preparing for some kind of woman battle and saunter over to the bar, ready to flirt with McHotterson so he'll let Meg sing.

CHAPTER SEVENTEEN

~Mark~

"I fold." Caleb throws his cards down in disgust and glares at Matt. "When did your luck get so fucking good?"

"The day I met Nic," he responds coolly and gathers the chips he just won. We're in the high-roller area at the Aria, next door to where the girls are partying. None of us wanted to be too far from them.

"God, you're whipped," Dom murmurs and bites on his cigar as he counts his chips. Will set us each up in here with twenty-five thousand dollars worth of chips and said good luck as we sat at two tables and got down to business three hours ago.

Any money we're lucky enough to walk out of here with will be donated to charity.

"It'll happen to you eventually, brother." Matt claps Dom on the shoulder and laughs when Dom's face tightens. "Trust me. Some chick is going to make you stupid."

"He doesn't need a chick for that," Will yells from the table next to ours then high- fives Luke.

Logan glances over at me and shakes his head with a rueful smile. He joined us about an hour ago after checking into the hotel.

"When can we go collect our girls?" Luke asks.

"Sick of us already?" Leo says and throws in some chips.

"Natalie's a helluva lot better looking than you."

"I won't disagree there," Leo says with a smile. "And you've got nothing on your sister."

"She's a pain in the ass," I murmur good-naturedly. "And you're a fucking saint."

"I'm no saint." He shakes his head. "And yes, she can be a pain in the ass, but she's my pain in the ass."

"That's so sweet," Dom taunts him. "Watch out, you're about to lose your man card."

Isaac smirks from next to Luke. "I think you pass your man card off to your wife when you get married. You're still a man, but you're *her* man."

"That's too deep to think about when I'm drinking, bro," Will responds and swigs his beer. "I'm not handing my man card off to anyone. Meg knows who the boss is."

All the guys burst out into laughter and shake their heads at Will as though he's just a stupid, stupid man.

"Sure she does," Luke says with a grin. "*She's t*he boss."

"Yeah." Will sighs and then gets a goofy grin on his face. "She is."

"See, you don't have that problem when both people in the relationship are men," Logan says with a satisfied smile.

"Not gonna happen, dude," Caleb says with a shake of his head, making Logan laugh.

"That won't ever be an issue for me either," Leo mutters with a scowl and tosses his cards on the table in disgust.

"Won't marry you, huh?" Caleb asks.

"Nope."

"Have you asked her?" Logan asks soberly. The more I get to know Logan the more I like him. He doesn't mince words.

"I've mentioned it a few times, but she insists that she doesn't ever want to get married, so no, I've never formally proposed." He looks miserable. His jaw ticks as he grinds his teeth and his tattooed hands are flexed on the table.

"Ask her," Nate says soberly.

"She'll say no."

"Maybe not," I reply and nod when he looks up at me in surprise. "She thinks you've been mad at her or something."

"She talked to you?"

"She came to my place one night when you were working late."

"I'm not fucking mad at her." He scowls and shakes his head, as if he's confused. "I can't think of anything *but* her."

"Ask her," Luke says again and then to the dealer, "I'm in."

Suddenly, all of our phones begin to chime and vibrate at once. We all glance at each other then check our phones.

It's from Meredith, and it's a picture of her gorgeous breasts. Jesus Christ, just a photo of her tits makes me hard. *Here's your boob pic, perv.*

I grin and then glance around at the others. Their jaws are all dropped, staring at their phones in fascination.

"Did everyone get a tit pic?" I ask.

The guys nod, but Logan laughs and shakes his head. "No, I got a photo of my man draped in all of your women." He shows it to all of us, making us laugh.

"I thought you said they'd be safe together," I say to Matt who is grinning like a loon and staring down at his phone.

"I said they'd be safe. I didn't say they'd make wise choices." He tucks his phone inside his pocket as we all begin to pack it in. "However, I think that's a sign that they've been left to their own devices for long enough."

"I'm marrying these tits," Will says in wonder as he continues to stare at his phone.

"Don't let Meg hear you saying that," Luke says with a laugh. "She'll kick your ass."

"I'm marrying her," he whispers and then grins, also like a loon.

The Montgomerys are a bunch of fucking loons.

We settle up with the dealers then head out. I'm ready to be with my girl. I couldn't be happier that she's having fun with the other girls, and it doesn't surprise me. She's funny as fuck and easy to love.

She's so fucking easy to love.

"I have a feeling Jax might be pissed at me," Logan confesses as we make our way through the casino toward the sky bridge back to the Cosmo.

"Why?" I ask.

"What the fuck did you do?" Will tosses over his shoulder to us.

"He doesn't know I'm coming," Logan says, "so I haven't been answering my phone today."

"Is he blowing it up? I hate it when that happens," Dom says.

"No, he's just called once and texted a few times, but I feel guilty for not responding."

"You could have just pretended like you were at home," I say and eye the man next to me.

"I'm a horrible liar."

"It's a text. He can't tell if you're lying."

He shrugs a shoulder and purses his lips. "I just hope I didn't waste a trip to Vegas."

"You're fine." I clap him on the shoulder and follow the guys into the club. We all stop short, in a line, and stare open-mouthed at the scene before us.

Meg is belting out a Britney Spears song on a karaoke machine. Brynna is lying on the bar with a wedge of lime between her perky, plump breasts and Sam is throwing back a shot of tequila, then takes the lime out of Bryn's breasts with her teeth.

"Jesus, my woman is doing body shots with your wife," Leo says to Caleb, his voice low and reverent. Caleb simply nods silently.

Jax and Natalie are on the dance floor, dancing to the noises coming out of Meg. Luke is watching her and laughing his ass off.

Jules and Mer are leaning back against the bar, their heads tipped back so the bartender can pour shots directly into their mouths.

Stacy is sitting on some strange man's lap and Nic is behind the bar, serving customers, throwing bottles in the air Cocktail-style.

"Is this really happening?" Dom asks when he can catch his breath from laughing.

"Why is my wife sitting in some motherfucker's lap?" Isaac asks. We've all crossed our arms over our chests, watching like it's a train wreck that we just can't look away from.

The air smells of sweet liquor and bad choices as the girls laugh and high-five each other. Mr. Grabby Motherfucker lays his hands on Stacy's hips and she automatically moves them away.

"Good girl," Isaac mutters. "I'm going to kill him."

"This is fucking awesome," Dom laughs. "So fucking awesome."

"My girl can sing," Will says with a grin.

"Dude, you're fucking drunk," Leo says with a smirk. "She's horrible right now."

"Fuck you, she's awesome," Will insists.

"Hey! Mr. Lovey Pants is here!" Meredith exclaims and points at Logan. "Jax! He's here!"

"Did she just call me 'Mr. Lovey Pants'?" Logan asks incredulously.

"Yeah, I think that's what they call you when you're not around," I inform him soberly.

"Well, I do have a lot of love in my pants," Logan says smugly.

"Dude, really?" Caleb snarls.

"He's going to fit in just fine," Dom laughs and doubles over when Stacy waves at Isaac.

"Baby! Hi! This is Stan." We all walk forward to claim our girls. "All of the chairs were gone!"

"I'm not Stan," he says and winks at Stacy.

"Who are you?" Isaac growls.

"Ted."

"He looks like a Stan," Stacy shrugs. "All of the chairs in the *whole world* were gone!"

"If you don't take your hands off my wife," Isaac says coldly, "I'm going to fucking kill you. My brother is a cop and I'll get away with it. I won't tell you again."

Ted pales and swallows hard, then smiles at Stacy and boosts her out of his lap. "Nice to meet you, darlin'." With that, he scurries away.

"I missed you so much!" Mer exclaims and launches herself into my arms. "It's been days and days since I saw you."

"I saw you about four hours ago, baby." I laugh and kiss the top of her head, then tilt her chin up so I can kiss her soft lips.

"Did you know Mr. Lovey Pants was coming?"

"I did. It was a surprise."

"Awww," she says and lays her head on my shoulder, watching her friend. "Look at them."

Logan and Jax are dancing, their foreheads pressed together as Meg and Will sing a horrible rendition of "I Got You Babe" by Sonny and Cher.

Luke lifts Nat in his arms and kisses her long and slow, making Jules gag. "Stop it!"

"No," Luke says then goes in for more kisses.

"Christ on a crutch, Williams, your room is right upstairs!" Nate wraps his arms around her, pulling her against him, but she continues to taunt Luke until finally Nate simply shuts her up by kissing her himself.

"There's a lot of kissing going on around here," Brynna murmurs.

"Let's go upstairs," Caleb says and takes her hand in his, leading her toward the door.

"I'm getting orgasms!" Brynna calls and waves at all of us. "Can we do that sixty-nine thing you're so good at?"

"Me too!" Jules announces. "Well, apagasms."

"Julianne," Nate murmurs in exasperation.

"What? I am!"

Sam and Leo are at the bar, Sam is in Leo's lap, but they're not talking to each other while Matt joins Nic behind the bar and eyes the apron tied around her waist.

"We're taking this with us," he informs the bartender and leads Nic out of the club without a backward glance.

"You can put Nat down, Luke," I say to my brother, but he simply shakes his head and kisses her temple.

"Nope. I'm taking her back to the room. Goodnight, everyone."

"They're dropping like flies," Meredith murmurs. "Did you know that when a guy has an orgasm it starts in his *spine?*" she says with wide eyes.

"Uh, I'm a guy," I say with a laugh.

"I know, but I didn't know that. Did you?"

"I guess that's one way to put it. I hadn't ever really thought about it."

"Thank you!" Jax says as he and Logan join us. "These drunk as fuck women were asking me all kinds of questions about sex. Men don't think about sex. We just have it."

"You were very informational, Doctor Dangerous," Meredith slurs, making us laugh.

"Were you now?" Logan asks him, pushing his glasses up his nose. "I want to hear all about this later."

Mer's hands roam up and down my back as she snuggles close to me, resting her head on my chest. She turns her face to rub her nose against my sternum and glides those sexy as sin hands down over my ass.

"I love your ass," she says so only I can hear.

She's hot as fuck tonight in another short dress, but this one is looser than the one she tortured me in last night. It's a red V-neck, showing off her amazing cleavage and hangs loosely from below her boobs to just above her knees.

"You sent me a boob shot," I murmur back.

"It was Brynna's idea. We had to remind you guys what you already have so you wouldn't fuck any of the whores that came onto you when you were away from us."

I laugh and push a loose tendril of her hair behind her ear.

"Well, first of all, we weren't going to forget what was waiting for us, and number two, we were too busy playing poker to fuck anyone who might have hit on us."

"Whores," she mutters, as if she's picturing the imaginary women in her head.

"Whores!" Stacy agrees then turns to her husband. "Can we go fuck now?"

"Don't have to ask me twice. Peace out, guys." Isaac immediately takes Stacy's hand and leads her out of the club.

"I'm going back to play poker," Dom says and waves at us as he leaves. "I'm on a winning streak."

"We're leaving too," Jax says with a smile. "Thanks for keeping the secret. It was a great one."

"You're welcome."

"See you tomorrow!" Mer calls after him. Sam and Leo are deep in conversation now.

"Want another drink?" I ask my already drunk woman, with no intentions whatsoever of actually giving her any more alcohol.

"Nope." She grins widely and bites my chin.

"What would you like to do, drunk girl?"

"Strip you naked right here and take advantage of your hot body."

I stare down at her then bust up laughing. "Yeah, that's not going to happen."

"Damn. You're no fun." She sticks her bottom lip out in a pout, and that's it. It's over.

I'm done.

I nod at Sam and drag Mer behind me to the elevator and punch the button to go up.

"Are you gonna strip me down in the room?" she asks and buries her face in my neck. "God, you smell good. You've always smelled so good. I could just keep my face right here for, like, twenty years and be okay with that. As long as you're naked."

"You're killing me," I mutter and bite my lip against the throb in my dick and the chills that Mer is sending through me as she nibbles on my neck.

No way in fucking hell am I going to make it up to our room without making her come.

The elevator finally arrives and is blissfully empty.

"Thank Christ." I push her up against the wall of the small car, push the button for our floor and then attack her. "You can't know how fucking sexy you are."

"You're the fucking sexy one," she replies and yanks my shirt out of the waistband of my pants then plants those hands on my abs. "Jesus, Mark, your body is incredible."

"You make me do shit that I would never do with anyone else. You make me forget myself." I hitch her leg up around my waist and tug her thong to the side, giving my fingers access to her wet pussy. "Your pussy makes me crazy."

"I want your cock, Mark."

"In a minute," I reply. "I want to make you come before we reach our floor."

"Oh God," she groans as her hips circle and push against my fingers, finally crying out, biting my shoulder as she erupts on my hand. "Holy shit."

The doors open and I scoop her up and carry her to our suite. "I'm not even close to done with you."

"Thank God."

Chapter Eighteen

~Meredith~

Am I going to throw up? I lie still and take stock of my stomach, head, body. All seem to be in working order. My stomach isn't rolling, which is a good sign because with the amount of alcohol I consumed last night, I should be violently ill. I never drink like that.

My mouth is as dry as can be, I'm sure I have dragon breath, and if I don't pee *right now,* I'm pretty sure my bladder is going to explode.

I roll out of bed and shuffle into the bathroom, take care of business, then splash water on my face and brush my teeth, scrubbing the foul remnants from last night out of my mouth. When I'm finished, I rub my eyes, then take a good look at myself in the mirror.

Holy. Shit.

Mascara is smeared down my cheeks, my blond hair is a messy tangle and I have hickeys on my breasts.

I close my eyes and feel myself go wet when I remember how Mark worshiped my breasts last night, his words of appreciation for the boob pic I sent him, how they turn him on.

Who knew a boob pic would have that reaction?

I want to go wake him up with my mouth on his body, but he can't see me like this so I start the shower and get in before it heats up, shocking my body awake. I wash my face and scrub my body then stand under the stream and wash my hair.

Just as I'm finally feeling human again, the door to the shower opens and Mark steps in and silently wraps me in his strong arms, hugging me close.

"Good morning," I murmur against his chest.

"'Mornin'," he replies, his voice still rough from sleep. He's warm and smooth and perfect for leaning on right now. "How are you feeling, baby?"

"Better now that I've scrubbed every inch of me." I grin up at him and feel my heart stumble when he returns my smile with sleepy blue eyes. "How about you?"

"I woke up missing you." He kisses my forehead and turns us so he's in the water. "And I think I smell bad."

"We got very dirty last night." I go to work washing him and watch my hands glide over his tight body, the muscles in his stomach, his amazing arms, his hips. "I see I put a few marks of my own on you last night," I murmur when he turns and I see the nail marks on his back.

"You were enthusiastic," he says with a chuckle.

"Back at you."

"I'm always enthusiastic when it comes to you."

"Back at you again." He spins back around and washes his hair, then leads us out of the shower and tenderly dries me off, his hands gentle and thorough, making my body come alive again. Instead of leading me back to the bed when we're dry, he guides me to the vanity and turns on the blow dryer and dries my hair, strand-by-strand, brushing through it with his fingers, quietly watching his own hands in my blond strands. He's quiet this morning, thoughtful, and he's taking care of me.

When my hair is dry, I turn the tables on him, blowing his hair dry. He watches me with amused eyes, his hands on my hips, until every hair on his handsome head is dry.

"Meredith." He takes the dryer from my hand and sets it on the counter, then circles his arms around my waist and tips his forehead down to rest on mine.

"Yeah?"

"I love you."

I grin and drag my fingertips down his face as he lays his lips on mine, gently sweeping them back and forth, nibbles the corner of my mouth, nuzzles my nose. My nipples pebble as his hands glide up to my ribcage, but he doesn't move farther up to cup them. He continues to simply kiss me, our naked bodies aroused and pressed together, against the bathroom vanity. When he kisses my nose and forehead again, I drag my hands over his hips and am about to circle his hard, thick cock when he catches my wrists in his hands and holds me away.

"I want to touch you," I whisper.

"Not yet." He nuzzles my nose again, a small smile on his lips to soften the rejection. "I just want to kiss you."

"Really?" I cock a brow and glance down at his cock. "That's not what it looks like."

Without another word, he turns and leads me back to the bedroom, lifts me onto the center of the bed and joins me. But instead of climbing on top of me and making love to me, he lies next to me, facing me, presses his hand to the small of my back and pulls me into him and claims my lips again with his, kissing me slowly. It's lazy and gentle. Our legs tangle, I bury my fingers in his hair and hold on as he sweeps those amazing lips back and forth across mine, then slips his tongue in my mouth, as though I'm a delicacy he wants to nibble on.

I love the different facets of this man. He can be crazy with lust, as he was last night, and make me feel like if he doesn't fuck me immediately he'll die. Or he can be like right now. Taking his time, seducing us both, basking in the love we feel for each other.

His fingertips draw circles on my back, over my shoulder and down my ribs, and then follow the same path again, sending shivers through me.

"Cold?" he whispers and tugs the covers over us, completely covering us, heads and all, without missing a beat. I drag my foot up and down his leg, loving the way the soft hair feels against the arch of my foot. His cock is pressed against my lower belly, pulsing with his need. I shift slowly, hitch my leg over his hip and tilt my hips, filling myself with him, making us both gasp. He cradles my face in his hand, his mouth shaped like an O as I barely move but contract my muscles around him.

"I love you too," I whisper. Our gazes hold, and we are connected in *every* way, from head to toe as we make slow, quiet love. "So much more than I can ever say."

His hand glides down my neck, over my breast and side to anchor on my hip, guiding my small movements. The angle has the base of his cock pressed against my clit, and I bite my lip as I watch him, knowing I'm getting so close.

"You're so fucking tight, Mer. God, so wet." He bites his lip too, but doesn't look away from me. "Are you close?"

"So close," I whisper. "Oh God, Mark, I'm gonna—"

"That's right." His hand tightens on my hip and that's all it takes to urge me over the edge. It's the quietest we've ever been, the sweetest lovemaking, so easy and lazy, but I have a feeling it's the most meaningful it's ever been. For both of us.

He blinks slowly and follows me over the edge, trembling with his orgasm, but not making a sound as his body shivers, clenches, sweaty and tight. His hand slips around to cup my ass and his lips are on mine again, nibbling lazily.

"Mine," he whispers against my lips.

***

"Nice of you to join us," Luke says dryly as we make our way out onto the patio near the pool. The tables are shaded by wide, colorful umbrellas and brunch is being served.

"They're in love. Leave them alone," Brynna says with a grin.

"How is everyone feeling?" I ask as Mark holds my chair out for me and I pick up my menu. Jax leans over and kisses my cheek, then shoves his orange juice in my hand, which I thankfully consume in two gulps.

The whole clan is wearing sunglasses, which makes me laugh. Except for

Logan, who has his trademark thick-rimmed glasses perched on his handsome nose. He winks at me.

"You're not hung over?" Jules asks in surprise.

"I was a little, but I'm fine now. Nothing a shower and brushing my teeth didn't fix."

"And maybe a little sex," Nic says with a wink. Matt kisses her temple and rubs his hand rhythmically up and down her back.

"So what's happening today?" Dom asks before stuffing a big hunk of waffle dripping with syrup into his mouth.

"Lazy day," Will says with a half smile. "I think we're all recovering from last night."

"I have a meeting," Leo says quietly.

"What meeting?" Sam asks with a scowl.

"The guys want to go over a few potential songs for the next album." He shrugs like it's no big deal, but Sam is clearly not happy.

"No," she says and shakes her head adamantly.

"No?" he echoes with a raised brow.

"No. We're here to celebrate with our family, not to work. You work enough when we're home."

"It's just for a few hours, Samantha."

We all share glances with each other, quiet as Leo and Sam glare at each other. Mark tenses beside me, so I take his hand in mine and squeeze it reassuringly.

"What is your problem?" Sam finally demands.

"What are you talking about?" He pinches the bridge of his nose and sighs in exasperation.

"You're moody. You work all the time. You think I don't feel you pulling away from me?" Her voice is edged with panic now, and Luke looks like he's about to speak up when Leo's hand drops and his head whips up to stare at her.

"Are you kidding me? I think we need to have this conversation later, when we're alone."

"No, we're going to have it now. Right here." She pulls her sunglasses off and throws them on the table. "If you're trying to break it off, just fucking do it, Leo. This distance from you is killing me."

"I don't want to fucking break up with you, Goddamn it!"

"Then what's wrong with you?"

"I want to marry you!"

We all sit in stunned silence, watching as Sam's mouth gapes open in surprise.

"You don't want to get married, I get it." Now he throws his glasses on the table, and the misery in his eyes brings tears to mine. "You've been saying for almost two years that you're happy with the way things are, and we don't need a piece of paper to let everyone know that we love each other. Fine."

He throws his hands in the air, then shakes his head. "I'll take you any way I can get you, Samantha, and that's the fucking truth. I love you, every damn day, I love you. I'm never going anywhere. You're it for me. But *I* do want to get married."

"I don't want babies," she whispers, her lips barely moving. Leo laughs and shakes his head.

"We're still on the same page there, these baby making machines are filling this family full of kids just fine without us adding to it, and people get married without having kids every day. But I get it, sunshine. It's not what you want."

"But it's what you want."

He just nods and clenches his eyes shut. I glance up at Mark to see his eyes riveted on his sister and Leo. The girls around us are sniffling, trying to do so quietly, but doing a bad job of it and all of us are quiet as Sam and Leo have their moment.

"Then let's do it."

"What?" Leo's head whips up again.

"Let's get married. We're in Vegas for Christ's sake."

"This isn't funny." His voice is angry again.

"I'm not trying to be funny." She's watching his face and a smile slowly spreads across her beautiful face. "Let's get married, baby."

"Why? And if you say because I'm moody and you're trying to placate me, the answer is fuck no. I already told you, this isn't an ultimatum."

"Because I love you, every damn day." She climbs into his lap and buries her face in his neck. "Because I want you to be happy, and because I'm just with you for your money."

That makes us all smile and Leo lets out a small laugh then holds onto her tightly, almost desperately.

"Really?"

She nods.

"When?"

"Today."

His jaw drops and he grips her shoulders to hold her away so he can see her face. "Today?"

"Why not? We're here. The people we love are here. Even the band is in town. We can do it tonight. Is this why you've been so moody? So distant?" She nuzzles his nose with hers and cups his face in her hands.

"I always work a lot."

"Yes, but you're not always a grouchy ass about it."

He sighs and tips his forehead to hers. "I guess it's been on my mind a lot lately. It feels right to take this step with you."

"I've been scared that you wanted out, but didn't know how to tell me."

"Never," he says fiercely. "I don't ever want to think about the possibility of not being with you. Nothing matters without you, sunshine."

"Honestly, I've just been so happy with the way things are, getting married really hasn't been on my radar." She grins widely and traces the tattoo on his upper chest with her fingertip. "But now that you mention it, I'm all for it. Let's do it."

"Mom and Dad aren't here," Mark says immediately.

"If this is what you want to do," Luke begins and when I look over at him I'm stunned to see tears in his eyes, "I can have Mom and Dad here in about four hours. I'll make the call."

"What do you say?" Sam asks, smiling at her man. "Will you marry me today?"

"This is so us," he whispers with a shake of the head. "Don't you want to do all that girly planning stuff?"

"Nope." She grins and kisses him hard on the lips. "I have my favorite shoes with me, my family is here, and I'm ready."

"Then let's do it." Leo turns to look at Luke. "Make those calls. I have some to make too."

"I'm on it." Luke rises but instead of pulling out his phone, he walks around the table to kiss Sam's head. "I love you."

"I love you too. Get Mom and Dad here so I can get married."

"Yes, ma'am."

"Wait, what about the kids? They're with your mom and dad," Natalie reminds her husband.

"Mom and Dad will take them," Caleb says immediately. "That won't be a problem."

"Oh my God!" Jules exclaims. "We're planning a wedding!"

"For today!" Meg says and hugs Will. "I don't feel hung over anymore."

"What do we do?" Stacy asks.

"The first order of business is the food," Will says, earning an eye-roll from Meg.

"I'm already looking into it," Matt says, his fingers flying over his phone. Dom is also fiddling with his phone.

"I've got license info here, man," Dom says to Matt.

"Great. I'm looking at chapels. I've got two to call."

"Who knew that Matt and Dom would turn into wedding planners?" Natalie says with a wide smile.

"We don't need all that," Leo says. "I'd be happy with a ride through the wedding drive-thru and Elvis."

"Oh, hello no." Sam shakes her head and laughs. "I may not need all the fancy trimmings, but the guests should at least have chairs to sit in rather than follow us through a drive-thru."

"It's too bad Alecia couldn't come," Jules says and shakes her head. "She'd have it all planned by now."

"I know, I invited her, but she had an event this weekend," Meg says with a pout. Dom clears his throat, catching my attention.

"I don't think I've met Alecia," I say and watch Dom's face. He glances up at me, firms his lips and returns to this phone.

"She plans all of our events. She's brilliant," Jules says. Dom's jaw ticks.

"You don't like her?" I ask.

"I don't know her well," he responds, not looking at me.

"Dom asked her out and she turned him down," Will informs me. "Bruised his ego."

"*Vaffanculo,*" Dom mutters.

"Did you just tell me to fuck off?" Will asks with a laugh.

"Close enough," Dom replies.

"You speak Italian *and* you're hot? How could she pass that up?" I ask sarcastically.

"You think I'm hot, *bella*?" Dom asks with a slow smile.

"Duh." I roll my eyes as Mark growls next to me. "Have you seen you?"

"Well, this is interesting," Dom says.

"Watch yourself." Mark's voice is low and hard. Dom shrugs and winks at me then turns back to his phone.

"You're awfully possessive," Stacy says to Mark while nibbling on a strawberry.

"Fuck yeah, I am," he agrees.

"Okay, Sam and Leo, you're with me. We're going to get your license." Dom jumps up and walks away without looking at the rest of us.

"Mom and Dad are on the way," Luke announces as he returns.

"Thank you." Sam hugs her brother and then she and Leo follow Dom, leaving the rest of us to simply stare at each other.

"Did that just happen?" Brynna asks.

"My sister is getting married. *Today.*" Mark murmurs.

"Never a dull moment around here," Logan says cheerfully. "What do y'all do for an encore?"

"Just wait until they get drunk," Jax says with a shake of his head. "You haven't seen anything yet."

"We need to get her flowers," Nat says.

"The chapels are full-service," Matt replies, his nose still in his phone. "And I just reserved one online for this evening."

"What should we do in the meantime?" Isaac asks.

"Get our girls recovered from last night so they can do it all over again tonight," Nate replies with a grin.

"I'm a mother," Jules replies primly. "I can't do it again tonight."

"Really?" Meg asks.

"Oh God, I better go nap now," Jules replies. "Wanna go nap, ace?"

"If that's code for sink inside you and lose my mind for a few hours, then yes, I do."

"Thank God you can read my mind."

CHAPTER NINETEEN

"You can't wear leather pants to your own wedding," Jules insists with her fists planted on her slim hips and a scowl on her gorgeous face.

"I'm marrying a rock star, Jules," Sam says with a laugh. "I think I could wear cut off shorts and a tank top and it would be okay. Besides, we're in Vegas. The JP will just be thankful that I'm sober."

"You plan on being sober?" Stacy winks at Sam as she stares lovingly at the red stiletto Louboutins in Sam's hands.

"Absolutely. Jesus, you guys. I had no idea that he wanted to get married."

"Seriously?" I ask and grin when I see a text from Mark come across my phone. The girls are all in Meg and Will's presidential suite on the top floor of the hotel. This place is bigger than my mother's old house. The guys have made themselves scarce for the next two hours until the wedding because, like Natalie said, it may be unconventional, but it's still bad luck for Leo to see his bride before the wedding. Jax and Logan chose to go with the guys because they'd both agreed they'd had enough estrogen for a while.

Pussies.

Is Sam nervous?

I glance up at her and smile at the dreamy grin on her face.

No, she's excited. Leo?

"We haven't talked about it since the beginning of things," she insists. "We agreed that marriage wasn't for us and never brought it up again."

"Well, I guess he changed his mind," Brynna says. "I love Leo, Sam. He's so great."

"Women all over the world are going to be in mourning when this news hits," Nic says with a shake of the head. "I'm not afraid to admit that I would have been one of them a few years ago."

Sam turns to her and chuckles. "And now?"

"Now you're my friends and I couldn't be happier for you. You deserve your happily ever after with your rock star." Nic hugs Sam close then pulls back with a gasp. "We need to find cake! Damn it, Sam! You can't get married without cake!"

"I'm sure we'll find something," Stacy assures her and then bounces on her toes. "Sam's getting married!"

"Where's my baby?" Lucy demands as she comes into the suite with Neil right behind her.

"Mom!" Sam runs to her mom and hugs her close, and I feel my heart catch, suddenly missing my mom something fierce.

Leo can't stop smiling. He looks like an idiot, Mark responds, making me laugh.

"I can't believe you decided to get married today." Lucy laughs as she pulls back to look Sam in the eye. "Are you sure?"

"Never been more sure."

"I'm heading down to hang out with the guys and scare my soon to be son-in-law," Neil says as he hugs his daughter. "But I wanted to come up and hug the bride first."

"I'm so happy you're both here," Sam replies with a grin. "I guess having Luke around for times like this doesn't suck."

"The boy is resourceful," Lucy agrees. "Okay, Neil, shoo. This is a woman-only zone."

"I'll see you all soon." He waves at all of us and heads out of the suite.

Your dad is on his way to you. Lucy is with us. I send the text to Mark and watch quietly as all of these beautiful women fuss around Sam, laughing and hugging and sipping diet sodas. Lucy fits right in, her face aglow in happiness. These women, this family, is magical. They've circled around Sam as if they're her sisters.

What I wouldn't give to be with my sister on her wedding day.

I tuck the sad thought away for now, determined to be happy for Sam, to concentrate on her happiness today.

Someday, she might be *my* sister-in-law.

The thought stuns me and makes me giddy all at once.

He's here. Miss u. Mark's text makes me grin and my heart light.

You'll see me soon. Love u.

I tuck my phone away and laugh when Jules continues to glare at Sam's black leather pants.

"She's not going to change her mind," I say to Jules.

"Black leather pants," Jules says again, pointing at the offending clothing. "How can she get married in these?"

"They'll look hot on her." I shrug. "The top is beautiful."

"You're wearing black leather pants?" Lucy asks with wide, stunned eyes.

"Yes. But look at the top!" Sam holds up a white tank top with a high neckline. It has large, white lace flowers and is cropped to hit her right above her pierced navel. "It's white."

"And the sexiest red shoes I've ever seen," Stacy adds.

"Well," Lucy says after a moment of consideration. "It's Vegas, last minute, and you've always marched to the beat of your own drummer. I think it's fantastic."

Sam sends Jules a smug grin. "See? It's fantastic."

"It's ridiculous." Jules shakes her head and sighs in exasperation as the rest of us chuckle at her. "You should be wearing a beautiful dress."

"It doesn't matter." Sam smiles and pulls Jules in for a big hug. "It doesn't matter what I wear, Jules. I could be in ratty old pajamas and it wouldn't matter. All that matters is that I'm marrying Leo. He's the best part. Not what I wear."

"Except the shoes," Stacy says fiercely.

"The shoes are always the exception," Sam says with a wink.

"I'm so happy for you," Jules says with a hoarse whisper. "We all know what you and Leo have gone through, and no one deserves to be together more than the two of you. Natalie will make lots of babies for you to spoil."

"Yeah, I will," Nat agrees with a grin.

"What are you doing about vows?" Meg asks. "Knowing Leo he'll want something original."

"We already wrote them."

"You did?" I ask. "You've barely seen each other today."

"We did it in the cab on the way to get the license. He writes songs for a living. This was a breeze."

"I can't wait to hear them," Nic says with a sigh. "It's all so romantic."

"When do you think you and Matt might get hitched?" Brynna asks.

Nic looks surprised by the question, then just shrugs. "No idea. Eventually, I'm sure." She bites her lip as if she's thinking about it for the first time. "There's no rush."

"Okay, ladies," Sam announces and begins stripping out of her casual clothes. "I'm getting dressed and getting married."

"Want me to touch up your hair?" Stacy asks.

"Yeah, can you make it all messy and cool like that night when Will proposed to Meg?"

"Absolutely."

Sam, Brynna, Stacy and Nic all file into the bathroom to primp. The rest of us went to our respective rooms earlier to change into something nicer than jeans and tank tops, although I'm beginning to think it wasn't necessary.

Not if the bride's wearing leather pants.

Lucy sits beside me and takes my hand in hers companionably. "How are you, darling girl?"

"I'm great. This weekend has been a blast."

"It sure sounds like it," she says with a chuckle. "I'm glad. You all needed it. A little play time is good for the soul."

"It is." I smile at the kind woman beside me. "Were you shocked when Luke called?"

"Between you and me? No." She cranes her neck to see into the bathroom. The noise is echoing in the vast space as the girls chirp and giggle.

"I'm surprised it took this long," Meg adds as she falls into a deep-cushioned couch and sips her soda.

"Sam's stubborn," Nat says. "I knew it would happen eventually, but I thought he'd have to work at it a little harder."

"I'm just thankful that Elvis isn't officiating," Jules says as she reapplies her lip gloss. "Are you almost done in there?" she calls into the bathroom.

"Coming!" Stacy calls back.

"Okay, who wants to place bets on who cries first during the ceremony?" Meg asks.

"Neither are going to cry," I reply with a smirk. "They're both too badass for that."

"Have you ever heard the song "Sunshine"?" Meg asks. "Leo wrote that for her. They wrote those vows together. There will be waterworks."

"I'm not betting against that," Nat replies.

"Me neither," Jules agrees.

"He wrote "Sunshine for her"?" I ask with a sappy grin on my face as Meg nods. "That's the most romantic thing I've ever heard."

"Still wanna bet?"

"Hell no."

"We have to go!" Nat yells back to the bathroom.

"I'm ready!" Sam comes walking down the hallway on her high red shoes, those black pants hugging her every curve and that white lacy tank is absolutely stunning, showing off her pierced navel.

Her hair looks messy in a classy, rocker way and her blue eyes are shining above blood-red painted lips.

"You're magnificent," I whisper and feel my eyes fill with tears. "Oh, Sam."

"Oh, my sweet girl," Lucy sniffs as she stands to hug Sam. "You're the most beautiful bride I've ever seen."

"Thanks, Mom."

"Come on," Meg says with a sniff. "Let's put my brother out of his misery and get you two hitched."

Sam smiles triumphantly. "Let's do it."

***

This might be the most beautiful wedding I've ever seen. And it's in Vegas. Amazing.

This particular wedding chapel offers an outdoor garden option. It's evening, just past sunset. We are sitting in ornate white iron chairs facing an arbor, covered in white twinkling lights.

"You're gorgeous," Mark whispers in my ear.

"Wait till you see your sister," I reply with a smile.

"It's a different kind of gorgeous," he says and brushes his knuckle down my cheek. "You take my breath away, M."

I take his hand in mine and kiss his palm softly.

We're all here. All of the Montgomery siblings and their significant others. Nat and Luke, Mark and I. Jax and Logan. Even Leo's band and their families are here, smiling and anxious to get this show started.

Leo, dressed in black ripped jeans and a black button-down shirt rolled on his forearms, escorts Lucy down the aisle to her seat, kisses her cheek and joins the justice of the peace on the small stage. The song "Sunshine" begins to play, signaling that we should all stand and turn to watch Sam, dressed in her unconventional wedding attire, walk down the aisle with her dad. Neil is smiling at his daughter proudly, clasping her hand tightly in his own, and I can't help but remember that my daddy will never walk me down the aisle. Mark won't escort my mama to her seat. Tiff won't stand by my side as I pledge myself to the man I love with my whole heart.

Will they know anyway? Will they be with me? Can they see how happy he makes me?

I inhale deeply as Mark wraps his arms around me from behind and kisses my head before whispering, "It's okay, M. Just breathe through it."

How does he always know?

I feel his chest move against my back in a long, deep breath and I do as he asks, taking a cleansing breath and refocusing on the here and now.

Sam's carrying a small bouquet of tiger lilies, her eyes are pinned to Leo's. I glance over at the groom to find him watching his bride, his jaw dropped in awe and love and everything in me goes soft at the romantic moment.

She passes her flowers to her mom when she hugs and kisses her before joining Leo on the small stage. He takes Sam's hands in his and whispers something down at her that makes her cheeks blush and her smile widen.

"Family and friends," the tall man begins as we reclaim our seats. Mark wraps his arm around my shoulders and pulls me close to his side. "It's my pleasure to officiate this special occasion. Samantha and Leo have asked that we make this quick, and I have to say, unconventional."

"Imagine that," Will says with a chuckle. We all smile and nod.

"This very special couple has decided to exchange rings as they recite their vows to each other. Samantha, please recite your vows to Leo."

Sam clears her throat and pulls a ring out of her bra, holding it up for all of us to see.

"Best storage system ever," Leo murmurs softly, making Sam laugh. She takes a deep breath, reaches for Leo's hand and looks up into his eyes solemnly.

"I promise you, Leo, until my very last breath, to fight for life, for joy, for us. To never take your actions, words and kindness for granted, and to keep leaving you secret notes when we are away from each other." Leo grins as Sam slips his ring on his finger and continues speaking.

"I vow to grow with you and not apart, to make my accomplishments, ours, and your challenges, mine. I will always love you deeply and honestly, as your equal and your partner. I fiercely want to grow old with you; so we can sit on our front porch on a warm summer's eve, so we can hold our frail hands together and laugh, so I can simply be with you, and know that I am home. I was born to tell you I love you, to be your wife, to be with you, forsaking all others, for the rest of my life."

I watch through tear-filled eyes as Leo swallows hard, takes a ring from his pocket and looks deeply into Sam's eyes.

"I promise you, Samantha, my sunshine, until my very last breath, to fight for life, for joy, for us. To never take your actions, words and kindness for granted, and to write you love songs as often as possible." Sam bites her lip, trying to keep her tears at bay, and failing.

"I vow to grow with you and not apart, to make my accomplishments, ours, and your challenges, mine. I will always love you deeply and honestly, as your equal and your partner. I fiercely want to grow old with you; so we can sit on our front porch on a warm summer's eve, so I can hold you in my arms, so I can simply be with you, and know that I am home. I was born to tell you I love you, to be your husband, to be with you, forsaking all others, for the rest of my life."

With the ring firmly on Sam's hand, he raises it to his lips and presses a kiss on her finger. Mark hands me a tissue and kisses my cheek as the officiant steps forward to speak.

"By the powers vested in me by the state of Nevada, it's my pleasure to pronounce you husband and wife. You may kiss your bride."

"Whoop!" Mark exclaims as we all clap and whistle as Leo bends Sam backwards and kisses her breathless.

"Ladies and gentlemen, Mr. and Mrs. Nash!"

"We did it!" Sam exclaims and throws her hand up to Leo for a high-five, which he happily obliges, then pulls her back in for a long, soft kiss.

"That was amazing," I whisper as tears continue to roll down my cheeks. "He has such a way with words."

"Told you," Meg says as she mops up her own face.

"Let's go eat," Will says, but holds his hands up as if in surrender. "To celebrate. We all need to celebrate."

"You all go," Neil says and hugs his wife close to his side, and it's in this moment, watching Neil cuddle his wife, kiss her tenderly on her temple as she continues to silently cry, that I realize I have this man to thank for the man Mark has become. What a wonderful example of what it is to be a good husband.

A good man.

"We need to get back to the babies," Neil finishes.

"Oh, stay just a little while longer," Natalie says with wide eyes. "The kids are fine."

Lucy shakes her head and hugs her new son-in-law tightly, then cups Sam's face in her hands and kisses her cheeks. "We want you all to celebrate. We'll have a party for the whole family after you're home. Have fun tonight. Enjoy yourselves."

"I am proud of you, baby girl," Neil says and plants his lips on Sam's forehead as he hugs her. "Have fun."

"Let's go celebrate!" Brynna announces, clapping her hands.

"Drinks are on Luke," Sam says sassily, smacking her brother on his arm. "He's loaded."

"So are you," he reminds her.

"I'm the bride. I'm not paying for anything."

***

"Why are you sitting over here all alone?" Logan asks as he joins me at the table in the corner of the semi-quiet bar we found off the strip. The music isn't too loud, the drinks are decent and there are enough pool tables to go around our lively bunch.

Not to mention, there aren't many people in here tonight, so the celebrity members of our group don't have to worry about being approached.

"I'm just watching," I reply with a smile and sip my drink. Mark is currently bent over a pool table, his back to me, making me drool. Dear God, what that man does to a pair of slacks!

"I've never seen anything like this group," Logan says with a laugh.

"I'm pretty new to it too. They're fun and welcoming…"

"And overwhelming," he finishes. I lean back and study the man next to me. His brown hair is messy, his green eyes lit with happiness and humor.

"I like you." I hold my glass up to clink with his. "I'm glad Jax found you."

"I like you too, gorgeous," he replies and tips his glass to mine. "And it was me that found Jax."

"Really?" I lean on my elbow and give him my undivided attention. "He never told me how you met."

"In the grocery store."

"Seriously? Picking guys up in the frozen pizza section works?"

"I believe it was over the bananas," he says and sips his beer. "I don't know, he looked up at me and something in me just clicked."

He's watching Jax across the room chatting with Natalie and Jules. I can hear them laughing. I don't reply, I simply wait for him to continue.

"I've had a different experience than Jax," Logan says and takes another swig of his beer. "My family is awesome. I never came out to my parents, they just always knew and accepted me for me."

"I'm happy for that," I murmur.

"Me too." He clears his throat and shifts in his seat. "I know that Jax's experience has been the opposite of mine, and to be honest with you, Mer, I want to hunt down his family and kick their asses."

"Get in line."

"I don't understand how you turn away someone as awesome as he is."

I follow his gaze to watch Jax tuck Nat's hair behind her ear. "He has an easy way about him," I say. "He's physically affectionate. Always has been. Like that, right there, when he tucked Nat's hair behind her ear?"

Logan nods.

"He's always doing stuff like that to people he knows and feels comfortable with."

"It took him until the second date before he'd let me hold his hand," Logan says with a rueful shake of his head.

"That's because he was trying to figure out if he could trust you or not." I bite my lip, unsure how much to say to this man who clearly loves my best friend very much. "Does he know you love him?"

"Yes." He sighs and swigs his beer.

"And Jax?"

"He feels the same." My heartbeat speeds up at the pure joy on Logan's face.

"Oh my." I sigh wistfully. "It's finally happened for him."

"And for me. Although I never had the issues with my family that Jax did with his, I've been selective about who I choose to have a relationship with. I've never told a man that I love him before."

"I'm so happy for you." I rub his arm soothingly, then lean in and kiss his cheek. "So happy for both of you."

"Mer, you need to know, I'm going to ask him to marry me."

I bite my lip as the tears fill my eyes. My gaze finds Jax again across the room. He's laughing and gesturing with his hands as he tells the girls a story. He's my friend, but more than that, he's my brother.

"Today is the day for wedding talk," I murmur with a soft smile.

"You don't think it's too soon?"

"I think it's wonderful."

"You do? I need to know you're okay with it." Logan rubs his fingers over his mouth. They tremble slightly. "You're his family, Mer. Your opinion matters."

"I love Jax with all my heart," I answer honestly. "He's one of the best men I know. But you know what, Logan? I think you're one of the best men I know too. You're lucky to have each other."

He lets out a gusty breath, as though he's been holding it during the whole conversation. "Thank you."

"I want to be in the wedding."

"We wouldn't have it any other way."

CHAPTER TWENTY

"You wanna talk about what the hell crawled up your ass and died before or after class?" Jax asks as he leans against my desk and crosses his arms over his chest. Little girls are filing in for their after-school ballet class, chattering and laughing, excited for class.

"I'm fine," I reply with a sigh.

Except, I'm not fine.

"We've been home for two days and you've been damn moody," he mutters then pushes his fingers through his hair. "Are you and Mark fighting?"

"No, we're great." It's not a lie. Mark and I have been fantastic.

"Something is wrong, KitKat." He tilts my head back to look me in the eyes. "If everything with Mr. Hot Tamale is so great, why do you look so sad?"

"I've just been in a funk since the wedding," I admit softly.

Jax tilts his head, watching me closely. "Why?"

I jerk my shoulder up in a shrug. "It's stupid."

"I doubt it."

I sigh and wave at a mom as she sits on a bench on the far side of the room.

"It just reminded me that Mom, Dad and Tiff are gone and if I ever marry Mark, they won't be here for it."

"That's not stupid."

"It's not stupid, but it's silly to still be brooding about it. That would just piss Mom off."

"You're grieving, sweetie. It's okay to be sad sometimes."

"Yeah." I blow out a gusty breath. "I'm starting to piss myself off, though, so it's time to shake this mood off."

"GGN tonight?" Jax asks.

"That would be fun! No plans with Mr. Lovey Pants?"

"I can rearrange things."

"Meredith." Our heads swivel toward the door at the sound of Luke's voice.

"What's up?" I grin at Mark's handsome older brother, but I feel the smile fall from my face when I see the look on his. "What happened?"

"Jax," he begins without breaking eye contact with me. "I need you to take care of things here. There's been a car accident."

I gasp and feel my heart speed up as my entire body breaks out in cold sweat.

"What?" My voice is a low whisper.

"There's been a car accident, Mer. Mark's on his way to the hospital."

I blink frantically as Luke and Jax continue to talk, but I can't hear what they're saying. My ears are buzzing. Or is that my head? Someone takes my hand and pulls me out of the chair.

"Meredith," Jax says sternly, making me meet his gaze. "Breathe, baby. You go with Luke. I'll take care of this last class and meet you at the hospital later."

I nod automatically as Jax passes my hand to Luke and he leads me out of the studio to his SUV, but I can't even feel my feet. I'm just following automatically. My face suddenly feels wet.

"Is it raining?" Is that my voice? Soft and hoarse and weak?

"Yes, sweetheart. Come on, get in my car."

Luke is talking, but I don't hear him. I lean my forehead against the cool glass of the passenger window, and I'm suddenly thirteen years old, sitting in Mrs. Yakamura's classroom.

"Meredith?"

Oh geez, did I do that bad on the stupid math test? Mrs. Yakamura is staring at me with really serious eyes, like I'm in trouble or something. I didn't do anything I can think of. I mean, she wouldn't know that I stole Tiff's favorite barrette this morning and put it in my hair after I got to school.

"Yes, ma'am?"

"I need you to go down to the principal's office, please."

The kids around me snicker and my tummy tightens with nerves. "What did I do?"

"You're not in trouble, but they do need you down at the office, sweetie."

"I'm not in trouble?" Why else would I be sent down there? This is the weirdest day ever!

"No. But grab your things. You won't be coming back to class today."

"She's suspended?" *My best friend, Amanda, asks with wide eyes.*

"No. They'll explain when you get down there." I grab my backpack and coat and shrug at Amanda when she does the what the heck is going on look. *When I move to pass by Mrs. Yakamura, she pulls me in for a strong hug, surprising me.*

"I'm so sorry, Meredith."

I must be in trouble. Why else would she be sorry? Oh my gosh, if my dad finds out that I got suspended from school, he'll be beyond mad. He might even take my dance lessons away, and that would suck the worst. He's always lecturing me and Tiff about being responsible and taking school seriously, and that it's okay to have hobbies but we need to be focused.

Blah, blah, blah.

I'm only thirteen, for gosh sakes. It's not like I'm going to college next year. Maybe I won't go to college at all. Maybe I'll just be a dancer. I'll be a dancer and fall in love with a handsome musician and he'll write me love songs and tell me how pretty I am.

Daddy tells me I'm pretty, but he's my daddy. He's supposed to say that.

Happy with my decision to marry a musician, I execute a perfect pirouette down the empty hallway on my way to the office. When I go inside, I'm surprised to see my mom and the counselor, Mr. Pritchett, waiting for me.

"Mom?" Her eyes are red and blotchy. Mine get the same way when I've been crying for a long time. "Mommy?"

"Oh, baby girl." She yanks me into her arms and smothers me against her breasts, holding onto me so tight I can barely breathe, and cries hard. She's shaking and sobbing against me.

Why is she crying? She only ever cries when she watches sad movies or when Grandma died. I start to cry too because she's scaring me.

"Come on, Addie," Mr. Pritchett says, pulling us toward his office. "Let's sit down for a minute."

"The police officer is waiting outside to take us back," she sobs.

Police officer?

"Am I going to jail?" I cry.

"No, baby, no. Of course not." Mom sniffs and wipes her cheeks dry, then pushes my hair back over my shoulders. Her lips are trembling. "Sweetie, there was a car accident today. Daddy's at the hospital now, but we have to get back as soon as possible because they don't think…" She can't finish the sentence.

"They don't think what?"

"You need to go see your dad, Meredith," Mr. Pritchett says quietly.

"Where is Tiff? Is she at the hospital too?"

Another sob escapes Mom's lips, but she firms her chin and swallows hard. "No, honey. Tiff isn't at the h-h-hospital."

"Where is she?" I whisper.

Mom shakes her head, takes my hand in hers and kisses it. "She didn't make it, baby."

I wrinkle my forehead in confusion. "Didn't make what?"

"Tiffany was killed in the accident, Meredith," Mr. Pritchett says. His eyes are full of tears too.

"What?" I pull away from Mom, yank my hand out of hers and bump into a chair. "What?"

"Come on," Mom says. "We have to get back now."

"I don't understand." I can't stop crying now. My whole body feels hot, like it does when you stand in the bathroom with the shower running hot on a summer day. I can't breathe. "I want Tiff! I want Daddy!"

"We're going to see Daddy right now," Mom says and pulls me out of the office, through the front doors of the school to the police car out front.

I want to ask why the police are here, but I can't talk. This can't be happening. What in the hell is happening?

Mom hugs me hard on the drive to the hospital. The tears have dried up, but I feel numb. This can't be true. Dad had to take Tiff to her dentist appointment this morning. They're fine. Maybe he took her out to lunch after the appointment and there's been a mistake.

The policeman's radio is loud with a deep, monotone man's voice listing numbers and ten-fours. When he pulls up at the hospital, he helps Mom and me out of the car. He has nice eyes. Sad eyes. He pats my shoulder and walks next to us into the hospital, up an elevator and down a hallway. It smells like medicine and cleaner and feet. I hate the smell of feet.

Why does the hospital smell like feet?

Mom leads us to a room where a curtain is pulled, blocking the view of the bed. She keeps my hand in hers as we walk inside and as we walk around the curtain, I see my daddy lying in a bed with tubes coming out of his mouth. He has a white and green hospital gown on. His face is all bruised. His hand is scratched up badly and his right arm is wrapped in gauze from his elbow to his fingertips.

"Daddy," I whisper.

"Go talk to him, baby." Mom guides me next to him. "You can touch him."

"He's hurt."

She nods quickly, tears spilling from her eyes again. "He is, honey. They're just keeping him with us until we have a chance..."

My eyes fly to hers. "He's going to die?"

"He is."

A doctor joins us. She has crazy red hair and freckles, but she has kind eyes too, like the policeman.

"Your dad was in a very bad car accident, Meredith."

"He's breathing," I point out desperately.

"With the help of this machine, yes he is. But sweetie, when we turn the machine off, he will pass away."

"How do you know?" I ask angrily. "You don't know! My daddy is strong! He's just scratched up!"

"Your daddy is strong, Meredith," the doctor replies when my mom can't. "He tried all he could to save your sister. He is a brave man. But you have to say goodbye to him now, honey. You can both take your time. Spend some time with him." She squeezes both mine and mom's shoulders and leaves. The policeman leaves after her, and we are alone with my dad.

"Mom?" I don't want to touch him. If I touch him, this might all be real, and it can't be real. "Mom, he just looks scratched."

"I know."

"I don't want to say goodbye." I shake my head slowly. I can't look away from him.

"Okay." She clears her throat and smiles bravely at me, then pulls two chairs by his bedside and motions for me to sit closest to his head. "Let's just sit for a while and talk. Let's tell stories. I bet he can hear us."

"What k-k-kind of stories?"

"Any kind. Happy ones." Mom takes Dad's hand in hers and bites her lip. She puts it up to her face, nuzzles her cheek into his palm the way she always does when we all sit and watch movies together. Tiff always steals all of the Sour Patch Kids.

"Remember when we took the road trip down to the beach in Oregon last year and Dad kept warning Tiff that she might get bit by sharks?" I smile at the memory as Mom snickers.

"He likes to torment you girls," Mom says. "You and Tiff collected about a hundred sand dollars on that trip."

"Ninety-six," I say proudly. "We were so close to a hundred, but then we had to come home."

Mom and I sit and talk for a long time. Daddy never moves, but I think he can hear. I finally get brave enough to reach out and lay my hand on his arm.

"He's warm."

"I think we have to say goodbye now, baby."

Tears cloud my eyes as I stare at this man that I love so much. "I don't want to."

"I don't either."

"Mama, why did this happen?"

"I don't know."

"Where's Tiff?"

She's quiet for a long minute.

"She's in the morgue, honey."

"Here? In the hospital?" I've seen Law and Order when Mom and Dad didn't know I was watching, so I know how the morgue works.

"Yes."

"Can we say goodbye to her too? Before we leave?"

"I don't know for sure. We'll ask, okay?"

I nod and stare at Daddy. I just want him to wake up. Just for a minute. Just to tell me that he loves me and that I'm pretty. So I can tell him I love him and that I will be responsible and I will take things more seriously.

I stand and lean in so I can whisper in his ear. His hair is bloody and his ear is all swollen and scraped up, but I ignore it and talk anyway.

"I love you so much, Daddy. You are my hero. I will watch over Mama. Don't worry, okay?" I sniffle and kiss his cheek, resting my lips against his scratchy stubble for a second. He used to always tease me with his stubble, rubbing it against my neck, making me giggle. I brush my nose over it for a second. "I love you."

I step away and wipe my nose on my sleeve and watch as my mom, rather than sit next to him, or lean in and whisper like I did, crawls on top of him, rests her head on his chest, wraps her arm around his waist, and just cries. It's the saddest cry I've *ever heard. So loud and long. She buries her face in his neck and holds on, crying for a long time.*

When it seems like she might have fallen asleep, she kisses his cheek, his neck and then his lips. Tiff and I always make gross faces when they kiss and stuff but this time it just makes me cry harder. When she lays her head back on his shoulder, she whispers to him. I can't hear all of the words, but I do hear love, forever, best time of my life.

Finally, when she's all done, she stands and leans over him. She kisses his forehead and next to his lips and presses the red call button.

A few seconds later, the doctor comes back with a bunch of other people. She has Mom sign some papers, and then the team of people unplug all of the machines and take the wires off him. I don't know what they mean or what they do.

They leave just the one that beeps with his heartbeat on and silently leave the room. Mom sits with him, murmuring to him, caressing his face.

"Love you so much, darling. You're not alone. You don't need to be afraid. Go see our girl. Go be with her now, and I'll see you a little later."

I'm crying silently. The beeps are getting farther and farther apart, until finally, there's a beep and then… nothing.

No more beeps.

Just me and Mama, crying.

***

The house is quiet. It's not quite dark yet. After Daddy was gone, we were escorted down to the morgue, which is nothing *like* Law and Order, *to see Tiff. They would only let me see her face. They wouldn't tell me, but I think her arms were really hurt because I wanted to hold her hand, but they wouldn't let me.*

My baby sister was really pale. Her eyes were closed like she was sleeping. But her hair was bloody like Daddy's.

I wanted to wash her off. They should have cleaned her up. They should have put a pillow under her head. I tried to make them put the barrette I stole this morning in her hair, but they said they wouldn't.

Mama said we would make sure someone puts it in her hair so she's pretty when we bury her.

Mom and I stand in the living room, looking around with blind eyes. Why does it look the same?

Dad's sneakers are by his rocking chair. Tiff's backpack is on the kitchen table. It smells like them.

"I'm going to bed," I whisper and trudge up the stairs to our bedroom and stop at the doorway. This is our *room. Tiff's and mine. We share a room, even though we could each have our own. Tiff's bed is made. Her side of the room is always cleaner than mine.*

"Meredith," Mom says softly. I turn to look at her. She looks... tired. Her eyes are swollen. Her shoulders are saggy.

"I can't sleep in there," I say quietly. "She isn't here to sleep with me."

"Do you want to sleep in the spare room with me?" she asks and offers me a watery smile.

"You're not going to sleep in your room?"

"Not tonight. Maybe tomorrow." I nod and follow her down the hall, past her room to the guest room.

"It's not even dark out yet," I murmur. "And we didn't have dinner."

"Are you hungry?"

"No."

"What do you want, baby?"

I shrug and bite my lip. I can't look her in the eye. I'll just cry again. "I guess we could just sleep."

I don't know where Mom got them from, but she pulls Daddy's T-shirts over our heads and we slide under the covers together.

"Daddy will hug us tonight, baby girl," she whispers brokenly. His shirts do smell like him, and it's like having him right here with us.

"Wait!" I jump from the bed and hold my breath as I run into my room to grab something off Tiff's bed, then run back in with Mom. Mom hugs me close, Tiff's ratty old bear between us, and we both cry together, missing Daddy and Tiff already. We cry for a really long time, until we fall asleep.

"Meredith?" The passenger side door opens and Luke is there, holding my face in his hands. "Jesus Christ you're pale, Mer. Come on, we have to go inside."

"Luke?" Sam is suddenly next to him. "What's wrong with her?"

"I don't know. She looks... *hollow.*"

"Should I get some help?"

"No," I reply hoarsely.

CHAPTER TWENTY ONE

"I'm okay," I murmur and move to get out of the car, but Luke holds me still for a moment, examining me.

"You're not okay."

"I need to get to Mark."

"Where were you, Mer? You were gone during that entire thirty minute drive."

"I was in the past." I firm my chin and do my best to not show him that I'm falling apart here. I don't matter. I need to get to Mark.

Luke swears under his breath and steps back to let me out.

"Her dad and sister," Sam murmurs.

"I know," he replies.

"I'm right here. I can hear you." I try to shake them off, but they flank me. Luke wraps his arm around my low back and Sam takes my hand, and we walk into the emergency room together.

"I'm glad you can hear me now because you couldn't five minutes ago," Luke says almost angrily. Why is he mad? Maybe he's just scared. God knows I'm fucking terrified.

"What happened?" I ask. Jesus, I wasn't even thinking clearly enough to ask what happened. "Is he dead?"

"I fucking hope not," Luke replies. Now he *is* mad, and Luke never gets mad. He takes one look at my face and then takes a deep breath and swears softly. "I'm sorry. No, he's not dead. I don't know how bad his injuries are. Isaac is on the way here too. He was on the job site."

"It happened on the job?" I ask incredulously. "How in the hell is there a car accident on the job?"

"Let's see if we can see him and I'll tell you what I know."

Luke leads us to the reception desk and flashes the woman behind the counter his million-dollar smile. "Hello. My brother, Mark Williams, was just brought in. Can you buzz us back?"

She taps on her keyboard and frowns. "I don't have record of him. When did you say he came in?"

"He should already be here."

"Could be they're still on the way. I do show that we're holding a room for an ambulance."

"We beat them here?" Sam asks disbelievingly.

"Check back with me in a while," the receptionist says with a smile. Luke leads us to the waiting room and I plop in a chair, trying not to think about the germs that I'm sitting on.

"Jesus, I hate emergency rooms," Sam mutters. "Do you know what kind of nastiness is on these chairs?"

"You and I are on the same page," I say absently as I rub my eyes. "Okay, tell me."

"All I know is a car hit him in front of the job site. Isaac called me and said they'd called the ambulance and to have us meet him here."

"Are his legs broken? Does he have internal bleeding? Is he conscious?" I'm getting shrill now. I stop and swallow, trying with all my might to keep my panic at bay.

"I don't know anything else," Luke insists. "We have to wait to see him."

"I'm sure he's fine," Sam says and risks coming in contact with the plague and sits next to me. "Honest. If it was horrible Isaac would have said something to prepare us. He would have called the whole family."

I nod my head. Right. She's right. *But if he's fine, Mark would have called me himself. He wouldn't have sent Luke.*

"I mean," she continues, "he works a really dangerous job. We've always known this. He's always climbing on stuff and working with sharp, dangerous tools and equipment. He could fall, get electrocuted, cut off his hand with that really big saw. At least he's not working on the fishing boats anymore."

"Sam," Luke says warningly.

"Fishing on those boats is the most dangerous job in the world! I swear, I still have stomach ulcers from waiting for days to hear that he was okay."

"*Samantha!*" Luke shouts, cutting her off. "I don't think you're helping."

Sam looks at me with wide eyes. The blood has drained from my head and my lips are trembling.

"Is that true? I never stopped to think that construction is so dangerous."

"He's careful," she insists, backpedaling. "Honest, Mer, he's really careful. He's never been hurt before."

"But it's possible."

"Hell, you could get hit by a bus crossing the street, Mer. Anything's possible."

I shake my head and stand to pace the room, which isn't easy with all of the people sitting in the cramped space. A couple people are sleeping. One man is holding his face. He obviously has a toothache. A baby is crying in his mom's arms.

Luke comes up behind me and rests his big hands on my shoulders. His hands are so much like Mark's.

"I can't lose him," I whisper.

"Meredith, I think you're overreacting, sweetheart. He's probably just scraped up."

I twirl and stare up into his clear blue eyes. "You don't get it, Luke. The people I love die. This isn't the first time I've been rushed to a hospital because of an accident."

"Not all of the people you love die," he says softly.

"The ones that matter the most."

"Mark isn't dead, Meredith." He grips my shoulders tightly. "He's not dead."

I nod again. I feel like that's all I've been doing, nodding like an imbecile. But then the image of my father in that hospital bed enters my head. My mom lying on him, keening in pain and agony and I shake my head in denial.

I don't know if I'm strong enough for this.

"He's here," Sam says as she rushes over to us. "The chick with the computer—"

"Is that her name?" Luke asks sarcastically.

"—said that the ambulance just got here. He's going to be examined and stuff before we can go back." She cups my face in her hands, not gently, and says, "He's *not* dead."

He's not dead.

"How long until I can see him?"

"She didn't know."

It's the longest fucking two hours of my life.

"I'm sorry," computer chick says with sympathetic eyes. "They've taken him back for some tests. As soon as he's ready you'll be the first to know."

"If you just tell him I'm here, he'll want me back there with him," I beg.

"You can't be in the area where the tests are being done. I promise, I'll call you back as soon as I get the okay from his nurse."

"His nurse and I are going to have some words," Sam says with a snarl. We both turn away just as Isaac comes running through the door.

"I couldn't get here sooner. I had to talk to cops and calm the crew down and…" He sees me and immediately hugs me close. "How are you holding up, sugar?"

"Not great," I reply honestly. "They won't let us back to see him. So you need to tell me if he's okay."

"I think so," he replies. "I don't think he passed out, but I didn't want to take any chances."

"How in the fucking hell does a person get hit by a car on a construction site?" I ask him angrily.

"Fucking looky-loo. Too damn busy checking out the house rather than watching what's happening in front of her damn car and going too fast. Mark was looking at his phone and just walking around his Jeep, he wasn't even walking across the street, and she hit him, full on. Sent him flying. Scariest fucking thing I've ever seen."

"Ms. Summers? You can go back with him now."

"Go ahead," Luke says. "Sam and I will wait here for our parents."

I nod and follow Computer Chick into the bowels of the ER. Someone is crying. She leads me to a room with a curtain drawn around the bed. I swallow hard and for a millisecond I consider running away, but instead I take a deep breath and walk right in and around the curtain.

And there is my man, in a hospital gown, his hair a little bloody, his face and arms scraped, and a big, fat smile on his arrogant face.

"Hey, M," he says.

I immediately burst into tears. I sit in the chair next to his bed and sink my head and arms onto his lap, crying big, gulping sobs.

"Shh…" He's rubbing my head now, my shoulders and back. "Hey, it's okay. I'm okay, baby."

"You could have died!" I cry into his lap.

"I am fine." He grips my shoulders and makes me sit up to look at him. "Look at me. Meredith."

I can't open my eyes. I feel so foolish. I know he thinks I'm overreacting. Everyone does, but they haven't been in my shoes. They don't understand.

"Meredith. Breathe. Breathe with me, baby." He scoots down in the bed and leans his forehead on mine. "Come on. You're having a panic attack. Breathe deep and slow, Meredith."

He calms me. My heart slowly returns to normal and my tears stop until I look up into his gorgeous blue eyes and I lose it again.

"Baby, I'm okay."

"I know. But I didn't know before, and it reminded me of Dad and Tiff, and oh my God, Mark, I can't do that ever again."

"Stop." His voice is brisk now. "Stop it before I call the nurse in here for you."

"Are you going to be okay?" I whisper.

"Yes. I'm scraped up, and I have a knot on my head, but I'm fine. They wanted to do a CAT scan to make sure I don't have internal injuries."

"Do you?" My heart stops again.

"No. I'm fine. I'll be sore as hell tomorrow, but I'll walk out of here as soon as Nurse Ratchet brings me my fucking papers and more pain meds."

"Why didn't you call me?"

He reaches for a rolling table at this bedside and holds up his phone. The screen is shattered.

I close my eyes in relief and I'm suddenly being lifted into Mark's lap.

"What are you doing?"

"Calming you the fuck down." He cradles me against him and rocks us back and forth. I wrap my arms around his neck and bury my face in my place in his neck, holding on tightly. God, I love him. He's everything to me. I can't lose him the way my mom lost Dad. I don't think I'd survive it.

And I *will* eventually lose him. Because I lose everyone I love.

As we sit here silently, I cling to him as I realize what I have to do.

I have to give him up.

I cup his face gently in my hands and kiss him softly. My lips linger on his for a moment as I breathe him in and my hands trace the strong muscles in his arms.

Finally, I pull away and climb off his lap.

"I love you more than I can ever tell you, Mark. But, I can't bear the thought of losing you the way I lost my family." I swallow hard as he frowns in confusion. "I just can't do this."

"Can't do what, exactly?"

"I can't be with you."

"You *are* with me, Meredith."

I shake my head and rub my forehead with my fingertips. Jesus, how do I find the words for this?

"I don't think I can be in a relationship with you." The last few words are said on a sob. His jaw drops just as the nurse bustles in.

"Okay, Mr. Williams…"

I leave as she's giving him his instructions and rush out of the ER, through the waiting room and outside.

Fuck me, I don't have my car.

"Meredith!"

Natalie runs out after me, catching up to me when I get to the parking lot and realize I don't have a ride home. He's going to come marching out here any second.

"I need to leave, Natalie."

"Is he okay?"

"Yes, he's just scraped up. He'll be fine." *This time.*

But what about the next time?

"Oh, good." She breathes a sigh of relief and then sobers when she sees the look on my face. "Where are you going, Mer?"

"I'm leaving. I just broke it off with Mark."

"Wow, talk about kicking a man when he's down."

"Fuck you, Natalie. You don't know me or what I've been through." It's not her fault, but I can't stop myself from going after her verbally, and I hate myself even more for it. "You haven't had to bury your parents and your sister and watch everyone around you that you love the most die!"

"Yes I have."

"And you haven't…" I stop, stunned. "What?"

"My parents both died when I was in college," she replies calmly. "I'm an only child."

I blink twice and feel about three inches tall.

"Scared you, didn't it?"

"I'm fucking terrified."

Nat nods and pushes her hair out of her face as the wind kicks up. "He won't let you just break it off, you know."

"He doesn't have a choice."

She narrows her eyes and watches me for a moment. My eyes fill with tears again, pissing me off even more.

"Why would you do this? Even a blind woman can see that you're completely in love with each other."

"I would rather give him up voluntarily," I begin and have to swallow hard against the bile rising in my throat. "Than have to lose him the way I did my sister and my dad. I watched my mom lay on my dad's chest and say goodbye to him, Natalie. I can't do that."

"I don't know how anyone can do that," she says softly, her own eyes full of tears. "What a horrible thing, Meredith. But you don't know that you would ever be in that situation."

"I don't know that I won't."

"You didn't strike me as a quitter."

My eyes whip over to hers. "I. Can't. Do. It."

She nods thoughtfully, then hugs me as Jax pulls his car up to us. "Think it over. A love like yours doesn't come along every day, you know. Love him. Let him love you. Make the most out of every single day, so at the end of it all, you can say you don't have any regrets, Mer. Life's too short for that, and no one knows that better than you and me."

She pats my shoulder and jogs back into the hospital. I watch her go then climb into Jax's sporty little car. "Take me home."

"Is he okay?"

"Yes." He eyes me, taking in my tears and my shaking hands.

"Are you?"

I shake my head and sob again. "Take me home."

CHAPTER TWENTY TWO

~Mark~

"Are you okay?" Mom rushes to me as I walk into the waiting room.

"I'm fine. Where did Meredith go?" Fucking hell, those pills have knocked me on my ass. My arms and legs feel heavy and my head is fuzzy.

"Jax picked her up," Nat says. "She's scared, Mark."

"I get it, but she's not getting rid of me that easy. I need your car," I say to Luke who just smirks at me. I growl at him and would advance on him if my feet would move.

"You need to fill those prescriptions and rest," Mom interjects, pointing at the papers in my hand. "I love Meredith to death, but you're in no shape to be running all over the damn world."

"Mom." I take a deep breath to calm my temper. "I need to fix this with her. She's not okay." I remember the feel of her in my arms, the trembling, the absolute despair rolling off her in waves. "She's not trying to be dramatic. Meredith isn't like that. She's hurting."

Luke takes the papers from my hand and rattles his keys in his hand. "You're not driving anywhere, Mark. Nat and I will take care of these and Sam will get you settled at home." He points outside and wraps his arm around Mom's shoulders. "Why don't you come with us, Mom?"

She continues to watch me and finally stands on tip-toe to kiss my cheek.

"We'll meet you at your house," Mom says.

"Why won't you all listen to me? I need to see Meredith!"

"Do you honestly think you're in any shape to charm her right now?" Sam asks with a roll of the eyes. "She'll still be around tomorrow when you're not all drugged up."

I glare at her, but she's right. My eyes are heavy and my body is in that in-between place of numb and pain. Every step out to Sam's car is agony and effort, making me embarrassingly tired.

By the time we make it back to my house, all I want to do is sleep. "Please call her," I say to Sam as she helps me stumble my way up to my bedroom. "Just call her and make sure she's okay."

"I will," Sam promises and helps me into the bed, not bothering to make me change out of the green scrubs the hospital gave me. I roll onto the mattress and immediately slip into a drug-induced sleep.

***

Fuck me, I'm sore. I wince as I sit up and try to stretch my muscles. I ache, which shouldn't surprise me since I've refused to take the pain meds over the past six hours so I can drive to Meredith's this afternoon. I rise from the bed and take care of business, then curl my lip in disgust when I see that I'm still covered in bloody smears. I crashed before I even had a chance to take a shower.

First thing's first. I need coffee.

As I descend the stairs, I hear voices in my kitchen.

"I tried to call her three times last night and once more this morning and she wouldn't answer," Sam says quietly, sipping coffee as I walk into the room. She's talking with Jax who also looks exhausted and worried.

"How are you feeling?" Jax asks.

"Like I got hit by a fucking car," I reply and pour myself some coffee. "But it doesn't matter. Talk to me about Meredith. Is she okay?"

Jax winces and shakes his head.

"No. She won't calm down. You're okay, but it's like a dam has burst and I can't get her to calm down. It's freaking me out." He rubs his hand over his face. "She cried for a long time, then slept for a few hours. When she woke up she went back to crying. Any time I go in her room, she makes me leave."

"Jesus," I whisper, staring down into the coffee in my mug. "I know she's still grieving for her mom, and this had to bring up bad memories for her," I mutter.

"It's just typical for her though," Jax adds, making both Sam and I frown in confusion.

"What do you mean?" Sam says.

"Meredith always pushes people away. She always has, for as long as I've known her. She couldn't shake me because I sunk my claws into her and didn't let go, but even that scares her sometimes. She's afraid of losing people she loves. So, the ones who fight back and stay are the ones she figures are around for the long-haul."

"Well I'm clearly going to fight back," I reply. "She's not shaking me off like this."

"Do you feel well enough to drive or do you need a lift?" Jax asks.

"You really should shower first," Sam says. "You look horrible."

"I'm fine, and I'll shower at Meredith's." I take a long swig of cooling coffee and grab my keys. "Will you be by later?" I ask Jax.

"Yeah. I'm going to go buy some juice and soup. I know it's not the flu, but I don't know what else to fucking do. She won't let me touch her. Here, you'll need a key."

I nod. "Thank you. I'll take care of it."

I'm moving slower than I usually do, which pisses me off because right now all I can think of is getting to Mer. The drive is quick, and before I know it, I'm at her place.

I walk swiftly to her room and pause by her door, listening to her soft sobs inside. Silently, I open her door and when I see her curled up on her bed, her hand over her head, crying in despair, my stomach falls to my knees.

I crawl onto her bed and pull her into my arms. "Meredith, everything is okay."

She gasps, surprised to see me, and stops crying long enough to take me in, but then starts to cry again.

"Stop. I can't be with you." She's not fighting me, not trying to get out of my embrace.

"Yes, you can."

"Mark, I'm going to lose you too, and I can't stand the thought of it." She's shivering. Instead of trying to talk some sense into her, I simply hold her. Kiss her hair, caress her shoulder and back, rubbing in big, soothing circles. We lie together for a long time, until she finally looks at me. Her eyes are still leaking, but she's not trembling any longer.

"I love you," I whisper.

"I love you too." She swallows hard and brushes her cheeks dry with the back of her hand. "You know what happened the day my dad and Tiff died."

"Yes, you've told me the story, baby."

She nods. "When Luke said there'd been an accident, and we got in the car, I was right back in that place, as if I was thirteen years old again, and the pain was bright and brand new."

I brush my knuckles down her cheeks, my heart breaking for her.

"I understand that you're okay. My brain computes it, Mark. You weren't hurt badly, thank God, and you'll heal quickly and everything will go back to normal."

I nod, watching her as she struggles with her heart.

"But I can't help the way my heart feels."

"How does it feel?"

"Panicked. Terrified. God, I'm so scared. I didn't know that your job is dangerous. It never occurred to me."

"Would it have changed things? Would knowing that there are hazards on my job have kept you from falling back into love with me?"

She bites her lip and wrinkles her brow, and I want so desperately to lean in and kiss her there, to comfort her, but I wait, letting her reason things out.

"I never fell back into love with you. I was *always in* love with you," she admits. "But maybe I could have prepared myself."

"Honestly, M, the injuries that happen on a job site are typically small ones. Hammer a thumb, trip on a board. We are very careful and have rules to keep us all from getting hurt."

She pulls away, turning onto her back and looks at the ceiling. "I think you should go home and rest."

My heart stills.

"Didn't you hear a word I just said?"

"I did."

"But you're still throwing me out."

She bites her lip and jerks her head yes.

I stand and walk toward the door, but stop and turn around and watch the tears run down the sides of her face into her hair. She doesn't want me to leave. She's just scared.

"Fuck this, Meredith. I remember exactly what it felt like ten years ago to stand on your porch and have you tell me that we were through. I refuse to go through that again. I am not giving up on this. I can't go a day, *an hour* without thinking about you. Without needing to hear your voice, see you smile."

I rub my hand over my mouth and pace away in frustration and then circle around again.

"I'm trying to protect myself!" She stands and faces off with me, her hands fisted at her sides. "You want me to stay with you, to love you every day, but what am I supposed to do when you die and you leave me?"

"I'm not leaving you!"

"Today. You're not leaving me today."

"Meredith, I can't promise you that nothing will ever happen to me because we don't know. I can't promise what I don't have control of."

"Exactly!" She points at me as if I finally get it. "You can't."

"No one can, M. Are you just going to be alone forever?"

"I'm not alone. I have Jax."

"Until he dies too," I reply coldly and hate myself when her face crumples.

"I have my studio."

"What if it burns down?"

"STOP IT!" She screams nearing hysterics again.

"Baby, you have to know that the chances of any of that happening are minute." I fight through her flailing arms and pull her tightly against my chest, tucking her head under my chin, and hold on with all my might. "Jax and I aren't going anywhere. Your studio is safe."

"I'm scared."

"Me too. Mer, I wouldn't survive losing you again. Your mom was the strongest person I've ever met. Next to you, and I'm surrounded by a lot of strong women, sweetheart." I tip her face up so I can stare down into her beautiful face. "You're so strong, baby. I love you more than I can ever tell you. I'm sure there are pretty words that would work, but I don't know what they are. I just know that what I feel for you is so big, there's no way I can let you go. Please don't ask me to. I can't say goodbye to you, M."

I lean my forehead against hers as she finally, *finally*, wraps her arms around me and holds on desperately.

"I love you so big," she whispers as she buries her face in my neck, the way she always does.

"As long as we have each other, we can do anything." I smirk at myself. Where the fuck is my man card? "I know it sounds cliché, but it's true, Mer. Something Luke said not long ago has stuck with me. He said that if Natalie ever tries to leave him, he's going with her because his life doesn't work without her."

I feel her grin against my neck and I take the first clean breath I've had since she walked out of the hospital room yesterday.

"That sounds like him," she mumbles.

"I get it." I tug her into my lap at the edge of the bed. "I feel the same way."

"Natalie is a lucky girl," Meredith says. *There's my smart-ass.*

"My life doesn't work without you in it, M." I kiss her temple and continue to rub her back, soothing us both.

"I'm sorry." Her voice is small and shaky. "I panicked. I've been panicking all night because I was worried and I was regretting not being with you to take care of you."

"Yes you did." Now that she's with me, truly with me, I feel my own trembles begin. "You scared me too."

Her hands glide down my arms, then she sits back and takes in my clothes. "You're in scrubs."

"My clothes were ruined."

"But that was yesterday." She bites her lip. "You have blood in your h-h-hair."

"I fell asleep as soon as I got home and I haven't showered. I bumped my head on the street. Bled like a stuck pig for a little while, but it didn't need stitches."

"Can you take a shower now?"

"Yes."

She stands, takes my hand and leads me to her bathroom. "You should be resting."

"Now you sound like my mother."

She blows her nose and turns on the shower then returns to me. "She's a smart woman."

"She is. She loves you, you know."

Fresh tears fill her eyes, but she simply smiles softly and nods. "I love her too. I love all of them."

They'll be yours before long, I think and drag my fingertips down her cheek. She grips the hem of the green scrub top in her hands and gently guides it over my head, then unties the drawstring on the matching pants and lets them fall to the floor.

I'm not wearing underwear.

"Me crying turns you on?" she asks in surprise, staring at my semi-hard cock.

"You stripping me down turns me on, Mer. Always." I chuckle and pull her shirt over her head. "That hasn't changed since we were seventeen."

"You're scraped up pretty good back here," she says when she makes me turn around. She presses a sweet kiss to my shoulder blade before leading me into the shower. She didn't set it too hot, not too cold, but just perfect so when it slides over the cuts and scrapes the stinging isn't too bad.

"I'm going to wash you," she informs me softly.

"I like it when you take care of me," I murmur.

Her hands glide gently over my body, cleaning the brown dried blood and dirt from my arms and hands, washing the blood out of my hair, and when all is said and done, and we're both dry, she examines me one more time.

"See? It's not so bad now that I'm cleaned up."

"You must be really sore."

So fucking sore.

"I'll be fine."

"Come on." She leads me back to her bedroom, pulls the covers back on her bed and motions for me to lie down.

"It's mid-afternoon, Mer."

She simply raises a brow. I sigh and climb onto the bed, and grin happily when she joins me. She picks up my right hand, kisses the scratches on my palm, then cradles her small, smooth cheek, nuzzling my palm. She works her way up my arm to my shoulder, kissing each red spot.

"Are you going to kiss all my boo-boo's?"

"Yes."

Finally, she straddles my lap and pushes her fingers into my hair, examining my scalp more closely than any of the nurses or doctors at the hospital did.

"You must have a headache."

"They gave me something for it," I reply and close my eyes on a sigh when she continues to soothingly brush my hair with her fingers. "You don't ever have to stop doing that."

She kisses my nose and then my forehead. Her warm, smooth, toned body is pressed to mine, her amazing breasts in my face, and I can't stand it any longer. I glide my hands up her thighs, over her ass and up her back, making her purr low in her throat.

God, that's a fucking sexy sound.

My cock twitches against her folds, sliding along her clit. She bites her lip and gazes down at me with lust-filled eyes.

"You're hurt," she whispers.

"I'm never too hurt for this."

I begin to flip our position, but she presses her hands on my shoulders, keeping me in place.

"No. Let me." She smiles slowly as she lifts up, reaches between us and guides me inside her slowly. God, every single time is like the first time. She's so fucking tight and sweet. "Don't move," she says.

"That's impossible."

"No it's not." She leans down to kiss me, caresses my cheeks and neck with her fingertips and begins to circle her hips effortlessly. "I'm sorry I got scared."

"Don't leave me again." *Ever.*

She shakes her head and kisses me, licks my lower lip and kisses me again, deeper now. My cock pulses inside her. I want to grip onto her hips and drive inside her over and over, but I wait, knowing that she's comforting us both.

Her hands glide to my arms and she holds on as she begins to ride me. Jesus, I'm not even moving and I'm not going to last.

"God, M," I mutter. "Your body is amazing." It's true. Her firm, round breasts, tight stomach, full hips all make me weak in the knees. But it's her heart that has had me in its grip for more than a decade.

"Love you," she whispers and tucks her face in my neck as she picks up speed.

"Can I move now?"

"Yes, please."

I roll her to her back without breaking our precious contact and cradle her shoulders and head in my hands, tip my forehead against hers as I move in slow, earnest strokes.

"Love you," I say, my lips against hers. "Always."

EPILOGUE

Three months later…

~Meredith~

"Why are you acting so weird?" I ask Jax and help one of the littlest girls tie her dance shoes.

"I'm not." He won't look me in the eye, which spells lie with a capital L.

"What's going on?"

"Nothing."

"Jax, something's up. Is everything okay with Mr. Lovey Pants?"

Strong arms wrap around my shoulders from behind and Logan presses a kiss to my temple. "Mr. Lovey Pants is fine."

"Hey, handsome." I grin up at the man that's quickly become a good friend of mine. He's perfect for my Jax.

"Hey, gorgeous," he replies flirtatiously.

"Get your hands off my man, potato chip," Jax growls with a glare, making me laugh.

"He only has eyes for you," I assure Jax and brush my fingertip over the ring on Logan's left hand. "I love the rings you guys chose. Marriage looks good on both of you."

They grin at each other, love and humor and understanding floating between them, making my heart catch. Their wedding was absolutely beautiful.

"I'm sorry that we scheduled this recital for the same weekend you're moving the rest of your things." I cringe and offer Logan a sympathetic smile.

"It's fine. My dad is keeping an eye on the movers."

"You didn't have to come," Jax says. "And you didn't have to hire movers. I don't have that much stuff."

"Well, with movers you didn't have to try to squeeze in time between choreography and dance recitals to pack your stuff, and I wouldn't miss this recital for the world." He smiles down at me. "How do you like your new kitchen?"

I smile widely as I think of my beautiful kitchen, complete with the insanely awesome and insanely expensive wine cooler I wanted. "I love it. You and Jax have to come for dinner soon. We'd love to have you."

"Sounds great. Have you told him?" Logan asks with a low voice, his blue eyes shining behind his sexy glasses.

"Tonight," I reply.

Logan kisses Jax's cheek, then mine, and grins. "Good luck with that. I'll be out in the audience with the others."

"I can't believe the *entire* Williams and Montgomery families came," I mutter and count heads. The little girls are all abuzz with excitement, admiring each other's pretty outfits and thrilled that they get to wear red lipstick.

"You know they love an excuse to get together, and they haven't missed one of the twins and Sophie's recitals yet."

"Except Mark." I scowl down at my quiet phone. "He never has to work on Saturdays, but he said something came up with work and he couldn't get out of it."

"Okay, it's time," Jax says and walks away, motioning for the girls to gather around him. I walk out onto the stage.

"Welcome, everyone, and thank you so much for being here today. I am Meredith Summers, the co-owner of Twinkle Toes, and on behalf of Jax and I, I'd like to say thank you so very much for all of your support. We love teaching your little ones and are honored that you've trusted this studio to bring them to dance. Your girls have been working very hard to prepare for today's recital. So, without further ado, let's get started."

I smile as the families applaud and walk down the steps to my mark in the audience, where the girls can still see me and I can lead them through their dances. As always, we start with the youngest ones.

As they file out and begin to move their tiny bodies to the music, one little girl on the end decides to freestyle it, singing with the music, skipping and dancing around the stage, making the parents, and me, laugh.

That little girl is going places.

Parents happily snap photos and ooh and aah over the girls' routines as each age group comes out on stage to perform two dances each. Finally, when all is said and done, I return to the stage.

"That concludes today's recital. Thank you again…"

There's a tug on my skirt. I glance down to see a tiny little red-haired girl holding up a red rose to me, which I take and smile down at her. She walks away, and suddenly, another girl appears with a rose.

I look up to survey the audience for Mark, thinking this might be his handy-work, but he's not here. I shrug, thinking nothing of it. Sometimes the dance instructors receive flowers after a recital.

As I try to thank the audience for coming, I'm interrupted over and over again, until my arms are full of beautiful, fragrant red roses.

Suddenly, all of the Montgomerys, Williamses, and Logan, with Jax now standing next to him, all stand and applaud enthusiastically and I'm at a loss.

"What in the world is going on?"

"Turn around, Miss Mer," Josie yells out from behind me. I turn and stop, stunned, at what I see before me.

All eight of the oldest girls are standing in a line holding signs that spell out *Will You Marry Me, M?* and Mark is on one knee, holding his hand out to me. I stumble to him, walking on numb feet and feel my eyes fill with tears.

"Are you kidding me?" I whisper. Mark laughs, his blue eyes dancing with happiness, and he flashes that naughty smile at me, making my knees go weak and my heart sing.

"Meredith," he says and the whole room hushes. "We waited a long time for each other. I don't think we even knew that's what we were doing. I will never stop loving you, Meredith A—"

"Watch it," I say, cutting him off from saying my middle name out loud. He laughs and kisses my hand.

"In a sea of people, my eyes will always search for you, my love. You are the best part of my life, and I can't imagine ever being without you again. So, in front of everything and everyone we love most, I'm asking you to believe in us and become my wife. I promise, I'll work every day making sure you never regret it."

Tears are streaming down my cheeks as I step forward and cup his face in my hand. "Of course I'll marry you, M."

He kisses my palm, then slips a beautiful round solitaire diamond engagement ring on my finger before standing and wrapping his arms around me. He slants his lips over mine, then kisses my cheek.

"You said yes."

"Damn right I did." I laugh. Everyone in the audience continues to applaud as Mark nuzzles my nose. "Is this a good time to tell you you're gonna be a daddy?"

"What?" He jerks back and gazes down in my eyes. "What did you just say?"

"I'm pregnant, babe."

"Holy shit." He kisses me again, harder this time and then lets out a loud, "Whoop!"

"What's going on up there?" Will calls out from the audience.

"We're getting married," Mark calls back and raises a brow at me, silently asking for permission to announce the good news. I happily nod and he smiles wide, never looking away from me and calls out, "And we're gonna have a baby!"

Applause erupts again, and I'm suddenly surrounded by people, being passed around from brother to brother, hugged and kissed. The girls are all crying and smiling and hugging each other until they can get to me.

"Congratulations, *bella*," Dom says happily as he hugs me close and then passes me to Luke.

"I'm so happy for you," Luke whispers in my ear. "If you need anything at all, you only have to call."

I nod with tears in my eyes and then am scooped up into Neil's strong arms.

"Welcome to our family at last, my sweet girl," he says with a wide, handsome grin. "It's about time. We've been waiting for you, you know."

"Thank you," I whisper.

"Your mother gave me her wedding dress to hold on to for you," Lucy says as she pats my cheek softly.

"She did? But how did she—"

"A mother knows." Lucy winks at me. "We'd better get you married before you can't fit into the dress anymore."

I glance over to where Jax and Logan are standing, hand-in-hand, laughing with Jules and Nate, who has a sleeping Stella on his shoulder. Will and Meg are congratulating Mark as Leo and Sam both enfold me in a group hug.

"Way to go, babe," Sam says smugly. "I've always liked you."

"Yeah, right." I snort as I laugh and she laughs with me. "I think the term is *tolerate*."

"I liked you. Now I love you. You're good for us."

Jesus, is everyone going to make me cry today?

"Proud of you," Natalie whispers in my ear, then winks at me and gives my arm a squeeze. "We'll talk later."

I'm passed from person to person, until finally, I'm back in Mark's arms and he's kissing me silly.

"Are you ready to be a part of this crazy family?" he asks with that naughty grin.

"I can't wait," I reply and press my face to his neck. "I can't wait."

THE END

Don't miss the final book in the WITH ME IN SEATTLE series, FOREVER WITH ME, releasing in the Fall of 2014!

WITH ME IN SEATTLE SERIES:
Come Away With Me and on audio
Under the Mistletoe With Me and on audio
Fight With Me and on audio
Play With Me and on audio
Rock With Me and on audio
Safe With Me and on audio
Tied With Me and on audio

Look what's coming in 2015!

From the *New York Times* and *USA Today* Bestselling Author, Kristen Proby, comes an all new series for 2015!

Mia, Addison, Riley, Camilla and Katrina have been best friends since elementary school. Five women have never been so different, yet it's their diverse personalities and their love for one another that have fused them together since childhood. Now they're all back home in Portland, Oregon. At a crossroads in their lives, they decide to take the chance of a lifetime and open their restaurant, Succulent, in the heart of the City of Roses. Playing a key role in the success of the business, each woman is determined that, not only is Succulent going to do well, it's going to knock Portland off it's feet. Specializing in titillating the senses with delicious aphrodisiacs, amazing music, an impressive wine cellar and an atmosphere that is as inviting as it is thrilling, Succulent is an experience, and one you won't soon forget.

Prepare to be seduced in early 2015 with book one in the Fusion Series, A **TASTE OF DELICIOUS**!

Made in the USA
Lexington, KY
21 July 2014